EMMA VISKIC is an award-winning Australian crime writer. Her critically acclaimed debut novel, *Resurrection Bay*, won the 2016 Ned Kelly Award for Best Debut, as well as an unprecedented three Davitt Awards: Best Adult Novel, Best Debut, and Readers' Choice. It was also iBooks Australia's Crime Novel of the year in 2015.

Emma studied Australian sign language (Auslan) in order to write the character of Caleb, whose adventures will continue in *Darkness for Light*, coming soon from Pushkin Vertigo.

PRAISE FOR THE CALEB ZELIC THRILLERS

'Outstanding, gripping and violent... a hero who is original and appealing'

Guardian

'An Australian thriller at its finest. A captivating read from first page to last'

Jane Harper, author of *The Dry*

'Terrific... Grabs you by the throat and never slackens its hold'

Christos Tsiolkas, author of *The Slap*

'Outstanding... Pacy, violent but with a big thundering heart, it looks set to be one of the debuts of the year and marks Emma Viskic out as a serious contender on the crime scene'

Eva Dolan, author of *Long Way Home*

EMMA VISKIC

AND FIRE CAME DOWN

PUSHKIN VERTIGO

Pushkin Press
71–75 Shelton Street
London WC2H 9JQ

And Fire Came Down was first published in Australia by Echo, 2017
First published by Pushkin Press in 2018

1 3 5 7 9 8 6 4 2

ISBN 13: 978-1-78227-455-1

Offset by Tetragon, London
Printed and bound by CPI Group (UK) Ltd, Croydon CRO 4YY

www.pushkinpress.com

For Meg and Leni

And fire came down from heaven and devoured them.

REVELATION 20:9

1.

The man cornered Caleb at the lights. Twitching and sniffing, talking in staccato bursts. A skeletal face and pupils like voids.

Caleb gestured to the empty pockets of his running shorts. 'Nothing on me, mate.'

Sniffy kept talking and twitching. Caleb ignored him. Thirty more seconds and he'd be in his flat and under a long, cold shower. It was an hour after sunset, and the day's heat still clung to concrete and asphalt, the pores of his skin. Stupid to have gone for a run, but last night's dreams had slipped into his waking hours again, plucking at his thoughts with their bloodstained fingers.

And now Sniffy was waving a piece of fucking paper in his face.

Caleb tried to skirt around him as the lights turned green, but the guy did a little sideways dance to block his way.

'Piss off,' Caleb said.

Sniffy shoved the paper into his right hand. A receipt of some kind, sweat-stained and crumpled. Something written on the back in thick letters. He held it up to the streetlight.

Caleb

33/45 Martin St Nth Fitzroy

His name, his address. The words were scrawled in lipstick, but there was nothing flirtatious about their jagged letters, the strokes flecked with lumps of flesh-like pink. Something cold slid down his neck.

He looked at Sniffy. 'Where'd you get this?'

Words scuttled from the man's mouth and disappeared into the shadows. Was that a W? And an O? Definitely an M.

'A woman?' Caleb guessed. 'A woman gave it to you?'

Sniffy gestured down the street. 'She said... and I...'

'Slower. What woman?'

'Tall, black...'

Kat.

Fear gripped Caleb's bowels. 'Where is she? Show me.'

Sniffy headed along the street, talking the entire time. A shambling gait like a sleep-deprived toddler. Step, shuffle, step. Past apartment blocks and pizza shops, around a corner into an empty side street. So slow. Why the fuck couldn't he go any faster? Around another corner into an unlit alleyway of rusting corrugated iron and jumbled cobblestones, the stink of stale piss. Caleb came to a halt halfway down it. Dark, no overlooking windows – a good place to get jumped.

Sniffy made his way to the back of the alley, where a thin shape stepped out of the gloom to meet him. Not Kat. Nothing like Kat. The woman's skin was so pale it looked translucent, a startling contrast to her short, dark hair. Black hair – Sniffy had been describing her hair, not her skin. Caleb let out a shuddering breath. Of course it wasn't Kat. She was five thousand kilometres away in Broome, not in a stinking Melbourne alleyway. And if he'd stopped to think for a second, he would have remembered that.

A quick exchange of money between the pair, and Sniffy shuffled away. Just a delivery boy. So who was the woman? She was young, probably early twenties, carrying a brown handbag and wearing a red cotton dress that looked as though it would smell of incense. Dark alley, vulnerable young woman – it had to be some kind of a con. Walk away. But he glanced at the crumpled receipt in his hand.

Caleb

'How do you know my name and address?'

Red launched into speech, but her face was deep in shadow. It was brighter out on the footpath – he'd be able to see her mouth there. And her hands.

'Move onto the street,' he said. 'It's too dark in here.'

She shook her head and pressed herself against the wall.

Well, he wasn't waiting around for someone to walk up behind him with an iron bar.

'OK,' he said. 'Find yourself another mark.'

He turned away, and she darted forward and grabbed his arm. Her trembling hand was slick with sweat. Impossible to fake that kind of fear. Or for him to feel like more of an arsehole. She was gesturing urgently, pressing her hands together and pulling them towards herself. A familiar movement, as though she was signing the word 'help'.

'You know Auslan?' he signed.

Red stared at him as though he'd performed a circus trick. Not a signer, then, just someone who'd learned a word. Which meant she probably knew more about him than his name and address.

'Help?' he said out loud. 'You need help?'

A rapid nod. 'I... and... said you'd help.'

'Who said I'd help?'

'...and... you...'

This was hopeless; he'd have to get her to write everything. He reached for his phone, but his hand dug into the empty pocket of his running shorts. Shit: no phone. Just him and his stupid desire to be alone when he ran.

'Have you got a phone?' he asked. 'Something to write with?'

She shook her head and attempted another sign. It was the wrong hand-shape, but it looked a lot like...

'Do that again,' he said.

Two fingers against two fingers, a twist of her wrists: 'family'.

Family? A brother he barely knew and an almost-ex-wife avoiding him in Broome.

'Anton?' he asked. 'Kat?'

More headshaking, more incomprehensible speech. Something about bees? No, that couldn't be right.

He tried for a gentle tone. 'Look, I can't understand you. My flat's around the corner. Do you want to go there? Or I can take you to the cops.'

Her eyes widened, staring behind him. He spun around. A man was pounding up the alleyway towards them. Thickset, with short, blond hair and a dark swirl of tattoos up his arms and neck. Caleb threw himself backwards and caught the edge of the blow on his forehead. Falling.

Down on his knees, head to the cobblestones. Up, get up. He levered himself to his feet. The man was dragging Red away, his arm locked around her neck. No thought, just motion: five steps and a fist to the man's kidney. Caleb's knuckles hit solid muscle. The man staggered and dropped Red, swung around. A calculating look as he took in Caleb's equal height but lack of kilos. His fist clenched. Caleb ducked the punch with reflexes born of a thousand playground fights. Quick, go for the kneecap. An awkward movement, mistimed, but his foot hit the side of the man's knee with a sickening jolt. Down like a felled tree.

Red. Where was Red? Caleb sprinted to the street. There she was, running towards Alexandra Parade. Good, there'd be people, lights, cars. He ran after her. Fitzroy Police Station was only a few blocks away – he'd get her there and work out what the fuck was going on. She was at the intersection, scanning for a break in the traffic.

'Stop,' he called, nearly at her side. 'It's safe here.'

Her head whipped around and she stepped back, her eyes focused behind him again. Shit, the blond man was only metres away, charging past him towards Red. She threw up her arms and stumbled backwards off the kerb.

Caleb lunged for her.

A fleeting touch of skin, then a flash of white, the smell of diesel and brake pads. She slammed against the van's bonnet. Into the air. Down.

An endless moment.

People were running. And he ran, too. Red was sprawled on the road, her arms flung wide. Blood. Blood everywhere. Bubbling from her lips and darkening her dress.

He'd been here before, seen the spreading pool, smelled its iron sweetness.

Her lips were moving.

'…the be… got the be…'

He made himself touch her cheek. Cold beneath the slick warmth of her blood.

'It's OK. Help's coming.'

Her eyes held his: sea green and rimmed with pale lashes. A fierce brightness that flickered, dulled and faded.

Then nothing.

2.

He made his statement in a soulless grey room at the Fitzroy Police Station. Eyes gritty, a dull ache squeezing his temples. The young policewoman questioning him was a hard read, with rigid lips and a tight jaw. She wasn't too impressed by him, either. She'd been through his statement twice now, querying each sentence, her eyebrows drawing together at his answers. He didn't blame her for her wariness. His image in the two-way mirror looked like it should be on a wanted poster: hollow-cheeked and unshaven, a wildness to his dark hair and eyes. Probably slurring his words too, exhaustion stripping all those years of speech therapy from his tongue.

He was going through the events for the third time when the constable stood without warning. A moment of confusion until she strode to the door. Right, someone knocking. Hopefully someone with a couple of painkillers.

It was a large man with granite-like features and close-cropped hair. Uri Tedesco: friend, life-saver, cop. Caleb had texted him from the station's sticky-handled public phone to explain why he'd stood him up for Friday night drinks, but hadn't asked him to come. A flash of anger that the big man had assumed he'd need help.

Tedesco shot him an unreadable look, then spoke to the

constable. The pair of them batted words back and forth, too fast for him to catch. Conversational ping-pong – his least favourite sport. He stared at the table until Tedesco waved to get his attention and said, 'You're right to go.'

The young cop wasn't looking too happy, but homicide detective trumped constable every time. Particularly a homicide cop who'd had the temerity to kill a bent colleague and stay in the job. Caleb gave her a nod and followed Tedesco through the station.

Outside, the air was like a sick dog's breath.

'You didn't have to come,' Caleb said.

Tedesco's gaze flicked across his bloodied running clothes. 'I was out of beer. Figured there'd be some at your place.'

———

Caleb showered while Tedesco got started on a beer. A long shower, with plenty of soap. He dressed and hunted for his hearing aids, finally found them under a book in the bedroom. They were small and pale, almost invisible beneath his dark hair. They amplified every unwanted sound and only gave hints of speech, had to be cleaned and replaced and adjusted and paid for. But without them there was nothing – no faint words or murmuring tones, just gaping mouths and guesswork. He never wore them on a run. Never took his phone or his notebook or even a fucking pen. Would Red still be alive if he did? Maybe. Probably.

Tedesco was out on the apartment's shitty balcony,

halfway through a stubby of Boag's. Caleb slumped into a chair and opened a beer.

'Not your year,' the detective said.

'No.'

Seven months since he'd stumbled blindly into an investigation that had ended with his best mate murdered and Kat badly injured. Since his business partner had betrayed him. Understatement was one of Tedesco's stronger suits. Caleb took a long drink, then put the bottle down. Enough. People having very bad years didn't have the luxury of drowning their sorrows, not if they wanted some semblance of a life.

A sudden realisation that it was January and the new year had begun. God.

Caleb nudged the bottle further away. 'What did you find out?'

Tedesco paused, probably consulting his inner censor. 'Not much. No handbag or ID. And no one's reported her missing.'

'She had a handbag. I told them. Did they look for it?'

'Nah, just shrugged and went home.' Tedesco drained his beer and set the bottle on the table. 'You definitely didn't know her? Not an old neighbour or something?'

'No.' He had a fierce memory for faces, but he'd never seen hers. Not in the street or in a shop, not even in a photo. Which meant she wasn't a local.

His phone buzzed in his back pocket. A message from Kat.

—*I've checked. No one thinks they know her. You OK? x K*

Damn. He'd gone straight to his phone when he got home. Standing in the entrance hall, hands still crusted with blood. It hadn't taken long: one text to his brother, Anton, in Resurrection Bay, and one to Kat. A description of Red and a bloodless version of her death, a plea for them to tell him if they'd sent her. Neither of them had. Kat's ring-around of her family in the Bay had been his last hope.

He resisted the temptation to prolong the exchange, and sent a quick reply.

—*Thanks heaps. All good. x C*

Tedesco waved. 'Any joy?'

Only the sight of that 'x'. A sympathy kiss, but a kiss nonetheless.

He shook his head, and Tedesco reached for a second beer. 'Guess that's that, then.'

Caleb roused himself. In the seven months he'd known Tedesco, he'd discovered that the man wasn't a big talker, sharer of secrets or believer in late nights. Caleb probably had one more beer and four more questions before the detective took himself home to bed.

'Have they got any leads on the guy who was chasing her?' Caleb asked.

Tedesco paused for another ethics committee meeting. 'No. No one else noticed him. They'll get her picture onto the news and do another doorknock tomorrow, see if they can jog anyone's memory.'

'That's it? A doorknock and a photo?'

'More than usual for a traffic accident.'

'It wasn't an accident.'

'Mate, half a dozen witnesses, one of them a QC, saw her step in front of that van.'

'So Red just decided to play with traffic on a whim? Her

death's got nothing to do with the big bloke chasing her?'

'Red?'

'Better than Jane Doe.'

Tedesco's grey eyes fixed on him. The detective was only a couple of years older than Caleb's thirty-one, but his Sphinx-like expression was aeons old. 'You're a country boy, you ever raise an orphaned animal?'

'I lived in town,' Caleb said. 'The only thing I raised was a rabbit.'

'I was eight the first time I did it. A spring lamb. He slept in my room so I could feed him. Did a good job of fattening him up, too. I called him Toby.' Tedesco tilted his head. 'Reckon you can guess how that story ends.'

Caleb stayed silent.

Tedesco drained his beer to the last couple of inches. 'Let it go, mate. It was a shitty experience, but the more I hear about it, the more I think you were just a mark.'

Tell him about today's break-in? The possible break-in, possibly today. A loose grip on time and specifics these days. There was no proof that anyone had been in his flat, just a bathroom door left ajar, a sense of stale air disturbed. He'd had the same feeling a few times over the past couple of weeks.

'She knew my name,' he said. 'Knew some signs.'

Tedesco lifted a shoulder. 'Good groundwork on her part. And everyone knows one or two signs.'

Not the people he met. A scant few people in his life knew any Auslan, and only two of them were fluent. His parents hadn't learned a word.

'You don't,' he said.

Tedesco smiled, the look of a smug student catching

11

a teacher in a mistake. He circled a fist in front of his face and then formed a diamond with his thumbs and forefingers.

Caleb choked on a laugh. 'Jesus, where'd you learn that?'

The smirk slipped from Tedesco's face. 'What? Why?'

Ant, it had to be Ant. Who except Caleb's brother would have taught a member of the force to call himself a pig's cunt?

'First lesson.' Caleb slid two fingers across his forearm. 'That's the sign for "cop". Second lesson, don't trust Ant. What were you trying to say?'

'That I –' Tedesco coughed. 'Never mind.' He finished his beer and stood. 'Bedtime.'

Caleb checked the time: 12.14 a.m. Long, long hours to go before dawn. Be a bit pathetic to beg Tedesco to stay and keep the monsters at bay.

He walked the detective to the door and paused with it half open. Red had known she was dying. That look in her eyes: desperation and pain, terror. He'd seen that look before. The memory of it lurked just beneath his thoughts, leaching to the surface in unguarded moments.

'Can you tell me if you find out her name?' he asked.

Tedesco shook his head. 'As my mum'd say – that'd just end in tears and a nice Sunday roast.' He slapped Caleb on the shoulder. 'Take care of yourself. And tell your shit of a brother to watch his back.'

Caleb wandered into the living room. He'd caught Tedesco's quick frown at his surroundings as they'd walked to the door. It was hard not to see the place through the man's clinical gaze: the hand-me-down orange furniture and un-vacuumed carpet, the patchy coat of white paint that Caleb had slapped on the walls in a burst of 3 a.m. energy. The thick layer of dust. Only the neat filing cabinets and organised desk saved it from being a hovel, and they didn't lend much to the ambience.

Trust Works had been shaky in the months after Frankie's betrayal, with no new clients coming in and plenty of old ones leaving. For some reason companies seemed reluctant to hire a fraud investigator whose business partner had been a lying, drug-addicted criminal. So he'd given up the shiny office and set up in the flat, taken on more quick-turnaround work: background checks and due diligence cases. Jobs that required hours in front of the computer and minimal human contact. Jobs he could do alone. Nothing was lined up for the next few days, though. Just him in the flat with the endless, empty hours.

A familiar darkness uncurled and stretched, ran its well-honed claws down his skull.

Move. Keep moving. He could outrun it if he pushed himself hard enough.

He was doing up his runners when he remembered the piece of paper he'd shoved in his pocket. Red had written his name on some kind of receipt. It could have her credit card details. He picked though the kitchen bin, found his blood-stained shorts beneath the banana skins and coffee grounds. He pulled out the receipt and turned it over. Only a cash payment for a train ticket, but written at the top was the station of origin – Resurrection Bay.

3.

Caleb exited the trees and shielded his face against the glare. The township of Resurrection Bay lay before him: silver roofs wedged between blue-green sea and bush, a dark metastasis of pine plantations spreading towards the west. A feeling of relief at the sight of it. Not his usual response to trips back home, but the air conditioner in his ancient Commodore had given out a few kilometres into the three-and-a-half hour drive. He'd fiddled with the temperature gauge, thumped the dashboard, then, skill set exhausted, wound down the windows. Nine a.m. and sweat was pooling in places that were better left dry.

He checked the fire danger sign as he took the turn-off into town, a fan of warm-hued warnings that ranged from 'moderate' to 'code red'. The needle was set to 'severe', two down from the worst rating. He sped through the outlying strip of struggling hardware stores and empty car yards. The tyre shop had closed since his last visit a couple of months ago, but the fried chicken franchise was still there, rebranded. He double-checked the name in the rear-view mirror: Alaskan Rooster. Was Alaska known for its fried chicken? If so, the Bay's inhabitants were yet to catch on.

He drove straight to his old family home, now his brother's place. Despite Ant's recent burst of home pride, the garden had succumbed to the heat, with a lawn that was more dirt than grass, and wilting silver birches. The house itself was unchanged: a two-storey blond-brick built by their father. There wasn't a room in the place that Ivan Zelic hadn't plastered and perfected. He'd recarpeted the master bedroom only months before his death four years ago, never mind the terminal prognosis or that his wife had been dead for a decade.

'If your best isn't good enough, try harder.'

It was cooler inside the house, the temperature of a low-to-moderate oven. Caleb dumped his overnight bag in the entrance hall and went through the usual check. No reason to think Ant was using again, but old habits die hard. There was washing powder in the laundry, food in the fridge, a new couch and coffee table. Everything was clean, far cleaner than his own place. No missing electrical goods or furniture. Their mother's old piano was still there, its curlicued paws standing on a dust-free floor. He'd spent hours beneath its keyboard when he was young, the rhythms vibrating through him as she played. He laid a hand on its flank and pressed a low note, felt it purr against his palm. Moving on, things to look at, places to snoop. Upstairs into Ant's room. Messy, but clean. None of the detritus that used to be scattered around Ant's lair like the bones of small animals – syringe caps and burnt spoons, scraps of tinfoil and cottonwool.

A moment to acknowledge the deep fucking relief, then he headed for the car. A town of three thousand – someone had to know Red.

He started near the railway station. The station itself had been unstaffed for years, but with a bit of luck he'd find someone in a nearby house who'd seen Red. With a lot of luck they'd know her name. He made his way slowly down the block, armed with the artist's impression that he'd screen-grabbed from the online news. There were a lot of doorbells and locked security doors. Since when had people started locking their doors around here? Not too enthusiastic about the trend. Waiting on the doorstep with the sun evaporating his blood, no idea if the bell was working or not.

He was missing a lot of words, too. People mumbling and chewing gum, leaving nothing but their intonation and expression to guide him. He'd turned up the volume on his aids, but no amount of amplification could make muttered sounds clear. It was good practise for him. He'd become slack working with Frankie, relied on her too much to fill in the gaps. Relied on her company too much, as well. Her snarky remarks and dark sense of humour. Her ability to see when he was flagging and give him a swift kick up the arse.

He stopped to wipe the sweat from his forehead and felt the ant-crawl sensation of someone watching him. A quick check revealed a kid doing wheelies on a BMX bike, and a mother dragging a screaming toddler along the footpath. Just twitchy. The streets of his childhood making him slip into old habits, a fist-clenching readiness born of long walks home from the school bus. He'd been the only local kid getting off that particular bus, the words 'Special

School' acting like bait to those with a scent for blood.

He headed down the hill towards the shopping strip that ran along the bay, a mismatched collection of bluestone terraces and 1970s bland boxes. There was a hard glare and the stink of rotten seaweed coming off the sand. He turned the corner into Bay Road and stopped: police tape was strung across the footpath, blocking his way. He detoured onto the road. Emergency hoarding covered the newsagents' windows, and two men were installing new glass in Dreamtime Crafts a few doors down – inside was a mess of splintered wood and broken pottery. A car crash? Hard to see how it could have involved two shops that were metres apart.

A flash of movement in the corner of his eye. An elderly man had come up behind him and was obviously under the impression they were having a conversation. He was pink-skinned and short, wearing summer pyjamas and a fetching Panama hat.

'…don't you think?' Pyjamas said.

'Sorry, what?'

'I said that it's a bloody shame. Where am I gunna get my papers now?' Each word was a hard little nugget squeezed through cat's bum lips. An easy read, but not a pleasant one.

'Do you know what happened?'

'Kids mucken about, they say.'

'Kids? Kids did all that?'

'Teenagers,' Pyjamas said. 'Should lock 'em all up.'

That seemed a little excessive, but who was Caleb to argue? He pulled out Red's picture and went through the motions.

Pyjamas shook his head. 'What's the girl done to her hair?'

Caleb stopped with the picture halfway back to his pocket. 'You mean you know her?'

'Of course. It's... What's the girl done to herself? Used to have lovely long blonde hair. Looks like a bloody dyke now.'

Blonde, of course. Red's hair had been far too dark for her fair skin and eyebrows. And that hacked style – all the hallmarks of a home-done cut. Not the sort of thing he'd usually miss, but he seemed to be functioning on low-power mode lately. No wonder no one had recognised her. People didn't look at faces, they looked at markers: the man with the beard, the girl with the glasses. The woman with the long blonde hair.

'What did you say her name was?'

The cat's bum squeezed out two syllables, possibly beginning with P. Or M. Or B.

'Sorry, what?'

'Mmmmma.'

Was that 'Paula'? Or maybe 'Mona'? Shit. A strong suspicion that admitting defeat was going to send this conversation down a long and circuitous path.

He pulled out his notebook. 'And how do you spell that?'

'I dunno, like that car she drives, I guess.'

A two-syllable name like a car. Mazda, Holden, Camry. Ah, Portia.

'Portia?'

'Yeah. Weird bloody name if you ask me.'

'How do you know her?'

'That greenie group of hers was hangin' around all last week, planting trees next door. Woke me up with their damn truck so I gave her a piece of me mind. Huffy little thing. Not a bad looker, though.'

'They're an eco group?'

'Nah, Australian. Most of them, anyway. Couple of 'em are pretty dark, might be foreigners. Not fussy either – got a few Abos workin' for them, too.'

Caleb took a moment. 'What do you know about Portia?'

'Oh, she's as white as white that one. No tar brush in that family.'

A shower after this, some antibacterial wash.

'Her surname?'

'Herst, I think.'

Hirst? Hearst? Hurst? He wasn't going to ask.

'Any idea where she lives?'

'Seen her goin' into the old mansion by the river. Lots of money, probably Jews.'

4.

The mansion stood on a small rise overlooking Red Water Creek. A gracious bluestone with wide verandas, the place had stood empty throughout Caleb's childhood, but someone had put some serious money into it recently. It had a new slate roof and iron lacework, and was surrounded by a lush garden that was a shock of green in the hard afternoon light. The plaque next to the wrought-iron gate read: *Hirst*.

Caleb parked outside and detoured to a towering river red gum that stood on the banks of the creek. One of the few scar trees still standing in the area. Its bark was a smooth, dappled white. An ovoid section showed dark against the pale trunk, taller than him and an arm-span wide: the mark where Kat's ancestors had cut away the makings of a canoe centuries ago. 'Old fella,' she'd said when they'd come across it in one of their hormone-fuelled walks as teenagers in search of privacy. Not a random route, he now suspected – she'd been guiding the gubba boy through her history, watching how he placed his oversized feet.

She'd been gone for four months now, had left just as he'd begun to see glimpses of her old self. She'd been hurt because of him. Tortured. Her arm cut and fingers broken, her blood flowing from her veins and pooling on a dusty warehouse floor. All while he'd stood and watched, helpless. But for some unfathomable reason, she didn't seem to blame him. They'd spent the three months after the attack slowly feeling their way back through the ruins of their past, not quite coming together, but inching closer. And then she'd left. A phone call from a friend, the suggestion of a road trip, and she was gone, leaving him reeling. She sent him chatty emails now, their Friday night arrival so regular that it spoke of a note in her diary. She never mentioned the things he was desperate to know but couldn't bring himself to ask: if her hand still hurt, if she could sculpt yet, if there was any chance for the two of them.

He pressed his palm against the tree, then headed for the house.

A discreet black intercom was set into the bluestone column beside the gate. Intercoms – even worse than doorbells. He pressed the button and waited. Pressed it again. The front door opened and a man in his mid-sixties looked out. Steel-grey hair and rimless glasses, dressed in a neatly ironed shirt and beige slacks. He gave Caleb a thorough up and down, assessing his clothes and income, his threat level. Caleb smiled and waved, added a little stoop for good measure. Too much? No, the man was heading over.

He reached the gate and gave Caleb another examination – eye to eye, but somehow looking down his nose. The short walk had left him slightly breathless.

'Isn't the intercom working?' he asked.

'I'm not sure. I'm looking for someone who knows Portia Hirst.'

21

A nano-expression crossed the man's face. Anger? Fear?

'I'm her father. Dean Hirst. What do you want?'

A flutter of panic: Caleb hadn't thought past confirming Portia's identity. He wasn't the person to be telling a father his daughter was dead. That was a job for the police, counsellors, a priest.

'My name's Caleb Zelic. I've just got a few questions about Portia.'

He passed his business card through the gate. People usually relaxed when they saw it, trust gained by a sans serif font.

Hirst frowned. 'You'd better come in.'

———

The house was cool inside, and smelled of wax and money. Hirst led Caleb to a small study that looked like an upmarket funeral parlour. The walls were built for artwork, but there was only one painting: Hirst and a younger woman with a teenage boy and toddler, none of them smiling. An echo of Portia in the woman's mouth and green eyes.

Hirst gestured to a chesterfield in a dark corner, but Caleb headed for a pair of stiff-backed chairs by the window. Hirst hesitated then followed, his breathing laboured. He obviously needed the Ventolin inhaler that was in his front pocket, its outline clearly visible, but he wasn't going to use it in front of Caleb. The type of man who associated physical weakness with a moral one. This was going to be a fun conversation.

'What's this all about?' Hirst asked. 'Why are you interested in Portia?'

That was a question best answered with a half-truth.

'She came to see me in Melbourne last night. I think she might be connected to a case I'm working on.'

'Who was she with?'

An odd thing to ask.

'No one.'

'Why did she come to you?'

So Hirst had let him in to quiz him about Portia. And not very subtly. This was a man used to asking direct questions and getting direct answers. Interesting speech patterns, too. Perfectly formed consonants one minute, flattened the next: the framework of a poor childhood showing beneath a thin veneer of sophistication.

'I don't know,' Caleb said slowly. 'We didn't get a chance to speak. Did she talk to you before she left town?'

Hirst lifted a hand. 'I haven't seen her for days.'

'She's been missing?'

'She's flighty. Changes degrees at the drop of a hat, changes jobs, changes homes. Running off for a couple of days is hardly something to be concerned about.'

And yet he'd let Caleb in to question him.

'Is Portia's mother around?'

'We're divorced, she's...' Hirst's words were lost as he pulled out his phone and frowned at the screen. He was already moving on from their conversation: things to do, people to intimidate.

'Sorry,' Caleb said, 'could you say that again?'

An irritated glance. 'She lives in Adelaide.'

'Does Portia work? Study?'

'She runs around planting trees and...' Another downwards glance.

'Sorry, can you look at me when you speak?'

Another flash of emotion crossed Hirst's face, this one easy to identify – anger.

'I beg your pardon?'

Frankie's first rule of interviews: don't piss off the subject.

Caleb took a breath and said the words. 'I'm deaf. I need to see your face when you talk.'

Hirst looked at him blankly, then leaned back in his chair. Caleb had the strong impression that his threat level had just been downgraded from 'moderate' to 'non-existent'.

'Ah well,' Hirst said. 'These things are sent to try us.'

Good to know.

Caleb pulled out his notebook. 'Can you give me a list of Portia's close friends?'

'I doubt she has any – she's only been here five months.'

'Where'd she move from?'

'Adelaide.'

'Why the move?'

'I beg your pardon?'

'It's unusual, a woman of her age moving from a city to a small town. Why the decision to move?'

Hirst didn't answer.

Caleb waited him out. Most hearing people panicked when they were dropped into silence, throwing words like grappling hooks to pull themselves out. He'd only met a handful of hearies who could last more than five seconds. Hirst lasted seven.

'Boyfriend troubles,' he said, the words strangled.

It was a long way to come to get away from a boyfriend,

around six hundred kilometres. Could the blond man in the alley have been Portia's boyfriend? The old, familiar story of misplaced trust?

'Well, if that's all.' Hirst stood, brushing off the legs of his pants.

'Sure. I'll just take a quick look at Portia's room and get out of your way.'

'I have to get back to work.'

Caleb tried the silence trick again, was rewarded after five seconds.

———

Hirst stood in the doorway while Caleb examined Portia's bedroom. It wasn't what he'd expected from her clothing – no Tibetan prayer flags or smell of incense, just plain white walls and a cream bedspread. The only decoration was a small photo of Portia as a ten-year-old, with an older version of the boy from the downstairs portrait. A handful of textbooks were arranged alphabetically on the desk next to it: *Economics and You, Journalism and Marketing, The Smart Way to Sell.* He flicked through them – words so dry they sucked the moisture from his eyeballs. No computer. Nothing much in the desk drawers, just pens and paper, a Myki public transport card. He picked it up. The receipt Portia had written his name and address on had been for a Myki card payment. So whose card had she used if hers was sitting in a drawer? And why had she caught a train? There couldn't be too many Porsche owners in the world who'd choose a four-hour trip in a crammed train over driving their car.

He turned to Hirst. 'Is her car here?'

'No.'

'It's a Porsche?'

Hirst's mouth thinned. 'Her idea of a joke.'

'Red?'

'White.'

There was more white in the wardrobe. Shirts separated from skirts, separated from dresses, all in white, beige and cream. Not a glimpse of loose-weave cotton anywhere.

'Finished,' Hirst said when Caleb closed the wardrobe door. It wasn't a question.

Caleb followed him to the front door but paused on the step. 'Where did Portia learn sign language?'

'Sign language? I have no idea.'

'Not from you?'

'Of course not.' Hirst closed the door.

Caleb drove the four blocks to Ant's place with the fan on full and the windows down, and arrived in a puddle of hot-stink ooze. Inside, straight into the shower. He turned the water to cold and closed his eyes. That was that. An unsettling twenty-four hours, but he'd discovered who Portia was. She could be buried by her family now, and mourned by people who actually knew her. It didn't matter who'd lent her the train card or the red dress. It didn't matter who'd sent her to him. It didn't matter that he'd seen the light in her eyes flicker and dull to nothing. He'd tell the cops what he knew and get on with his life. With something, anyway.

He was dressing, still damp, when the overhead lights began to flash: someone ringing the doorbell. He opened the door to a woman in her mid-thirties. She had the look of a salesperson about her, with mussed brown hair and a cheap pantsuit, a black briefcase that looked as though it had come free with a budget laptop. Putting her money into the late-model silver Volvo that was parked on the road.

'Hi, I'm...'

Damn, his aids were still in the bathroom; this would be a short conversation.

'Sorry, I'm not interested.'

'No, no.' An expensive smile that matched the car, not the suit. It didn't quite reach her eyes. 'I'm...'

An awkward moment as she juggled her mobile phone and briefcase, then she held out her hand. She had an unexpectedly firm grip. A waft of perfume, something sweet and cloying – jasmine.

She pressed her phone to his chest.

Fire

Pain

Falling

5.

On the floor, muscles spasming. A gasping breath. And another. Jasmine was standing over him, watching him writhe. A man was there too, a bit older, with a thin face and baggy eyes. He was going through the overnight pack Caleb had dumped by the front door.

Move. Get up. He managed to raise his head a few millimetres from the floor.

Baggy-eyes glanced at Caleb with disinterest. 'Nothing,' he said to Jasmine. He dropped the pack and headed down the hallway.

A waft of perfume as Jasmine knelt beside him, still holding her phone. No, not a phone: some kind of stun gun. A fucking powerful one.

She held it up. '...again... ?' An expressionless face and hard mouth.

He swallowed and tried to get his tongue to move. 'What?'

'Answer or... stun you again, OK?'

No, not OK. Not OK at all.

He nodded.

'...where... she... ?'

'What?'

Jasmine brought the phone closer.

'Wait. Can't. Hear.'

She touched the phone to his chest. Worse this time. A sledgehammer to his heart, ribs crushed and splintered. It took minutes for his brain to switch back on. Hours.

Baggy-eyes was back, looking at his watch. '...get a move on.'

Jasmine nodded and turned to Caleb. 'What did... and...?'

'Slower. Can't. Hear.'

No stun this time. They dragged him by his feet to the bathroom at the end of the hallway, his head bumping on the terracotta tiles. Water in the bath. Why was there water? Baggy-eyes hauled him to his knees in front of it and shoved his head down.

Water in his mouth and nose. Flailing panic. Air. He needed air.

And up. Coughing, dragging in ragged breaths.

Jasmine was standing next to him, talking. Asking more questions? He twisted towards her, but Baggy-eyes yanked his wrist up his back and pushed his head down again. Trying to brace himself, muscles like over-cooked pasta.

'Wait. Deaf.'

Underwater. Hadn't caught a proper breath. Chest aching, pressure building in his head. Getting darker.

And up. A fist in his hair, Jasmine turning his head towards her. She was kneeling beside him, her hazel eyes focused and unblinking; a terrible sense that she could do this for hours. '...she give you?'

What had Portia given him?

'Nothing,' he said. 'She wanted help, that's all.'

'What help?'

'Don't know. Didn't have time.'

'What did she give you?'

'Nothing.'

Jasmine nodded at Baggy-eyes.

'No. Wait.'

Baggy-eyes hauled him over the edge of the bath and into the water. Longer this time, lungs burning. He was going to inhale. Up again. Coughing, gagging, fire in his throat.

'Nothing,' he said quickly. 'Search the house. Nothing.'

A tiny nod – she believed him, thank fuck. They'd go now.

'...speak to?' she said.

'What?'

Baggy-eyes' grip tightened on his wrist.

'No, wait,' Caleb said. 'Say it again.'

Her eyes narrowed, but she repeated the words. 'Who else did she speak to?'

'Don't know. Didn't have time to talk. Don't know anything.'

'That's right... keep out of it. Understand?'

He nodded.

'...and no cops, or we'll be back... much worse... Understand?'

'Yes.'

'Good.' She patted his cheek and got to her feet.

They were going.

Baggy-eyes pressed his head towards the water. No. He pushed back. A knee in his spine, his wrist wrenched higher. And he was under. Much longer. Too long. Pain in his chest. Going to inhale, going to –

6.

He was lying on his side, coughing, retching. A small pool of vomit was on the floor in front of him. They'd gone. Get up, lock the door. He tried to stand, but his legs felt boneless. He gave up and crawled to the door, slid the bolt across. He leaned against it. Cold now, his teeth chattering, the sour stench of vomit on his clothes. Another smell, too – urine. Christ, Baggy-eyes had pissed on him. No, there was a dark stain at his crotch. He must have pissed himself when Jasmine stunned him. Jesus, fuck. Had they noticed? Laughed about it? He struggled to his feet, stripping off his clothes with thick fingers. Into the shower, the water as hot as he could handle. Hotter.

———

He toured the house, locking windows and doors that had never been locked. Signs of Baggy-eyes' prying were everywhere – half-open drawers and cupboards, a tipped vase – but there was no damage or wanton destruction. A nice change. People usually trashed his things when they searched them.

He retreated to the kitchen and hunted through the cupboards before remembering that Ant didn't drink alcohol these days. Tea, then. He switched on the kettle and found a dubious-looking box of tea bags at the back of a cupboard. A few moments to gather his thoughts, then he'd go to the police. He'd have no problems describing the pair. Every freckle and hair was etched in his mind.

'No cops, or we'll be back.'

Just scare tactics, he'd never been in any real danger. But his body hadn't quite got the message, his hand trembling as he poured the kettle. The tea bag rose limply to the surface, flotsam on a pale brown tide. Tea was Kat's drink, the correct blend required for every occasion, from heartache to joy. If she was here now, she'd insist on loose-leaf tea, add honey to soothe his tremors. An ache at the thought of her. Stupid. Should be thankful she wasn't here to witness his disintegration.

The overhead lights began to flash: someone ringing the doorbell. On his feet, heart thumping. He made his way slowly down the hallway to the front door. No spy-hole, no chain. His father had never felt the need for security, couldn't have imagined cowering behind a door, too afraid to open it. The lights stopped, then started again. Caleb grabbed the cast-iron doorstop and flung open the door.

Ant was standing on the front porch, wearing a grimed fluoro-orange jacket and overalls, a white helmet tucked under one arm; soot-streaked and sweating, his eyes more bloodshot than brown. 'Took you bloody long enough. What did you lock the door for?' He pushed past Caleb and dumped his helmet on the floor, switched to signing. 'What are you doing with the doorstop?'

'Ah, weights.' Caleb demonstrated with a couple of wobbly bicep curls. 'Why are you wearing a CFA uniform?'

'Because I'm in the CFA. We had a grassfire out on the highway.'

His little brother, a person consistent only in his unreliability, working as a volunteer fireman. That was going to take a little while for him to absorb.

Ant yanked off his gumboots, showering the tiles with dirt. 'You down for the weekend? You can help me paint the eaves. And the window frames. Actually, I need help pulling out that dead gum in the backyard, too.' He kept up a steady flow of Auslan as he stripped down to his shorts, a feat requiring Olympic-level flexibility and determination. He paused mid-sentence, his eyes on the floor. 'Why's the floor wet?'

The terracotta tiles were damp where Caleb had scrubbed them fifteen minutes ago. And a bit blotchy; probably shouldn't have used bleach. He'd have to remember that the next time he pissed himself.

'It'll dry soon,' Caleb said.

Ant gave him a long look. 'I'm going to shower. Grab me a Coke while you work out what you're going to tell me. Make it good – it's been as boring as batshit around here.'

———

Caleb took their drinks to the upstairs balcony and angled his chair towards the street. A good view from up here: rooftops and trees, a glimpse of the sea. No door-to-door salespeople driving silver Volvos. Not that Jasmine and her mate would use the same car again – they were too good for that. Their plan had been flawless. Jasmine coming to the door alone, the little dress-up act with the shitty suit and briefcase. The way she'd got him down and was inside the house within seconds, nothing to excite the neighbours, nothing to show the police except for a few blistering marks from the stun gun. Had to admire their style. No, he didn't. Didn't have to admire anything.

Ant appeared in the doorway wearing a lime green T-shirt and a purple sarong decorated with yellow butterflies. Caleb's own navy T-shirt and black shorts suddenly seemed funereal. 'Brave colour choice,' he said.

Ant dropped into a chair and opened his Coke. 'Not many people can get away with it.'

'Not any.'

Ant raised his can in salute. He'd filled out over the past two years, wiry now instead of skeletal, a summer tan hiding most of his old track marks. Something else different about him today, like one of those magazine spot-the-differences. Inappropriate clothing, check; relaxed sprawl, check; cigarette...

No cigarette.

'When'd you give up the smokes?'

'Five weeks ago.' Ant pushed up his sleeve to reveal a nicotine patch.

Ant had been a pack-a-day smoker since he was fifteen, clinging to the habit even after quitting smack and booze. Only one thing could have prompted him to give up now – sex. Or maybe not just sex, but something deeper. He'd been with his current girlfriend, Etty, for over a year now, a record for him. Caleb had initially assumed Etty was another of Ant's happy fuck friends, but since then he'd caught glimpses of a steely centre. And she seemed to be around a lot whenever Caleb visited.

'Etty asked you to give up?' he asked.

'No, but she's an ex-smoker, so I felt like an arsehole lighting up every two seconds in front of her. Bloody hard to give up, though – I keep reaching for my fags. Walking down the street, groping myself, mothers pulling their children away. I'm a mess.'

He didn't look a mess. He looked fit and happy, grinning with an easy charm that seemed to have skipped Caleb's genes and those of untold generations of Zelic men.

Ant drained his can and sat back. 'OK, spill. What's up?'

Caleb bought time by drinking his lukewarm tea. They'd barely spoken in the last few years of Ant's addiction. Their adult relationship was exactly seven months old: a rickety construction built on a few honest moments and a memory of childhood closeness. Hard to know what its load-bearing capacity was.

'C'mon.' Ant kicked the leg of Caleb's chair. Kept kicking.

It was probably worth telling him. Despite Ant's similarity to a kindergartener on red cordial, he knew everything that went on in town. And he wouldn't stop kicking the chair until he got what he wanted.

'A couple of people came to see me,' Caleb said. 'About the woman who died.'

He went through everything, doing a little light editing along the way: no need to mention the fear and helplessness. Or lying there in his own piss.

'Jesus,' Ant said when he'd finished. 'Trust you to poke a stick in a hole.' He scanned the street. 'You locked up again, right?'

35

'Yeah. But don't worry, they're hired hands – probably halfway back to Melbourne by now. And they're too professional to try the same trick twice.'

But confident enough to do it once. Park in front of the house and walk up to the door in broad daylight, no attempt to hide their faces from him or anyone else. Only people who were seriously connected – or stupid – would do that.

They weren't stupid.

Ant waved to get his attention. 'Why do you think they're from Melbourne? They could be locals.'

'Gut feeling. They were wearing suits, driving a nice car.'

Ant smoothed imaginary lapels. 'Some us have been known to suit up for court. Having stolen the nice car.'

True, but his vote was still on them being from the city.

'So who knows you're looking into her death?' Ant asked.

'Half the town by now, but Jasmine didn't know... She kept talking when I couldn't...' He coughed. 'She didn't know I'm deaf.'

'Shit.' Ant rubbed a hand across his face. 'Well, I guess that crosses off anyone who knows you – it's usually the first thing people say about you.'

Excellent.

Caleb finished his tea and wondered if one of Ant's nicotine patches would wake him up a bit. So tired. More than just ebbing adrenaline: as though his batteries had been drained.

'I found out Red's name,' he said. 'Portia Hirst. You know anything about her?'

Ant sat up. 'Portia? Shit, really? I thought you said she had dark hair.'

'She dyed it. So, you know her?'

'Only by sight. Met her father once. Did a bit of work on his place a few years back.'

'You robbed it?'

'*Work*.' Ant jabbed his arms into an X-shape. 'I *worked* on his place.'

Caleb could apologise. Or they could both accept the fact that Ant had stolen anything and everything during his decade-long addiction to heroin, and move on.

'What do you know about them?'

Ant shrugged. 'He's big money and likes you to know it in a quiet sort of way. Mr Alpha Male. He grew up here as a kid, moved back about five years ago to retire. Spent a squillion doing up that mansion of his.'

'And Portia?'

'She's an interesting one. Bit of a study in contrasts. Zipped around in a car that cost more than most houses around here, but she spent a lot of time on that conservation group of hers, too – Coast Care. Planting trees and stuff. Bloody things curl up and die straight away. No talent for it whatsoever. Guess she was trying to impress the old man, but he's got his head so far up his arse I don't know how well that went. Actually I probably do, seeing as trying to live up to someone else's expectations is an unachievable and self-defeating goal.'

Caleb realised he was gaping and closed his mouth. 'Um, how do you know all that?'

'Mate, that cabinet downstairs isn't just filled with *your* school prizes.'

It mostly was, but that competition was for a different decade.

'I meant about Portia.'

'People tell me things. It's the sex appeal, you wouldn't understand.'

One of many things in life he didn't understand. His head dropped forward, then jerked upright. Sleep. Hours and hours of it. He looked at his watch: 3.48.

'Want your jarmies?' Ant said.

He pressed a hand to his chest. 'The stun gun fucked up my chi or something.'

'Toddle off then, have a little nanna nap.'

'We'll be back.'

He had to take his aids out to sleep. Anyone could come in. Break down the door with a sledgehammer and he'd be oblivious.

'No,' he said. 'I'm moving into a motel. I don't want to risk them coming back while you or Etty are in the house.'

'I thought you weren't worried about a return visit.'

'Just being cautious.'

Ant examined him, frowning. 'Yeah, OK, but stay here tonight, you look like shit. You'll sleep better if I'm keeping an ear out for you. I'll tell Etty not to come over.'

Be fucked if he was going to be babysat by his baby brother. His CFA-volunteering baby brother. He got to his feet; a long way up, the world a little unsteady once he was there.

'No, I'm off.'

'What? Now? Don't you want to stick around and heckle me about my clothing choices?'

'Next time. I've got to get to the cops.'

7.

He drove with the car doors locked and the windows open a bare crack. Just being cautious. He wiped the sweat from his forehead with the back of his arm – he might have to consider buying a car with working air-conditioning if he got any more cautious. A flash of white caught his eye as he passed the EezyWay service station: the low-slung shape of a high-priced sports car. He slowed and did a U-turn. A Porsche 911 was parked in front of the mechanic's bay. Hard to believe that there'd be two white Porsches in a place like the Bay.

He got out and crossed to the car. The front was staved in, the windscreen shattered. The rear window, too, a little unusual in a head-on collision. The driver's door opened after a brief tug of war. Deflated airbags hung like dead sea creatures. A scatter of broken glass across the seats. And something else. Something that didn't belong: small and grey, the size of rat shit. He picked one up – a shotgun pellet.

The mechanic's bay was a concrete cave of sweat and grease. Two mechanics were hard at work, an older man in the back corner and a young Koori bloke by the window. Caleb headed for the window. The mechanic was in his early twenties, with pale brown skin and dark hair. Jai Johnson, according to the embroidered name patch on his overalls. Excellent stuff, there should be more embroidering of names on clothing. Possibly a legal requirement for names like Jai, all air and no form.

Jai gave him a friendly grin. 'Hi, y'after a service?'

An idea, sudden genius. 'Do you do air conditioners?'

'Sure. Take about a week, maybe two depending on parts.'

A moment to pick up the pieces of his dashed hopes. 'Do you know anything about the Porsche out front?'

'Portia's car? Yeah. I'd save your money, mate, it's stuffed. I had to tow it here.'

'You know Portia?'

Jai shrugged. 'A bit.'

'When did she crash?'

'What do you mean?'

'Did it happen recently? A while ago?'

'Yesterday.'

'Do you know what time?'

Jai pulled an oily rag from his back pocket and wiped his hands. 'What's this about?'

'Portia's dad's worried about her. She didn't go home after the accident.'

Jai jerked back. 'Fuck, mate, I didn't do nothin' to her. Didn't even see her, she got a lift with a friend.'

'No one's suggesting you did anything. She was seen in Melbourne last night. I've just got a couple of questions, then I'll leave you alone.'

'I dunno.' Jai glanced towards the older mechanic. 'I've gotta get back to work.'

The man was watching them, thin-lipped.

'Jai's helping me out,' Caleb called to him. 'Just be a minute.' He turned back to Jai. 'What time did Portia crash?'

'Around one, I guess.'

According to the Myki receipt, Portia had been at the station by 4.12 p.m. Which meant that she'd got a lift into town, dyed her hair, changed her clothes and reached the station all in the space of about three hours.

'Do you know who she rang for a lift?'

'No.'

'Wild guess?'

'Dunno. I barely know her.' Jai glanced at his boss. 'Look, I'm sort of on probation here, mate. I've really gotta get back to work.'

'Last question – where did she crash?'

'Out on Snake Gully Road.'

It took Caleb a moment to place it: about ten kilometres west of town, the back road to the disused quarry. A strange place to be driving an expensive sports car.

'Where on Snake Gully?'

'Couple of kays down it,' Jai said, turning to the car.

Caleb pressed a business card into his hand. 'Text me if you think of anything else.'

Jai shoved it in his pocket and bent over the engine.

———

Caleb parked in front of the police station, bunker-grey with a neat garden of palms and pine bark. Its windows were too high to give occupants a view of Red Water Creek opposite. Then again, maybe the cops didn't want a daily reminder of how the creek got its name back in the 1840s. Twenty-three Koori women and children chased into the water by officers of the law; guns used, machetes, axes. A small massacre by local standards.

The twelve-year-old constable behind the front desk listened to Caleb's story without comment, then handed him a slew of forms to fill in. He retreated to a plastic chair in the empty waiting room and went through them. Always a pause when faced with the fourth question: marital status. Impossible to know which box to tick. Not divorced and yet not married – in a precarious third state, somewhere between inhalation and exhalation, wondering if the next breath would ever come.

He held his pen over the box. Left it blank.

———

He was eventually admitted into a dull grey interview room that contained a scratched plastic table and two chairs. It had to be deliberate, the soul-killing atmosphere of these places; no one could choose that shade of grey by accident.

The door opened as soon as he'd sat down, and a uniformed man holding a clipboard strode in. Pale and stocky, with a face like a farmer squinting into the sun. Caleb retrieved the memory from dusty vaults, added a few kilos, deducted some hair – on the football team with Ant before Ant had decided that his Saturday afternoons were better spent smoking dope. A name tag was pinned to the cop's shirt: Sergeant J. Ramsden. John Ramsden. This was off to a good start; maybe this name-tag thing was catching on.

'Zelic,' Ramsden read as he sat down. 'Any relationship to Anton?'

'Brother.'

Ramsden gave him a suspicious look. 'No, his brother's retarded.'

Frankie's second rule of dealing with cops: never smack one down when asking for help.

'He's deaf,' Caleb said. 'And that'd be me.'

'Deaf? Really? You sound normal.'

Frankie's first rule: never punch one.

'Do you need him here to help you?' Ramsden asked. 'Or can I just talk slowly?'

Caleb unclenched his jaw. 'Just sound normal.'

A hard stare for that. 'Tell me about this girl. Portia, is it?'

Caleb told him about Portia and Blondie; the smashed car and shotgun pellets. Ramsden asked for clarification as he spoke, noting each answer on his clipboard. Not a total fuck-knob then, just a partial one.

'Right,' the cop said, slipping his pen in his pocket. 'I'll let Melbourne know and send someone to talk to the father. Appreciate your help.' He was getting up, getting ready to leave.

Do it. Tell him the whole, humiliating truth.

'There's more,' Caleb said, then went quickly through Jasmine and Baggy-eyes' visit.

'They attacked you in your brother's house?' Ramsden

asked when he'd finished. 'That opens up a few possibilities, wouldn't you say?'

'No, Ant's clean. He's been clean for two years. And they were asking about Portia.'

'They mentioned her by name?'

'Yes. No. I mean, I don't know. I couldn't really understand...' Fuck.

Ramsden looked unimpressed. 'And it wasn't the man from the alley?'

'No.'

'You piss anyone off lately? Sleep with someone's wife?'

'No.'

'You got form?'

'No.'

'You sure about that? Seem to remember your name being mentioned. Not in a court summons?'

'Probably the newspaper. I was part of an investigation that –'

'Took down a bent cop. Yeah, I remember now. Your partner was dirty, wasn't she? Ex-cop. Frankie Reynolds, right?' Ramsden sat back in his chair, eyes narrowing. 'There were whispers that case was connected to a gun death we had down here last year. A man in the dunes over by Res Point. You know anything about that?'

Caleb stared at him. Fuck, fuck. How had anyone made that connection? No one was supposed to know about it. The desperate struggle, his face in the sand. The hard edge of the gun beneath him; grasping it, turning, pulling the trigger.

The spray of blood.

He swallowed. 'No.'

'You sure about that?'

'Yes.'

Ramsden waited just long enough to show his doubt.

It was an educational experience, talking to the police these days. A growing understanding of Ant's twitchiness whenever a cop walked past, and why some of their darker-skinned friends crossed the street.

'I'll get someone to take a formal statement. We'll give you a ring if we need anything else.'

'Text,' Caleb said. 'Don't ring.'

'What?'

'Text me, I can't...' He cleared his throat. 'I don't talk on the phone.'

'Bit precious, isn't it?'

'Bit deaf.'

A faint blush crept up Ramsden's broad face. 'Right. Well. Let us know if you see them again, or if you hear...' He coughed. 'If you, ah, discover anything else about Portia. In the meantime, I'll tell the boys to keep an eye out for your assailants.'

'Pulling out all the stops, then?'

Ramsden's shoulders slumped. And Caleb took in his out-of-season pallor, the stain of a long-ago meal on his shirtfront. Not just a dickhead – a tired dickhead at the end of a very long, possibly endless, day. A fleeting feeling of kinship.

'Mate,' Ramsden said, 'I don't want to be an arsehole, but we're a bit pushed around here. We've got meth-heads stabbing their loved ones, a pack of kids trying to start a race riot, and some dickhead burning down buildings in the middle of the hottest summer on record. A dunking in a bath doesn't really make my top ten. So if I were you, I'd pull my head in and start checking the door before you open it.'

Caleb met his bleary eyes. 'Noted.'

8.

The police station's waiting room was empty except for a
neatly dressed woman with grey-streaked black hair. Caleb
did a little double take. Maria Anderson was Resurrection
Bay's first Koori doctor, owner of the local medical clinic,
and his mother-in-law. A day of treating weeping wounds
and fractured limbs, and she looked as though she'd
stepped from the pages of a magazine. One titled *Modern
Amazon*, or *Powerhouse Weekly*. He'd been a bit scared of
Maria when he'd first started dating Kat. Still was. But
she'd slotted him into her family without hesitation, giving
him dishwashing duties and clear feedback whenever he
did anything stupid. His separation from Kat had put an
end to the dishwashing.

'Hi, Maria.'

'Caleb, I didn't realise you were in town.' Her once-over
made him want to spit-wash his clothes. 'Are you all right?'

He smoothed his T-shirt. 'Yeah, good. Just trying to
report a break-in.'

'Trying to?'

Damn. She had the homing instincts of a ballistic
missile.

'I was butting heads with Sergeant Ramsden a bit,' he
admitted.

He expected a rap across the knuckles, but she nodded. 'Ah, yes. I've had some experience of that myself.'

'Why? Has something happened?'

'We had some trouble at the clinic last night.'

Significant trouble if she was talking to the cops about it. As a community leader, Maria worked hard at maintaining a good relationship with the police, but it was a relationship weighed down by two hundred years of history.

'Are you OK?' he asked.

'Yes, quite all right, thank you.' She went to add something, but hesitated.

God, he hated it when she did that. Indecision from Maria was right up there with birds falling from the sky and plagues of locusts.

She glanced towards the desk and stood. 'They're calling my name. Do you need my assistance before I go?'

He stiffened.

Assistance.

'Assistance?' he asked.

'If you're having trouble dealing with the police.'

'Do *you* need assistance?'

She looked at him. 'Very possibly, but point taken. Take care of yourself, Caleb.' And she swept inside.

———

Sweat formed on his forehead as he walked outside. The sun was dipping towards the horizon, but the day refused to give up its heat. The few nearby pedestrians were moving with surprising quickness – stepping briskly across the road, clutching their bags to their chests. He stopped dead, scanning the area for danger, but there was no stun-gun-wielding couple, just a young woman striding down the footpath towards him. She was swinging her arms and ranting with the spit-mouthed aggression of someone on a bad meth high. He stepped off the footpath just in time for her to stagger past. She had sunken eyes and cheeks, pale skin like thawing chicken. He realised with a start that he knew her – Jen, or Jan, used to work at the IGA. Chatty, with a sweet smile that could appease the grumpiest shopper. Christ, she couldn't be more than twenty-three. He watched her go, along with everyone else on the street. No, not everyone: the kid across the road was looking at him instead. Around fifteen or sixteen, with sun-baked skin and a brown rat-tail, a black backpack dangling from the handlebars of his BMX bike. He was holding up his phone, directing it at Caleb. He caught Caleb looking at him, shoved the phone in his pocket and pedalled lazily away.

There'd been a kid hanging around on a BMX when he was doorknocking this morning. No big deal, every boy too young to drive rode a BMX around here. But not too many of them went around taking photos of strange men outside police stations.

Caleb ran to his car and followed.

———————

He lost Rat-tail when the kid ducked down a walkway near the foreshore, so he cruised slowly down Bay Road and up the next street. Early Saturday evening and people were sprawled on verandas and in front gardens, clutching beers and fanning themselves. A young bloke was getting the night off to a good start by vomiting outside the Trawler's Arms Hotel. And there was Rat-tail leaning his BMX against the pub's red-brick wall. He left the bike unlocked and walked into the Arms with a loose swagger and an even looser hold on his backpack, no backwards glance. That was a kid who'd never been jumped because he'd forgotten to check his blindspots. More than just cocky – a kid with some kind of protection.

Caleb gave it thirty seconds, then followed him inside. An icy chill to the air, the smell of ancient beer and sweat. He paused to let his eyes adjust to the darkness, the two lone windows and pallid downlights doing little to relieve the gloom. The place hadn't changed much since his own underage drinking days. It was a long, L-shaped room with bolted-down tables and a crowd of red-faced men. He glimpsed Rat-tail disappearing into the toilets and headed for the bar.

Kat's cousin Mick was serving: a barrel-chested man with deep brown skin and the words *FUCK COPS* tattooed across his knuckles. Going on fifty; fit, but with a stiff-kneed gait courtesy of twenty-five years on the local footy team. He looked oddly naked without his gaggle of young daughters hanging off him.

'Cal, mate.' Mick glanced at the ceiling spots and shifted into the light.

They shook hands, a quick choreography of thumb, hand, fingertips.

'Don't usually see you in here,' Mick said. 'You slummin' it?'

'Getting some local colour.'

'You calling me coloured?'

Once upon a time, that comment would have turned Caleb's bowels to water, but he'd realised years ago that Mick's tough exterior hid a soft and gooey heart.

He smiled queasily and settled on a bar stool. 'You see that kid who came in ahead of me? Ratty brown hair?'

'No, mate, never seen a kid in here. What with the strict liquor-licensing laws an' all.'

'By "kid", I mean a young man who is clearly over eighteen years of age.'

'Yeah,' Mick said. 'That'd be Luke. What's he done now?'

'Hard to say.'

Rat-tail Luke emerged from the toilets and headed to a table of equally underage mates. No backpack – interesting. Was it under the table, or had he given it to someone? Caleb stood up to check, and Luke looked across the room at him. Not the respectful gaze of a youngster greeting his elder, more an I'll-smash-a-glass-in-your-face look. Caleb sat back down.

Mick was smiling. 'Friendly little bugger, isn't he?'

'What do you know about him?'

'You drinking or what? Trying to fucken work here.'

'You got Boag's on tap?'

'Nah, VB. That do ya?'

Not in any known universe. 'Ah, yeah. Just a pot, thanks.'

A hint of a smirk was on Mick's face as he expertly pulled a beer. 'Luke's a Blundon, eldest of the three. Not the sharpest knife in the drawer. You see the damage on Bay Road?'

'That was him?'

'Him and his mates. Stole a car and rammed it into a couple shops. Haven't been charged with anything yet, but Luke's been braggin' about it all over town. Like I said, not too sharp.'

Caleb took a token sip of the VB. 'They drunk?'

'With it enough to remember which stores are run by blackfellas. It's the latest in a string of bullshit – busting windows and throwing rocks. Threw a fucken pig's head through Aunty Eileen's bedroom window last week. Not to mention the fire last night. Though the little cunts might not have done that, I suppose. Guess you've heard all this from Kat, though, hey?' Mick squinted at him, an expression reserved for the drunk and the hopeless, the irredeemably stupid. 'Or maybe not?'

Caleb avoided his eyes by taking a long drink of the VB.

'What's the story?' he asked when he came up for air. 'Did something set them off?'

Mick shrugged. 'Dogs need a reason to lick their balls?'

A philosophical question he'd never before pondered. 'Guess not.' He pulled Portia's photo from his pocket. 'You know this woman? She's usually got long blonde hair.'

Mick peered at it. 'She's the one with the car, yeah? Portia with the Porsche.'

'You didn't happen to send her to me, did you?'

'No, mate, never spoken to her in my life. Why? What's up?'

'Bit of a complicated case. You ever see Luke and his mates with her?'

'Nah, reckon she'd be out of their league.' Mick's

attention shot to someone behind Caleb: a look laser-focused and unforgiving.

Caleb turned. A familiar beer-gutted figure was weaving his way through the tables towards the door, a brown sports bag hooked over his shoulder: Dave McGregor. McGregor wasn't a standout in terms of local fuckwits, though he definitely made the team. He was a year older than Caleb, but signs of his boyhood self lingered in his slit-eyed expression, ready to beat fear into anyone unable to hit back. No reason to think he had Rat-tail's black backpack stuffed inside his sports bag – except for the unusual sight of a McGregor carrying anything other than a grievance.

McGregor headed out the doors. Caleb watched him through the window as he swaggered over to a beefed-up Holden ute parked by the kerb, its iridescent-green duco shining in the fading light. He took off in a cloud of burnt rubber.

Caleb turned back to Mick. 'Luke and his mates – they have anything to do with Dave McGregor?'

'Why d'you ask?'

'Dogs and balls.'

Mick laughed. 'Yeah, I dunno. I keep away from fuckwits like McGregor unless it's necessary.'

If McGregor had any sense of self-preservation, he'd keep it from being necessary. Of the two stints in jail that Mick had done in his early twenties, one had been for car theft and the other for a fight that had left a loud-mouthed bigot with a permanent limp. Since then he'd had the calming influences of age and fatherhood, but Caleb still wouldn't want to get between him and his loved ones.

Caleb stood, leaving the VB unfinished. 'I'm off. If you see Luke Blundon with anyone interesting, can you let me know?'

'Sure. You staying in town?'

A good question. He should probably go back to Melbourne and hunt for more work. Forget about Jasmine and Baggy-eyes. Forget about writhing on the floor in his own piss.

Forget about the light in Portia's eyes fading to nothing.

God, please yes. Please forget about that.

'Yeah,' he said. 'For a day or two. Give my love to Pauline and the kids.'

'Do it yourself, the house is all of ten metres from Ant's. And I stock Boag's.'

A pity offer. Hard to refuse, even harder to accept.

'Thanks, mate. Sounds good.'

9.

Caleb spent the next morning holed up at the Happy Rest Motel on the outskirts of town: a row of brown-brick units frequented by travelling salespeople and budget-conscious adulterers. It had static-producing beige carpet and a sagging mattress, walls the colour of morning urine. And good wi-fi.

He sat on the bed, his laptop irradiating his crotch, and trawled through the internet for any mention of Portia. She might not have had many friends in the Bay, but she'd had at least one – the owner of the red dress and Myki card. If he could find that person, he might be able to discover who Portia had been running from and why. *If* he could find her.

For a young woman, Portia had kept a low online profile. No blogs or vlogs or conveniently tagged photos of all her friends, just a couple of social media sites with private settings. A surge of hope when he found a newspaper photo of her with a group of people, but it was from her university days in Adelaide. A prize-giving ceremony, Portia the recipient of something called the Harrington Memorial Award. So she'd been an all-round high-achiever. It was a good photo. Portia and her teacher surrounded by a group of applauding students. She looked like a different person from the trembling woman he'd met in the alleyway: her smooth blonde hair falling to her shoulders, make-up carefully applied. But the spark in her eyes was the same. That fierce light he'd seen flicker and dull.

The breath caught in his throat.

He pushed the laptop onto the bed and stood. Time to get moving. Portia's crash site was only a ten-minute drive away; it wouldn't be too bad in the car if he kept the windows down.

A few kilometres out of town, his foot eased automatically on the accelerator. He could smell smoke. Around here was old-growth forest, no trucking tracks to use as an escape route. He glanced at his phone. No coverage either, which meant no fire alerts. Caught between native forest and the pine plantations up ahead. Hard to know which to fear most: the eucalypts exploding, or the conifers flaming like funeral pyres.

He turned the bend into sudden brightness as he entered a wide firebreak between the bush and pines. People in bright orange jumpsuits were standing guard over half a dozen neat bonfires, alert but not frantic. Just the CFA taking advantage of the still weather to do a late-season burn-off. The fuel load was heavier than usual this year, the undergrowth flourishing after a long, wet winter and then baking dry in the endless summer. He nudged the car faster.

Snake Gully Road was a dirt track hemmed by tall pines. Caleb drove slowly along it and stopped short of the 'couple of kays' that Jai had estimated for the scene of the crash. It was a heavy heat this far from the sea. A thick scent of pine needles mixed with baked earth. The trees grew close around here, their branches spreading to block the sky. No undergrowth, just a deep layer of needles smothering the ground. Kat hated the plantations, called them living graveyards. A not unreasonable response.

He found the crash site fifteen minutes down the track. A trail of red shotgun shells led to a larger cluster in the middle of the road. The tree Portia had crashed into was marked by a deep, pale gash. It was easy to imagine the scene: the gunman accelerating behind her, the blast of the shotgun, the rear window exploding. Portia slewing off the road and into the tree. How had she escaped? She would have been terrified. The shock of the crash, the shotgun blasting, hands trembling, scrambling to get away.

Pressure squeezed Caleb's chest.

He'd been facedown in the sand. The bullets missing him by inches. A dull thud as each one ploughed into the ground beside him. He'd crawled. Across the dunes towards the beach, breath rasping in his throat. Over the crest of the hill, searching desperately for a weapon. Then the shadow of the man falling across him, dark shape of the gun in his hand. Raising it towards Caleb. Aiming.

Stop.

He was in the pine forest, not on the beach. Get it the fuck together.

He wiped the sweat from his forehead and went to examine the cluster of shells in the middle of the road, his legs only a little wobbly. There were more pellet holes further into the forest, red shells scattered among the pine needles. So the gunman had followed Portia into the trees and then backed off. That was odd. Why not go in close and finish the job? Caleb followed the pellet marks into the forest and turned to look back at the road. There were large craters in the trees in front of him, half a dozen shotgun shells at his feet. Orange shells, not red. A moment for him to work it out. Two people shooting: one from the forest, the other from the road.

Portia had shot back.

He headed into town, a little faster this time, his mind clicking through possible scenarios. Good-deed-doing, sports-car-driving Portia standing in the middle of a pine forest, blasting away with a shotgun. Or, more likely, standing with someone else who was blasting away with a shotgun. But who? The friend who'd given her a lift? Maybe he should talk to her father again, see if he could jolt a name out of him. That'd be a good conversation.

'Sorry I didn't tell you that your daughter was dead. By the way, did she know anyone with a shotgun?'

This was where Frankie would come in handy. Thirty years on the force and a brain like a steel trap meant that she understood with instant clarity things that took him weeks to figure out. Things like, why would someone shoot at a young woman who planted trees for a hobby? And, why had Portia come to him for help? And, how could you be so wrong about a friend that it felt as though your guts had been ripped out? He could still feel the heart-stop of shock when he'd realised that Frankie had betrayed him. That she'd been working for bent cops the entire time he'd known her. That she'd handed Kat over to a killer. The fact that she'd come back to save him and Kat didn't wipe the slate clean, only blurred the lines of her treachery a little.

He ran past her house sometimes. The mail was always cleared, the lawn mown, but the lights were never on. He had a sense that she was keeping a hand on her past life in the hopes that she would return to it one day. And she probably would. She was too smart to have left any incriminating evidence, and the clearest accusation against her – murder – would topple to self-defence at the nudge of a good lawyer. Then again, the police were probably the least of Frankie's worries: she had a talent for making enemies.

Caleb exited the trees into the blazing sunlight of the firebreak. The CFA volunteers were still there, keeping close watch on their fires. And it hit him – there was no phone service out here. So how had Portia rung her friend for a lift? More to the point, how had she rung Jai Johnson for a tow?

10.

According to the bored young man Caleb bribed at the EezyWay service station, Jai lived in Bellville, the old mission settlement on the outskirts of town. Previous governments had herded the local and not-so-local Koori population into the Mish over the past two hundred years, but it was owned and run by the community now. Home to thirty or so families, it was a miniature suburb of small houses and wide, dusty roads, a few towering gum trees. It had been a dry area until a few years ago, kept alcohol, drug and problem-free by a band of fierce-eyed aunties. Alcohol was still banned, but even the aunties had been unable to stop the tide of methamphetamine flowing in from the town.

The streets were almost empty in the late afternoon sun, but a few kids were running under hoses in front yards, dogs circling their legs. There was freshly scrubbed graffiti on the community centre, a couple of boarded-up windows. It looked as though Rat-tail Luke and his mates had been at it here, too. Maybe as a warm-up for the destruction in town.

Jai's address turned out to be a grey fibro house set in a square of immaculate lawn: Aunty Eileen's house. Caleb had never been inside, but he knew the garden well. Eileen was the leader of the fierce-eyed aunties. She'd raised a couple of generations, and most of the local kids, black and white, had felt the sharp edge of her tongue. He'd only had one run-in with her, but it had been a memorable one. Fourteen and hanging around with a group of older kids in his failed bad-boy phase – apparently also his stupid phase – he'd gone along with the idea of 'borrowing' Aunty Eileen's car. She'd hauled the lot of them in off the street the next day and set them to work in her garden as punishment. Two weeks of it, height of summer. Even the toughest of them, Gerry Harrison – sixteen years old and already with a record – had put his head down and done the work without whingeing.

She probably wouldn't remember Caleb. Hopefully wouldn't.

The house had a security door, but no bell. He rattled the door and it opened.

'Hello?' He stuck his head inside. 'Jai?'

A dark shape hurtled down the hallway towards him, a glimpse of fangs and fur. Caleb slammed the door, which bowed as the beast hurled itself against the mesh. He stood back. The mesh might have been strong enough to stop most dogs, but that animal sure as fuck wasn't a normal dog.

A shadowy figure appeared in the doorway, and the thumping stopped.

'I'm looking for Jai,' Caleb said. The door didn't open. 'I can't hear you. Can you open the door?'

No, bad idea. That would remove the only barrier between himself and the animal.

The door swung open to reveal Jai and a muscled

brown dog. The animal was snarling up at Caleb, its thick chest heaving with each rhythmic bark. A moment to be thankful that he couldn't hear lower registers.

'What do you want?' Jai said. He was holding the dog's collar with a worryingly casual grip. No friendly grin this time.

'I've got a couple more questions about Portia.'

'Yeah? Well you didn't fucken tell me she was dead. Had to hear about it on the radio.'

'Yeah, sorry. Her father didn't know. I didn't want him finding out the wrong way.'

But Jai's attention had gone to something behind Caleb. The dog bared gums like slabs of liver. Caleb turned to see an old Hyundai driving past: under the speed limit, no passengers, nothing unusual.

Jai watched it turn the corner. 'Bit hot out here,' he said, his eyes still on the road. 'You'd better come in.'

Caleb stepped into the hallway, resisting the urge to cup his balls as the dog turned its dark wedge of a head towards him.

Jai caught his glance. 'Don't worry about Jaws, he won't hurt you while I'm here.' He considered his words. 'Just don't pat him.'

'Good tip.'

Caleb followed Jai through the house, staying well back from the dog's stiff tail.

It was hotter inside than out, the rising air trapped beneath a low ceiling. The walls were crammed with children's paintings and shelves of toys and handmade dolls. The dolls were the size of newborn babies, with dark woollen hair and skin of soft brown cotton. Some were new, others loved to fraying pieces. No sign of the children who'd played with them. Empty bedrooms to each side, no scattered toys or clothing, no rumpled beds.

Jai led him into the kitchen, a wide room with a cracked lino floor and ceiling-high cupboards. A folded blanket lay by the back door, an ice-cream container full of water by its side. Aunty Eileen was sitting at the formica table sewing something by hand, the electric fan by her elbow set to high. She had to be in her seventies by now, her cropped hair more white than grey. Soft folds of flesh spilled from her floral dress, but she'd obviously lost a lot of weight recently and her skin had the yellow tinge of long-term illness.

'Caleb about Portia,' Jai said by way of introduction. He clicked his fingers: Jaws padded to the blanket and lay down, but lost none of his alertness.

Aunty Eileen gave Caleb a benign smile. 'Have a seat, love. Make us a cup of tea, will you, Jai? Kettle's boiled.' Her acceptance of Caleb's presence was strangely casual, as though she'd been expecting him. 'Jai said you'd been around asking about Portia. Sad business that, surviving one car accident and dying in another.'

'They weren't accidents – she was being chased.'

Aunty Eileen examined him with eyes as dark as river stones. 'News reports didn't mention that. Not that it's got anything to do with my grandson. All he did was tow her car.'

Grandson. The word was a flag planted firmly in the ground. A bright red flag with a skull and crossbones.

'Dunno what it's got to do with you, either,' she said. 'Were you friends with her or something?'

'No.'

'Then why are you goin' around asking questions about her?'

Because she'd come to him. Because he'd seen the light in her eyes flicker and fade to nothing. Because if he crawled back to his flat now, he might never come out.

'I'm looking into it for her family.'

A ripple in Aunty Eileen's calm expression. 'Her poor father. The man's lost both kids now.'

Both kids. The family portrait in Hirst's empty mansion, Portia and the unsmiling teenage boy. God, how could you keep going?

Jai set a mug of tea in front of him. The visitor's cup. Plain white and pristine, it was a stark contrast to the lumpen handmade thing that Aunty Eileen cradled between her hands. She and Jai were sitting close together, mirroring each other's body language. A tight little pair. Caleb might be able to trip Jai up, but Aunty Eileen was a veteran of uncomfortable conversations. He'd have to go in hard.

'Tell me about the shotgun.'

Jai flinched. 'Shotgun? What shotgun?'

'Jai, I know you were in the car with Portia. I know you had a shotgun. And I know it'd take a forensics team five seconds to confirm all that. So tell me what happened.'

'I didn't, I haven't –'

Aunty Eileen put a hand on Jai's to silence him. This was it, she was going to kick Caleb out.

'What's your family name, love?' she asked him.

He blinked. 'Sorry, what?'

'Your surname. What is it?'

'Zelic.'

'Ah.' Her look of surprise was almost convincing. 'I knew your father way back when. He worked on the community centre for us. I was sorry to hear of his passing. His heart, was it?'

'Lungs.' All those years working with asbestos, the deadly fibres worming their way inside. There'd been a time when Caleb had worried that they might have wormed their way inside him, too.

'You married one of Maria Anderson's, didn't you?'

'Kat.'

A growing realisation that Aunty Eileen knew exactly who he was and where he slotted in. Probably knew who everyone in town was. At least, everyone who touched the lives of those around her.

'How d'you get on with Maria?' she said.

'We, ah, yeah, good.'

'Yeah? She scares the shit out of me. Smart woman, though.' She picked up her mug but didn't drink. 'She told me once that you're pretty sharp.'

That didn't sound like something Maria would say.

'Really?'

'Yeah, so sharp you were in danger of cutting yourself.'

That was more like it.

'She also said you're the stubbornest person she knows. Thought she'd taken out that prize years ago, so well done.' Aunty Eileen set her mug on the table: decision made, ready for action. 'Jai got himself into a bit of strife a while back. Bad strife. He's sorted himself out now, but he's on probation, can't afford to get involved with anything, even as a bystander. Cops aren't too fond of him.' She fixed

Caleb with her river-stone eyes. 'You understand what I'm saying, yeah?'

'Not too fond' could mean a lot of things when it came to the local cops' interactions with the Koori community, none of them good. In the past twenty years there had been two deaths in custody, a lot of late-night raids in the Mish, and some unexplained clumsiness involving Indigenous prisoners in the holding cells. A cocky, young Koori man with a record would have real reason to be nervous.

'I understand,' Caleb said.

'Good. So he'll tell you what happened, then you'll piss off and leave him alone, not mention his name to anyone, yeah?'

Caleb nodded.

Aunty Eileen angled her head towards her grandson. 'Go on, then.'

'Yeah, um.' Jai rubbed his hands on his jeans. 'I was with Portia when it happened. We were driving, coming home. Next thing I know, Portia's flooring the car, and I look around and see a motorbike right up our arse.'

A sinking feeling. 'What kind of motorbike?'

'A Harley.'

Bikies. Of course, because that was just what this shit sandwich needed to taste better. There was no local chapter, but the Geelong-based Copperheads were a regular presence in town, the yellow snake on their jackets glimpsed in pubs and on the street, sometimes outside the homes of people who suddenly found the ability to pay outstanding debts.

'There was this big bang,' Jai said, 'and we were going

off the road. Hit a tree. The guy kept shooting, glass flying everywhere. I thought we were goners, but then Portia pulls a fucken shotty from under her seat and starts firing back.'

'Portia had the shotty, not you?' Caleb tried to keep the disbelief from his tone.

'Yeah. You can ask her father if you don't believe me – it was her grandad's. He used to hunt with it.'

A believable explanation, and easily checked.

'OK. What happened then?'

'The guy took off and we walked back into town. Took forever.'

'Did you get a look at him? See his jacket?'

'Nah, I was too busy trying not to shit myself.'

'What did Portia say?'

'Nothing, just to tow the car and keep quiet about it.'

'Jai. You've been chased down and shot at, Portia's pulled out a shotty – you don't just stroll back into town without asking a few questions.'

'Mate, I fucken asked them, I'm just sayin' she didn't answer.'

Damn. An actual witness, but he knew almost less than Caleb.

He scratched around for a few more questions in the vain hope that he'd learn something. 'What were you doing out on Snake Gully Road?'

'Helping Portia with her trees. She's got – had one of her plantations out there. Roped me into digging holes.'

'Sounds like you knew her pretty well if you were helping her do all that.'

'We weren't sleeping together, if that's what you're

getting at.' Jai was sitting back in his chair now, his limbs relaxed, breathing even. If he'd been romantically involved with Portia, he was a sociopath with a great political career ahead of him.

'Was she sleeping with anyone?'

A shrug. 'I dunno. We weren't mates or nothin'. Portia pretty much kept to herself, y'know?'

None of this was sounding like the flighty young woman that Portia's father had described. Then again, families often held on to outdated images of their members: the father-of-three always a frightened preschooler to his big sister, the businesswoman forever a tantrum-throwing teenager to her mother.

'Did she ever mention a big, blond guy?'

'Nuh.'

Caleb grasped at his last straw. 'Did she have anything to do with Dave McGregor?'

'That cunt? Sorry, Nanna. I dunno, I doubt it.'

The whole conversation had raised more questions than it had answered.

He passed Jai another business card. 'Text me if you remember anything.' He got to his feet. 'Thanks, Aunty Eileen.'

'Pleasure, love. Come back anytime you feel like doin' some weeding.'

So she had remembered.

'See you out,' Jai said, standing up. Jaws padded to his side.

Caleb paused. The dog, the empty bedrooms, the clear sense that Jai was here on guard duty – things must be bad if Aunty Eileen felt the need for protection. And if Rat-tail

Luke had anything to do with it, she'd know all about him.

'Mick Anderson said you'd had a bit of trouble around here.'

Aunty Eileen gazed at him. 'Did he now? I wouldn't concern yourself about it, love.'

'Was it Luke Blundon and his mates?'

'It's...' Her words were lost as she lowered her head.

'Sorry, what was that?'

She looked up and focused on his right ear; he resisted the urge to check that his hair was still covering his aids.

'I forgot you have trouble hearing,' she said. 'You work hard at that, don't you? Why? Be easier just to tell people to speak up.'

Caleb kept his face blank. 'He said that Luke and his mates threw a pig's head through your window.'

Her dark eyes were unblinking. 'Just kids mucken about.'

'But why? Is someone putting them up to it?'

'Kids can be arseholes. Worse than adults, sometimes. You'd know that – you used to cop a bit of shit as a youngster. Must've been hard facing up to your father afterwards. He was a real man's man, wasn't he? No one ever got the better of him.'

It took Caleb a moment to get the words out. 'Thanks for your help. I'll see you later.'

He left, felt the dog's hot breath on the back of his legs as he walked down the hallway, the swish of air as Jai shut the door firmly behind him.

11.

Two blocks from the motel, the warning snap of pain in his chest. Pulse drumming and jumping, mouth dry. Shit, not now. Pull over. Handbrake on, engine off. And breathe through it. Nothing to worry about, just an aftershock of his little freak-out in the pine forest. Inhale, two, three, and exhale, two, three. The touch of the gun beneath him. Grabbing it, turning, squeezing the trigger. The warm spray of blood. Not real, just a memory. Push it away. Grip the wheel and keep breathing.

He headed for Ant's, in need of distraction and movement, nearly kept driving when he saw the car parked outside the house. Shit, Etty was here: he'd have to talk, smile, be human. But it was here or the motel. Alone in the tiny room, long hours of the evening pressing down, trying not to think about blood and fear and death. A shudder ran through him. He turned off the engine and got out.

He rang the bell instead of walking straight in, something he'd learned to do years ago after witnessing more of Ant's love life than he was comfortable with.

Etty opened the door and gave him a bright smile. She

was small and wiry, with chin-length brown hair and an almost visible buzz of energy.

'Cal, hi. Howareyougoing?'

It took him the usual few seconds to untangle her words.

'Good, thanks. And you?'

'Ohgreat,I'mreally. . .' She chatted easily as they walked through the house, not seeming to mind that she was delivering a monologue.

He followed her into the sunroom off the kitchen, a small room with wide windows and polished floorboards. Ant had got rid of the mangy beanbags he'd once furnished the room with, and in their place was a plump brown sofa and matching armchairs. He was sprawled on the sofa, drinking a can of Coke, tousle-haired and glowing – a strong suggestion of recent, outstanding, sex. A burnt-orange sarong this time, bordered with bright green elephants. Possibly a nod towards the takeaway Thai meal sitting on the coffee table in front of him.

'Helpyourselftodinner,' Etty told Caleb and went to Ant. She stayed standing, but they both found excuses to touch each other as they spoke; the brush of a hand, the stroke of a finger. Caleb suddenly found the takeaway containers deeply fascinating: a box of congealing pad thai, and something green and oily. A total lack of hunger, but a quick check revealed that he hadn't eaten since breakfast. Slipping. Eating regularly was on the must-do list, right up there with showering and getting out of bed in the morning. He grabbed the pad thai and wondered if he should take it into another room. His bedroom, perhaps. The one he'd slept in as a child, with its lone, single bed.

Etty waved to get his attention. 'I'llcatchyoulater. I'moffto haveashower.' She gave him a wide smile and bounded from the room.

'See you,' he said about three seconds too late.

'You can tell her to slow down, you know,' Ant signed lazily. 'She won't be offended.'

'It's fine, I get most of it.'

'You're doing better than me, then.'

He sat opposite Ant and poked at the pad thai with a plastic fork. Maybe it'd look more appealing if he reheated it.

Ant was frowning at him. 'You OK?'

'Had better weeks.' He thought it through. 'Had worse.'

'Yeah. How were the cops yesterday?'

'Very friendly. I spoke to your old footy mate, Ramsden. He sends his love.'

Ant stiffened. 'Why was he talking about me? What did he say?'

Nine years since Ant's six-month stint for possession, but he still seized up at the idea of his name being mentioned in a police station. They should talk about that sometime. Or not. Avoidance was a family tradition, and one Caleb hated to break – why change something that had kept generations of Zelic men miserable?

'Figure of speech,' he said. 'Don't get tickets on yourself.'

He chased a cashew around the container while he thought about his next step. Dave McGregor was probably his best bet. Which wasn't saying much: a man who might have picked up a backpack that belonged to a kid who might have been following Caleb. It was a long shot. A very long shot – a telescopic sight needed for it. But it was a choice between following up on McGregor, or asking the Copperheads if they'd put a hit out on Portia.

'What's Dave McGregor up to these days?' Caleb asked.

Ant shrugged. 'Dunno. Although I hear he's got himself a girlfriend.'

'A girlfriend?' His mind baulked.

'Could be inflatable, I guess.'

'What about that swish new ute of his? Any idea where he got the money?'

Ant drained his can of Coke and set it on the table. 'Strangely enough, no. We don't exactly hang out.'

'If you had to guess?'

'Insurance scam? No, not bright enough.' Ant laid the can on its side and started spinning it around. 'Hey, maybe he won TattsLotto. I mean, someone's got to win it. Did you hear about Jerry Hays? Won fifty grand on a scratchie. Left his job and reckons he's going to move to Italy and buy a castle. Don't think he's quite worked out the exchange rate yet.' He caught the can as it flipped off the table.

God, it was like trying to converse with a labrador.

'What about bikies?' Caleb asked. 'Have you ever heard about him being connected to the Copperheads?'

'Who? Jerry?' Ant said out loud, his eyes on the can. He was tilting it back and forth, possibly judging its aerodynamic qualities.

'Dave McGregor.'

'Mate, you've really got to let that go, you know. So he made you cry a couple of times. You were ten, move on.'

'Fuck you, Buddha, this isn't about that.' Caleb stabbed his fork at the noodles. 'Anyway, I got back at him.'

'Eventually.'

'Didn't ever see you fronting up to him.'

An incredulous expression crossed Ant's face. 'Why the hell would I? I had you to scare him off. Anyway, Mum always told me to leave the fighting to you.'

'Seriously? Mum hated me fighting.'

'Yeah, but she loved me more.'

The ugly truth about survival at the bottom of the playground food chain had been a fraught issue between Caleb and his mother. Eleanor Zelic had cried the first time he'd come home with a bloodied face and bruised knuckles. Cried, and then yelled at his father for encouraging him. A shocking enough event for the memory to still be clear. Standing in the kitchen, noise but no words, the movement of her lips meaningless – so around five or six years old, just after the bout of meningitis that had taken his hearing. She hadn't usually been a shouter, but she'd yelled so loudly that day that he'd torn the weird new hearing aids from his ears and discovered the joys of silence.

Ant had gone back to spinning the Coke can.

Caleb put his hand out to stop it. 'Concentrate for a minute – is there any connection between McGregor and the Copperheads?'

'I doubt it. Why do you want to know, anyway?'

'There's a chance he's connected to Portia's death.'

Ant was fully focused now. 'Then aren't you worried that looking into him might get you another visit from your stun-gun mates?'

'We'll be back.'

'No.'

'But you –'

74

Caleb looked away and dug through the remaining noodles for a piece of broccoli. He jumped as something hit his chest and bounced to the floor. The Coke can.

'Shit,' he said, wiping a sticky trail from his T-shirt. 'What did you do that for?'

Ant's expression was pure innocence. 'Oh, I'm sorry, I thought we were pretending to be two-year-olds. My bad.' He got to his feet. 'Now, if you'll excuse me, Etty's out of the shower and I need to persuade her not to get dressed.'

Caleb took the remains of the pad thai into the kitchen and sponged down his T-shirt. He was in the hallway, halfway to the front door, when the overhead lights began to flash. Heart thumping, palms damp. He peered up the stairs, but Ant's bedroom door was closed; probably not a good time to ask him to pop down and call out, 'Who is it?'

He went out the back door and around the side path, stopped at the front of the house. A brightly coloured car was parked on the road: an old Volkswagen Beetle with a lurid, swirling mural that covered every panel and hubcap with entwined limbs and bodies. Art in some people's eyes, a criminal offence in other's.

The knot in his heart eased.

Kat was home.

12.

She was wearing denim shorts and a yellow halter-neck top, her hair tucked beneath a straw hat with a band in the black, red and yellow of the Aboriginal flag. She turned as he crossed the parched lawn towards her. Clear blue eyes against sienna-brown skin: a face more familiar than his own.

He tried to wipe the inane grin from his face. 'You're back.'

'Looks like it.'

Go for the kiss? Stupid not to. He bent down, did it slowly enough for her to choose whether to offer her mouth or cheek. Cheek. She smelled of salt and sun and lazy Sunday mornings, and he couldn't think of a single thing to say. Kat seemed to be having the same problem, shifting from foot to foot, looking away. She took off her hat and folded it in her hand. Her hair. Jesus, what had she done to her hair? All her beautiful curls, shorn. What remained clung tightly to her scalp in dark whorls. He made an involuntary sound, felt it in his throat, something between a sigh and moan.

'What?' she said.

'Your hair.'

Her hand went to her head. 'What do you think?'

That he wanted to cry. Probably shouldn't say that. Definitely shouldn't. Be supportive, use positive words like, like… Shit, total blank. 'Wow.'

She shoved her hat under her arm so she could sign. 'Want to take a minute to reconsider that response?'

'No – I mean, yes. I mean, it looks good, really good. You look good.' Shut up. Now. He clasped his hands behind his back.

'Just good, huh?' But a familiar glimmer was in her eye.

'Lost for words. Too busy wondering how it was possible for you to look even better.'

'Put the shovel down, you're only digging yourself deeper.' And she brushed past him into the house.

Kat sat at the kitchen bench while he set about struggling to find a single thing he needed: cups, tea, milk, cool-headedness. Eventually he sat next to her, tea made, stale biscuits produced. She did look good. Bright-eyed and glowing, a lot of long brown leg showing beneath those shorts. A sense of the world righting itself. Apart from a two-year stint studying in the US, this was the longest Kat had ever spent away from the Bay. His ties to the place had frayed over the years, but Kat's were multi-stranded and indestructible: friends, family, land, history, all keeping her securely tethered.

Should he start with the big question first or lead up to it with some nonchalant 'how was the trip' conversation? Who was he kidding – he couldn't pull off nonchalant.

'Are you back for good?'

'I'm –' She turned to the doorway.

Ant was there, phone in hand. His frown changed to a wide smile. 'Kat!'

They hugged and kissed each other's cheeks.

'You look great,' Ant said. 'Love the hair. Cal didn't tell me you were coming back. You staying long? How long have you been back?'

'It was all a bit last-minute. I got in a few hours ago.'

They were signing for his benefit, but their attention was on each other. Falling, as always, into the roles they'd established when they'd first met: Ant as besotted fourteen-year-old, Kat the indulgent big sister. They'd somehow managed to sustain their mutual affection through the grimmest years of Ant's addiction – something Caleb couldn't say for himself.

Ant pulled out a stool and sat down. 'So, how was Broome?'

Caleb stopped trying to be subtle with his leave-us-alone gestures. 'Go away, Ant.'

'But I've got –'

'Fuck off.'

'But –'

Caleb gave him the look. The one learned from their father, easily channelled. Ant stood up and left.

'Look at you two bonding,' Kat said. 'It warms the heart.'

She'd slipped into their usual pattern of mixing sign with the occasional spoken sentence, a system so finely tuned it barely required thought. Her hands flowed easily as she signed, the terrible stiffness gone from her broken fingers. But something wasn't right – some subtle difference he couldn't quite catch.

'Are you down here out of fraternal love?' she asked. 'Or are you working?'

If she'd been in town a few hours, she would have already spoken to a dozen people. Which meant she'd been given a complete rundown on his activities, possibly including his diet and bowel movements. The old Caleb, the stupid Caleb, the Caleb who'd let his marriage fall apart, despite repeated warnings, would have shut down the conversation immediately. The new and improved Caleb was open and communicative.

'I'm looking into that woman I texted you about,' he said. 'Her name's Portia Hirst. A couple of people stopped by to ask me about her, not very politely, which is why I was a bit jumpy when you rang the doorbell. No harm done, though, so I think they were just after information.'

She paused. 'Thank you for that very detailed report.'

'I aim to be open and communicative.'

A smile for that, the kind people give three-legged dogs. She settled back to drink her tea and recrossed her legs. His eyes followed the movement. She'd obviously been spending a lot of time in the sun, but she didn't have any sandal lines. No tan lines on her shoulders, either. Skinny-dipping. Memories of their once-frequent trips to Lantern Cove just out of town, the water cool against his hot skin, Kat's body soft and warm. He drank his tea while he composed himself.

'What about you?' he asked when he'd drained the cup. 'Are you back for good?' And if Ant walked into the room now, he'd sit on him until she'd managed to answer.

'Yeah, I'm back for good.'

He didn't bother trying to hide the stupid grin this time.

'I sent you an email this morning. You haven't read it?'

'No.' His grin faded. Why email? A text would have been easier if she was jumping on a plane at short notice. Unless she'd needed to tell him something that required a long explanation. Something that couldn't be handled with predictive text and a few emojis.

'Are you OK?' he asked. 'You're not sick, are you?'

'Jesus, Cal, straight to code red. No, I'm fine.'

He breathed again. Then thought of the next worry on the list. 'And have you, um… Is there someone else?'

'No. I am both single and well. I'm a little worried about you, though. You should pace yourself, you know. Work your way up through the different stages of panic.'

That was good. Very fucking good. Except for her use of the word 'single'. Was there an un-said modifier there? Semi-single? Single with the hope of upgrading to married?

'Can you maybe précis the email for me?'

'Did you hear about Mum's clinic?'

'I ran into her yesterday – she said there'd been a bit of trouble.'

Kat gave a humourless laugh. 'Trouble, yeah. Someone burned it down Friday night. That's why I'm back. Well, one of the reasons.'

'Jesus. Is everyone all right?' Now he was feeling even more of a dick about how he'd handled that conversation with Maria.

'Yeah, it happened pretty late, so the place was almost

empty. But it's totally gone. She'll have to rebuild.' Kat's face was pinched.

A Koori-owned business destroyed in the middle of a spate of racially directed vandalism. But it didn't feel like the work of fifteen-year-old boys riding BMXs. The clinic was one of Kat's father's designs: beautiful but highly functional, with tiled floors and mud-brick walls, metal shutters on the windows. You'd have to know what you were doing to burn it down.

'Is it connected to the other vandalism?'

'Mum thinks it is, but the police say not. They're looking into some of her more volatile patients. There have been some intense conversations between her and the cops.'

'I'll bet. How's she doing?'

'You know Mum – in full flight, trying to find new rooms, shifting patients to other doctors. I don't think it's hit her yet. She's turned half the house into a temporary clinic while she hunts for a place to rent. Speaking of which, I'd better get going.' She slid from the stool.

'You don't want to stay for dinner? Catch up properly?'

Her eyes flicked away. 'Not today. Mum's got me cleaning out the spare room.'

He rallied from his disappointment and walked her down the hallway. At the door, he asked the question before he could second-guess himself.

'What's the other reason you're back?'

'What?'

'You said the fire was one of the reasons you're back. What's the other one?'

She squared her shoulders as though steeling herself. 'It's time for me to face up to a few things.'

His eyes went to the soft skin of her inner arm, to the knife scar that ran along it in a thin, ridged line. More scars marked her fingers where the surgeon had repaired her broken bones. Her hand looked strong now, but it was too clean. That was what had been bothering him: there was no paint under her nails, no ink staining her skin, none of the usual nicks and scrapes and calluses. She still wasn't sculpting. Sorrow rose over him like a wave.

Kat caught the direction of his gaze and shoved her hands in her pockets.

He dragged his eyes away. 'Um, when can we catch up again?'

'I'm not sure.' She was speaking now, her hands still hidden. 'I'll be pretty busy with the clinic and everything. But I'm down here until my uni work starts up. Are you going to be in town?'

A sudden solidifying of his plans for the next four weeks. 'Yes.'

'Great. I'll text you.'

She gave him another kiss on the cheek and headed down the path. She didn't look back.

———

Ant was waiting for him at the bottom of the stairs, shifting restlessly, with the look of someone about to deliver bad news. A moment of heart-stuttering fear before he remembered that the sum total of people he cared about were either in this room or driving away in a pornographically decorated car.

'Timing,' Caleb said.

'Yeah, sorry. I just came in to say that your detective mate, Tedesco, called.'

An unexpected sentence. Ant and Tedesco had met a few times now, their initial wariness settling into something like acceptance – two strange dogs sharing a yard – but there was only one reason that Tedesco would be ringing Ant, and it involved dubious lessons in Auslan.

'I hope he scared the shit out of you,' Caleb said.

'What? Why?'

Caleb circled his fist in the sign for 'pig'.

Ant grinned. 'Oh yeah, I'd forgotten about that. I gave him a little lesson that time you were running late. He's a quick learner, yeah?' His smile faded. 'But this was about... He asked me to give you a message.' His hands fell to his sides.

'Am I supposed to guess?'

'A woman was taken off a street in Melbourne this morning. Kidnapped. Tedesco said the cops are pretty sure it was the Baymar brothers.'

God. If the Baymars were involved, it wasn't going to end well for the poor woman. People taken by the Baymars tended to turn up in small pieces, often in their loved ones' letterboxes.

'How's it connected to Portia?'

'Portia?' Ant shook his head. 'It isn't.'

He held back a sigh. 'We can keep playing twenty questions, or you can give me the message. Whichever's quickest.'

Ant shifted his feet. 'Look, it might not mean anything, but she was taken outside a house in Brunswick. Eight Mary Street, Brunswick.'

Frankie's address.

A feeling of stillness, no breath, no thought.

'...might not be her... know she fucked you over, but... friends for ages...'

'OK,' he said. 'Thanks.'

13.

He ran out along the dirt path towards the cliffs, through a grey-tinted world of boulders and scrappy bushes, a pallid quarter-moon guiding the way. His pace was off, gears not quite meshing. So many goodbyes. Parents, friends, children: all gone or never been.

He'd first met Frankie back in his early days as an insurance investigator. Twenty-four years old and a few months into a job with a large company, struggling and trying hard not to show it. Frankie had been the investigating officer on his first big case. She'd been efficient, rude, hungover and totally incomprehensible. It had taken her all of ten minutes to ask what the hell was wrong with him. So he'd told her. He'd braced himself for the inevitable cringing apology, but she'd just said, 'For fuck's sake, why didn't you say so?' and written down everything he'd missed. After that, she'd slowed her scattergun speech but gone on treating him with the same cranky dismissiveness she did everyone else.

And it was important to remember the rest.

That she was an addict, only looking after herself. That she'd been working for the man who'd killed his best mate, Gary. That she'd almost got Kat killed. Hold on to those thoughts, keep them close.

The Baymar brothers. God.

He took the inland path back to town, down a road dotted
with listless houses and wilting vegetable gardens. Old
grazing land around here, but no cattle these days, the
earth stripped bare by generations of hooves. A dying
land. Dead. He slowed as he reached the next house, a
double-fronted red-brick with a railing of smooth, white
stone that looked like a graveyard fence. Dave McGregor's
house. Some subconscious urge had brought him here.

The treeless yard was a tangle of blackberry bushes and
old sheds, a few rusted-out cars up on blocks. No lights on
inside the house, no sign of McGregor's iridescent green
ute. Caleb was pretty sure McGregor lived alone these
days, his brothers scattered around town or in prison,
parents long gone. If the house was empty, Caleb could
pop in for a quick look around. Many, many reasons not
to do it: the place could have an alarm, McGregor could
catch him, it was illegal. Then again, why the fuck not?

He walked up the middle of the potholed driveway,
composing excuses in his head. The front door was locked.
All the windows were closed, a fact explained by a hulking
new ducted air-conditioning unit. He tried the back door:
locked. It looked pretty lightweight, the plywood showing
beneath the peeling white paint – he could probably break
it down with a couple of kicks. That would definitely be
crossing a line. Not to mention giving McGregor a heads
up that someone had been snooping around. Frankie's
first rule of – No. No more of that.

Caleb stood back and gave the door a good kick. The
plywood cracked. Another couple of kicks. And another.

And another. Punching, kicking, thumping, a howl building in his lungs. He pounded the splintered wood, leaving bloody marks on the peeling paint. The door swung inwards. On his hands and knees, chest heaving, vision blurred. Get it together. Now. Frankie wasn't worth that kind of pain, so get it the fuck together and get inside the house. He wiped his eyes on the back of his arm and stood up.

It was dark inside, the hulking shape of a refrigerator just visible in the shadows. He hesitated, then switched on the overhead light. The kitchen was a wide room with greying floorboards and beige walls that had probably once been white. An old wooden table was pushed against one wall and heaped with pizza boxes and beer cans. At one end sat a laptop, a sheet of address labels lying next to it. He fired up the laptop on the off-chance he could get into it, but even McGregor wasn't stupid enough to use PASSWORD as a password. Caleb checked the address labels: only one was left, addressed to an A. Anderson, with a PO Box in the Sydney CBD. He took note of the name without much hope – it might as well have been A. Nonymous. The label had been printed on a cheap ink jet, but there was no sign of one in the kitchen. Maybe in another room.

He had a quick poke around the living room but found nothing except more beer cans and a giant plasma-screen TV. Into the master bedroom; the smell of stale cum and weed. The decor was a strange combination of 1950s housewife and contemporary porn, with net curtains and black satin sheets. A scratchy-looking black bra was hanging from the bedpost – looked like the rumour of a girlfriend was true. A passing thought, happily dismissed. Not Portia: the lingerie was the wrong colour and too cheap. He hunted through the wardrobe. A lot of new clothes, some with their price tags attached. No brown sports bag.

Headlights flashed across the window.

He froze. McGregor's green ute was pulling into the driveway. Shit, the room was lit up like a department store window. He flipped off the light. The ute stopped in front of the house and McGregor got out, looking towards the bedroom.

A surge of energy. Good. Let him come. Let him come in here with his fists and his smirk and his strut. Caleb widened his stance, his hands clenching. McGregor turned back to the ute and pulled something from its tray. Heavy, needing two hands to lift it – a crowbar.

14.

A quick scan of the room. Doona, shoes, TV. Nothing he could use in defence against a weapon that would smash bones and pulp flesh. A second's hesitation, then he ran. Down the hallway and through the kitchen, past the battered back door. He sprinted across the darkened yard to the fence and pulled up short. Fuck, a thicket of blackberry bushes. He glanced at the house. McGregor was silhouetted in the doorway, the crowbar resting against his shoulder.

Caleb slipped behind the shed and skirted around it to the front yard. He started across the stretch of land towards the gate, shadows looming. The gravel was loose underfoot. Walk slowly, gently. A flash of light to his left. He stopped. McGregor was standing at the rear corner of the house, sweeping his phone light over the yard. Shit. The front gate was too far; he'd have to scuttle back to the sheds and hide until McGregor gave up.

Fuck that, he wasn't cowering from Dave McGregor. He eyed the ute: McGregor had jumped out of it pretty quickly, there was a chance he'd left the keys in the ignition. Caleb crept closer to it, picking up his feet and placing them carefully. Eight more steps. Six. Shit, he couldn't see McGregor's light anymore. Where'd he gone? Focus. Four more steps. Two. At the ute. The keys were in the ignition. One hand on the door, easing it open.

The inside light came on.

A flash of movement. McGregor was pounding up the side of the house towards him. Quick, into the ute. Engine on, into reverse, go.

———

He scrounged a few coins from the ute's floor and texted Ant from the public phone at the old service station outside town. With any luck Ant would be near his phone, in a lift-giving mood and not currently having sex. It wouldn't take long to walk back into town, but staying off dark roads seemed like a smart move. McGregor would go into meltdown at the loss of his shiny new baby. Understandably – the ute was a nice ride, able to handle a quick reverse down a gravel driveway pretty well. A sudden desire to laugh. Adrenaline, not an inappropriate reaction to doing something seriously stupid. Had McGregor recognised him through the net curtains? It'd get ugly he if had, but it wouldn't be a waiting game – he'd be outside Ant's house right now, smashing up Caleb's car with a crowbar.

He shifted the ute behind the service station and turned on the air-conditioning. The vehicle couldn't have been more than three months old, but McGregor had already christened it with his own brand of slobbishness – beer cans and burger wrappers in the footwell, a dirty T-shirt, even a crumpled child's drawing.

A child's drawing? Caleb picked it up and smoothed it on his lap. A photocopied flyer: a crayon drawing of a tree, the name Coast Care printed above it. Coast Care. Portia's tree-planting organisation. A bit of an unexpected thing to find in Dave McGregor's ute. No contact information was printed on the flyer, but someone had scrawled a local address across the bottom in blue pen.

Lights flashed as Ant's battered white Toyota pulled in behind him. Caleb shoved the flyer in his back pocket.

'Thanks for coming,' he said as he got in the car.

Ant switched on the overhead light and examined him. 'You're going to have to help me out, here – I'm not up on the latest parenting techniques. Am I supposed to do the whole "I'll pick you up no questions asked" thing? Or demand to know what the hell you were thinking when you stole Dave McGregor's ute?'

'The first one.'

Ant's eyes dipped to Caleb's bleeding knuckles. 'Was it McGregor you punched? I'm asking in a completely non-judgemental way, you understand. I just want to know if I should be organising your funeral.'

A cold ache as Caleb remembered why he'd battered down McGregor's back door.

'Just an accident,' he said. 'Do you feel like a quick detour on the way back?'

Ant nodded in approval. 'Nice segue. A little abrupt on the turn, but full marks for the boldness of the manoeuvre. I'd give it a seven.'

The address on the flyer turned out to be a vacant lot between a kindergarten and a house. It was a deep block filled with weeds and a few rows of newly planted saplings, a green shipping container sitting by the back fence.

Ant stood next to him and surveyed the land with the look of a disappointed prospector. 'OK, I give up. Why are we here?'

Caleb showed him the flyer. 'I found this in McGregor's ute with the address handwritten on it.'

'And?'

'And it means that there's link between McGregor and Portia.'

'A pretty tenuous one.' Ant hopped onto the car bonnet, signing with hands as loose as a yawn. 'Give me a hoy when you've finished.'

A hundred or so eucalypts had been planted in rigid lines at the front of the block, their leaves curled and beginning to brown, the soil dry. No sign of any fresh weeding or digging, the shipping container locked, a scattering of rubbish blown up against its doors. Looked as though Coast Care was finished now that Portia was gone. Which meant he wasn't going to find any handy workers to interrogate.

He did a methodical sweep of the block, stepping over broken bottles and old tyres, but found nothing except the promise of backbreaking work. Which might explain Portia's commitment to the project if she was trying to impress her father, but didn't give any clue as to why Dave McGregor would be interested in it.

Caleb returned to the car. Ant was lying on the bonnet now, possibly humming, his foot tapping to some internal beat. He didn't react when Caleb smacked his foot. 'Why would McGregor be interested in a tree-planting scheme?'

'He wouldn't.' Ant beat out a few more bars. 'You know, sometimes flyers are just flyers and arseholes are just arseholes. It doesn't all have to mean something.'

'That online philosophy course going well, is it?'

'Yes, fuck you very much. I'm getting straight HDs.'

Not surprising. Ant had twice the brains of most people he knew, himself included. As child he'd excelled at everything: insults, schoolwork, excuses. He was probably right about the flyer. There was no sign of any significant connection between McGregor and Portia, and no sign of anything at all between him and Jasmine. And although McGregor had money coming in, it wasn't big money, not the kind you killed over.

'I guess it could just be McGregor being a perv,' Caleb said. 'Portia was pretty.'

Ant sat up and stretched. 'Popular, too. She always had a string of people wanting to talk to her.'

'Really? Her father said she didn't have any friends.'

'Well, let's all hope that fathers aren't always right about the failings of their children.' Ant paused. 'So, what now?'

'Back to the motel, I guess.'

'You're not going back to Melbourne?'

'Not yet.'

'But soon, yeah?'

Caleb gave him a long look. 'I'm sorry, is me being in town cramping your style?'

'Definitely, but I meant, it's Sunday night, shouldn't you be heading back to Melbourne? I thought things were wobbly with Trust Works. Shouldn't you be concentrating on the business instead of stealing cars and punching inanimate objects?'

'Thanks for the unsolicited advice. Working in a bottling factory gives you a lot of insight into running a business, does it?'

'Well, yeah, it does actually – I'm a manager now. But I wasn't giving you business advice, I was pointing out that you're being an obsessive fuckhead.' Ant jumped from the car bonnet and dusted the seat of his pants. 'If you've finished with your current episode of OCD, let's go. I'm getting hungry.'

15.

He woke early and spent the post-dawn hours chasing outstanding invoices for Trust Works. Nothing to do with Ant's little lecture the night before, just standard procedure for a small business owner. Particularly one who only had funds to see him through the next three months. He sent the last sternly worded reminder, then checked to see if Kat had texted. Checked again after his shower. Then after breakfast. After he'd checked for the sixth time, he went to see if his old grey Commodore was still in one piece.

It was sitting outside Ant's place, looking the same as always: dusty and a bit saggy, but undented by crowbar or fist. A little sigh of relief. He patted the dashboard and headed for the motel, only getting as far as the corner before he realised the petrol warning light was blinking. Shit, how long had that been on for? Another item to add to the long list of things he struggled to remember these days.

He drove to the EezyWay petrol station and filled the tank, watching a grey-haired couple at the next bowser squabble over a newly purchased map. Rough surf and distance from Melbourne meant the Bay didn't get many tourists. Those who did come wandered around looking bemused at the lack of artisanal bread, then left for somewhere better. The EezyWay seemed to earn most of its money by selling them the petrol to get there.

Which raised an interesting idea. Ant's house was only two blocks from the EezyWay. If Jasmine and Baggy-eyes had driven down from Melbourne like Caleb suspected, they would have needed fuel for their return trip. Were they cool-headed enough to half drown him, then stop a couple of blocks away to fill up on premium unleaded? Yes.

He hung up the pump and went to speak to the cashier. Vicky Graham was at the till, a tiny woman with limbs as angular as origami. She was an old school friend of his mother's, and eternal winner of the Bay's annual Christmas cake competition. The poor woman, working here – the EezyWay's owner was a man whose stinginess was trumped only by his racism.

'Caleb, love, how are you?' Vicky remembered to slow her speech halfway through the question, creating the odd feeling of a movie being played at half speed.

He dredged the names of her adult children from his mind and asked after them, got the full rundown on their many activities and offspring. There were times when he felt his family had made a pretty poor showing in the whole go-forth-and-multiply thing. Immigration, family feuds and premature death had all lopped limbs from the family tree. Just he and Ant remained, and sometimes neither of them felt like a sure bet.

He waited until Vicky had paused for breath, then jumped in. 'I'm looking for a couple who might've filled up here on Saturday. They drive a silver Volvo. She's around thirty, with messy brown hair. He's a bit older, with a thin face and baggy eyes.'

'Oh yeah, they were in here. Or at least, she was.'

No, that was too easy. 'You sure?'

'Yeah, perfect description.' Her eyes widened. 'Is this for your work? Are you investigating them?'

'I'm not sure. Did they pay by credit card?'

'Cash.'

Damn. 'You don't need to check?'

'How many people d'you think pay cash for a full tank around here? It's all on plastic and a prayer.'

'Did she say anything to you? Where she was heading? Where she was from?'

'No, just shoved the money at me like I was a leper.' Vicky's speech accelerated as she grew more indignant. 'I mean, it's not that... pretend... human being... CCTV...'

The last words leapt out at him. 'Did you say you've got CCTV now?'

'Yeah, about a month ago.'

'Bert spent actual money?'

'I know, right? Festival of the Moths when he opened his wallet. But insurance insisted.'

'Can I have a look at the tape?'

She caught her lip between her teeth. 'I should probably ask Bert first.'

'Just a quick look.'

She glanced around the empty shop, then lifted the countertop. 'You and your brother – I could never say no you. Charmers the pair of you.'

He ducked around to her side. 'Thanks, Vicky.'

She pecked slowly at the keyboard, pausing every few

keystrokes to turn to him. 'Saturday, you said? About what time? You and Anton should come over for dinner while you're in town. You look like you could do with a feed.'

Despite her own apparent ability to live on air and water, Vicky had an overwhelming need to feed people. She'd delivered truckloads of food to him and Ant during the long, slow months after their mother's death. A lot of mums had fed them that year, but Vicky had out-cooked them all: macaroni and cheese, cupcakes, pasties – children's food, despite the fact he'd already been eighteen, Ant fifteen. Caleb had a feeling she'd still be doing it if Ivan hadn't put his foot down.

She tapped the screen. 'There you go.'

True to form, the system that Bert had installed was the cheapest on the market, with fuzzy black-and-white images, but Jasmine's profile was instantly recognisable. Caleb clicked through the images. She kept her head down and angled away from the camera, obviously aware of its presence. Damn.

He switched to the external camera: grainy shots of bumper bars and numberplates. And there was Jasmine again, climbing from a Volvo – a clear shot of the licence plate. Finally, something to work with.

He wrote it down. 'Perfect. Thank you.'

'Have you cracked the case?'

'Couldn't have done it without you.'

'Oh, you.' She beamed. 'You can thank Bert for finally installing the cameras. I don't know why he didn't do it years ago – we catch at least one runner a week now, and it's stopped the vandalism.'

'Vandalism?'

'Oh, it's been terrible. I don't know what the town's coming to. It was just a few windows smashed at first, but then they broke into the mechanic's bay and wrecked a couple of cars.'

Similar to the vandalism in town and on the Mish, but possibly not related – Bert was whiter than Omo.

'Do the cops know who did it?'

Vicky's mouth pulled down. 'No, but I reckon it's the same kids who smashed up the shops in town. The little shits. I hear they were hooning around Boongville last night, scaring people.'

He froze. Boongville was what some people called the Mish. The kind of people who adorned their cars with bumper stickers saying *Keep Australia White* and *Love It Or Leave It*. People like Bert. She must have misspoken, a slip of a tongue coached by childhood chants.

'I, ah –' He cleared his throat. 'I think most people call it Bellville.'

'Oh.' Her hand fluttered to her mouth. 'I'm sorry, darling, I keep forgetting you married one of them.'

He walked outside, considering his options. Frankie would have slipped the licence number to an old colleague, but his choices were limited to by-the-book Tedesco and the sixteen-year-old computer whizz, Sammi, who'd helped him out last year. He wasn't sure how far Sammi had ventured into the shady areas of cyberland, though he'd lay good odds that she knew some friendly hackers. But while tracing a car rego could be said to be on the murky side of ethical, involving a minor definitely was.

He texted Tedesco.

—Can you trace the owner of this car? Wouldn't ask, but important.

He paused before pressing send. It would be very handy to know if he could trust Sergeant Ramsden, and Tedesco would know the right people to ask. A fair chance he'd do it, too: Tedesco might have qualms about dealing out information, but he wouldn't leave Caleb swinging in the wind if he was up against a dodgy cop.

—Dealing with a cop in Res Bay. Sgnt John Ramsden. Any word on him?

He turned for his car, then paused as a young Koori woman stepped out of the mechanic's bay in front of him. She was wearing a crisp nurse's uniform, her dark hair pulled into a sleek ponytail. Shit, Honey Kovac: Gary's lover, and mother to his child.

A sensation of falling. The gut-wrench moment of remembering once more that his best mate was dead.

Honey faltered as she saw him, probably still nervous that he'd expose the paternity of her baby. It was understandable, given that her husband was an uptight prick who'd kick her and her children out at the first hint of a scandal. Caleb stopped so she could slip past him, then saw the bruises on her face. Her cheek was swollen, her right eye puffed almost shut. Fresh injuries, maybe a day old.

He spoke without thinking. 'Jesus, what happened?'

She glared at him. 'What's it to you?'

Hard to say, really. Some unfocused but desperate need to know that a part of Gaz lived on and was happy.

'Did your hus– Did someone hurt you?'

'A couple of little turds threw rocks at my car, if you must know. Smashed the windscreen and made me run into a pole. It's costing me a fortune to get fixed.'

'Was one of them Luke Blundon? About fifteen, with a little rat-tail in his hair?'

A look of surprise. 'Yeah.'

So the boys had graduated from vandalism to physical violence. This was feeling more and more like organised attacks, not just random acts of mayhem.

'Was it personal,' Caleb said, 'or were they going for anyone?'

'A couple of gubbas chucking rocks at me? Why would I take that personally?'

Always incapable of saying the right thing around Honey. He tried again in the full knowledge that he'd probably fuck it up.

'I meant, was it a racial thing?'

'I didn't stop to ask.'

'What did the police say? Did you tell them who it was?'

'Jesus, what is it with you? Just leave it alone, will you.' She brushed past him.

'Wait, do you want a lift home if your car's being fixed?'

She turned, her expression hard. 'Look, we're not friends – I fucked your mate, that's all. I don't want my husband connecting me to you and Gary. And I sure as hell don't want to be part of any white-guilt thing that you've got going on. So just piss off and leave me alone, will you?' She strode towards the street.

Movement in the corner of his eye: Jai Johnson was standing at the entrance to the mechanic's bay, wiping his hands on a rag. His stance had a protective readiness, as though he was prepared to run to Honey's aid if needed. Caleb nodded at him, but Jai just gave him a cool stare and disappeared into the bay: whatever the young mechanic had overheard, it obviously hadn't improved his opinion of Caleb.

His phone buzzed in his pocket. He grabbed it quickly, but the text was from Tedesco, not Kat.

—*Asked around. Ramsden can best be summed up as not too bright, but clean.*

That pretty much confirmed Caleb's opinion of the man. He thought through his words, then replied.

—*Thanks. Appreciate it. Anything on my other question?*

A brief pause, then his phone vibrated.

—*Police officers are prohibited by law from using official data for private use.*

It was a polite fuck off, at least.

16.

He drove straight through to Melbourne and reached the city in the glorious fifteen-minute period between the end-of-lunchtime rush and the end-of-school rush. Despite it being a school day, Sammi had come through with the car rego details within minutes: a business called Transis, its offices in the leafy suburb of Elsternwick.

It was a busy thoroughfare, with a strange mix of Edwardian houses, designer shops and sleek apartment buildings. He pulled up outside number 104 and sat staring at it. Not the shiny office block he'd been imagining. He checked Sammi's message again, but there was no mistake – the address registered for Transis was a multi-storey carpark.

———————

Heading for his flat, he slowed to a crawl on Smith Street: a late lunch before facing the stale emptiness of his apartment. He found a parking spot within seconds and recovered from the shock by ordering a hamburger at the first place he came to, a diner called The Creed Feed with a worrying fondness for deconstructed food and quirky serving platters. When he'd first moved to Melbourne as a wide-eyed nineteen-year-old, the only things you could get on Smith Street were hep C and smack. You could still get both of those, but these days you could get a decent feed, too. The jury was still out on The Creed Feed, but at least burgers were pretty un-fuck-up-able.

He grabbed a table by the window and opened his laptop. Hard to tell from Transis's website what the business actually sold, though it ticked all the superficial boxes for legitimacy – it was a registered business, had a board of directors, local phone numbers, email addresses. But he'd learned the hard way that even when things appeared perfect on the outside, they could be a suppurating mess within. The trick was to look and keep looking. And if you didn't find anything, look again.

'If your best isn't good enough, try harder.'

The only address he could find was the one listed on the car registration. Had someone forgotten to change the company details after a move? No, the carpark had rusting drip marks and cracked concrete. There hadn't been an office block on the site for more than twenty years.

Caleb jumped as a hand deposited his meal on the table: a small hamburger in the centre of a gleaming hubcap. Skewered with a blade of lemongrass. His heart sank.

The waiter said something, his words lost in the depths of his glossy black beard.

'Sorry, what?' Caleb asked.

Beard pointed to the extra table setting. 'Anyone else?'

'Just me.' He averted his eyes as the waiter removed the spare cutlery.

'Just me' wasn't showing any sign of becoming 'us'. It was nearly twenty-four hours since he'd spoken to Kat.

Was that a long time in the scheme of things? God, a teenager again, not knowing if the lack of contact meant 'piss off' or, 'I'm presently busy, but please do continue to pine for me.'

He took a bite of the burger, then put it down and peeled off the top. Jesus Christ – guava. An overwhelming urge to look around for the cameras that were surely capturing his reaction. There were no obvious recording devices, but a man was walking past the window, talking to himself and sniffing, scratching at his pock-marked skin.

For a moment Caleb thought it was Sniffy, the guy who'd taken him to Portia in the alleyway. He'd forgotten about Sniffy. A possible witness to the attack on Portia, maybe even a friend of hers. He might know why Blondie was after her. How to find him? His clothes had held the deeply ingrained dirt of someone who lived without whitegoods and running water, so he was probably homeless. Which meant he was a local. He'd have a small territory and stick to it. People would know him.

Caleb grabbed his laptop, left the burger.

———

It took him an hour and fifty dollars' worth of 'donations', but he finally tracked Sniffy to the park next to the Fitzroy pool, only a few hundred metres from where Portia had died. The young man was slumped on a bench, staring at the dry grass. Younger than Caleb had thought, only seventeen or eighteen.

'Hey,' Caleb said, 'remember me?'

Sniffy looked up. His eyes were focused, breathing

steady. At that delicate pivot point between hanging out and tripping. 'Yeah, sure. You got ten bucks? Me mum's sick and I lost my wallet. I need to buy a train ticket home.'

'You gave me a message from a woman a few days ago. Took me to an alleyway to see her.'

A real spark of recognition this time. 'Oh yeah, the chick in red.'

Caleb held up a ten-dollar note. 'What do you know about her?'

'I didn't take nothin'.'

Interesting response. So Sniffy had stolen something from Portia. Her missing handbag? It wasn't a big stretch to image him hanging around to see if he could rip her off, then ducking in to grab the bag after the fight. And if he'd taken it, he might still have her phone and all its lovely electronic information.

Caleb kept his voice even, trying to suppress the flare of eagerness. 'Where's her handbag?'

'Dunno.'

'There's a reward for anyone who finds it.'

Sniffy's eyes skittered away, then back to him. 'I might've found something. Just lying in the street, y'know. But I gave it to my sister. She loves it. It's her favourite thing.'

'I'll give you fifty bucks for it.'

Sniffy led him to a Victorian terrace a few blocks away. Wire fencing with a decade's worth of creeper growing up it, doors and windows boarded shut. The young man slipped through a gap-toothed wooden fence in the side alley and climbed in a half-open window. Caleb followed him, then stopped. It was a place of deep shadows and hidden corners – he wouldn't be able to understand a word Sniffy said; wouldn't know if someone was creeping up behind him, ready to slip a knife between his ribs. He should go outside and get Sniffy to bring the bag to him.

And risk never seeing him again.

Other options? Give up, or get help. Ant would come if he asked. That'd be good, that'd bring their relationship to a whole new level.

He followed Sniffy deeper into the gloom. Up a staircase of broken treads and railings, past rooms with huddled shapes lying on bare floorboards. A stink of unwashed bodies, shit and piss fermenting in the heat. He let Sniffy get ahead of him, then stopped to pull out his wallet. He slipped most of his money into his shoe and tucked his near-empty wallet into his waistband in case he needed a diversion.

Sniffy came to a halt on the third floor and pulled a stick from his pocket. He levered open a piece of hoarding to reveal a small attic with exposed beams and baking air. Sunlight streamed in through a large glassless window. The tension in Caleb's neck eased a little. A mattress lay on the floor, heaped with sheets. Magazine pictures were stuck to the walls, of birds flying, on the ground, in trees. The bundle of sheets unwound itself and a girl appeared. Fourteen or so, with pale skin and thin limbs. She stared at Caleb and pulled the sheets up to her chin. He hadn't considered that Sniffy's sister might actually be real.

Sniffy was speaking to her, no hint of aggression in him now, his face gentle, hands open. Caleb edged towards the wall so he could see them both. The girl eventually climbed from the bed and pulled a brown cotton shoulder bag from under the mattress. On one side was a delicately embroidered lyrebird, its tail feathers outstretched. She gave the bird a little stroke and passed the bag to Sniffy, a slight tremble in her lower lip.

Sniffy thrust the bag at Caleb. 'Money.'

Caleb ran his hands down the bag, not taking his eyes from Sniffy. He felt a couple of small bumps inside, nothing bulky, definitely no phone. 'And the rest,' he said.

'There's nothin' else.'

Caleb waited.

Sniffy only lasted three seconds before pulling a Myki card from his pocket. He dropped it into the bag. 'Happy now?'

'What did you do with her phone?'

'Wasn't one.'

Was he lying? No, Portia had known that Blondie was after her; dumping her phone was what anyone with a sense of self-preservation would have done.

'Hey,' Sniffy said, 'there's money on the card. Over ten bucks, twenty. More than twenty.'

Caleb gave him the fifty he'd promised and showed him the empty insides of his wallet. The girl was looking at Portia's bag with open longing.

'How old are you?' he asked her.

Sniffy moved between them. 'What's it to ya?'

'Nothing. Just that she looks young. Too young to be here.'

Sniffy stepped in close: the smell of rotting gums and chemical breath. 'Better off here with me, than other places by herself.' He jabbed a finger into Caleb's chest. 'You got me?'

Hard not to. 'Sure.'

'Then fuck off.'

———————

Caleb waited until he was safely outside, then examined the bag. The small bumps he'd felt turned out to be a lipstick, a hair clip and a cough drop. He shook the bag, but nothing fell out: no notebook or hidden messages, no mysterious matchbooks.

Maybe he'd get some information from the Myki card. Or maybe the entire day had been an expensive exercise in futility.

———————

The foetid air inside his flat was laced with the smells of other people's cooking. Straight to the kitchen to wash his hands and drink a couple of litres of water.

That squat. Ant had been around the same age as Sniffy the first time their father kicked him out. Seventeen and on the streets. It hadn't occurred to Caleb to ask Ant to come and live with him in Melbourne. No, that wasn't true. He'd thought his brother had needed to learn a lesson, and he'd left him to learn it. And Ant had. He'd learned the best places to score and the easiest places to rob. The lowest forms of humanity to befriend. What else had Ant done to feed his addiction? Caleb's mind shied away from the possibilities.

He poured another glass of water and sculled it. A flash of movement reflected in the window. He whirled around.

A pale face and spiky grey hair.

Frankie.

17.

Frankie. Alive. Standing in his kitchen, looking the same as always. Tall and angular, wearing a black T-shirt and scuffed Doc Martens, her hair purple-tipped and wild.

Like waking from a nightmare into bright sunlight.

His vision blurred as he stepped towards her. 'Frankie. God.'

And then he remembered: Kat, the blood, the pain.

He drew in a tight breath. 'Get out.'

'Minutes five,' she signed. 'First –'

'Get. Out.'

She placed a handful of photos on the kitchen bench beside him and signed, 'Look photos first. If still want me to go, I go.'

Far more fluent than her usual attempts at Auslan. She'd obviously practised that sentence, spent a bit of time looking up the signs, trying to work out the syntax. He glanced at the photos despite himself.

No. That wasn't possible.

He snatched them from the bench. It was the warehouse – his blurred shape in the foreground, Tedesco beside him, Kat and her captors facing the camera. It didn't make sense. There'd been no eyewitness that night, just victims and attackers, some survivors. But there was the darkened room from his nightmares, the high ceiling and stacks of boxes. A good lens. A very good lens. A clear shot of Kat's broken fingers and twisted mouth, the stark fear in her eyes. On to the next image, the photographs fluttering in his hands. A glimpse of the knife gleaming in the darkness. The next photo: the blade against Kat's wrist. Kat struggling, him standing helpless.

The photos dropped from his hands. Something was trapped inside him, its panicked wings beating against his ribs. He walked out of the kitchen to the front door, down the stairs, bumping into walls and balustrades. Dying. Had to be dying, couldn't breathe. And outside, dragging in a single ragged breath. Walk. One foot, and then the other. Don't stop.

———

He returned to the apartment block after dark, a dull exhaustion blanketing his thoughts. If someone had been lurking in the warehouse that night, why hadn't they helped Kat? Because they'd been incapable of it, like him? Or because they'd been in on the whole thing? Some unidentified member of the gang still walking around, unpunished?

He reached the landing and stopped. A crack of light beneath his door. Frankie was waiting for him, just as he'd expected. He composed his expression and went in.

She was sitting on the couch, the photos tucked away. Fear flashed across her face when she saw him. A strange response – she had the upper hand, as usual.

'Who the fuck took those photos?'

'Help me,' she said. 'And I'll tell you.'

He sat opposite her, fighting the temptation to pace. Seven months of being on the run had put a dull pallor to her skin and new lines around her eyes; she was looking every one of her fifty-seven years. No, fifty-eight – she'd had a birthday. She was leaning back into the couch, a portrait of a woman in control, only the tightness of her mouth betraying her tension. But there was no scent of alcohol, no tremor to her hands. Probably on a nice, steady dose of smack, courtesy of whoever she was working for these days.

'Love what you've done to the place,' she said. 'That one shitty coat of paint really sets off the cobwebs.'

Back to speaking, confident that he'd put in the effort to understand her. He hated that she was right.

'I thought the Baymar brothers had you.'

She blinked in surprise. 'Just a misunderstanding. All sorted now.'

Misunderstandings with the Baymars were usually fatal. How the hell had she talked her way out of that one?

'Tell me about the photos,' he said. 'Who took them?'

'I need something first.' She lifted her hand, a casual gesture, almost perfectly executed. 'Nothing major, just my stuff from the office.'

'The cops took everything.'

'I don't mean my computer – just bits and pieces, crap from my desk. Nothing the cops would have bothered with.'

Bits and pieces. There was no way that Frankie had broken into his flat, ended seven months of silence, for a few Post-it notes and a couple of leaking pens.

'Your coffee loyalty card?' he said. 'Your favourite mousepad?'

She dropped the nonchalant act. 'OK, fine, it's not crap, it's important. But it's important to me, not to you. So give me my stuff and I'll piss off. You'll never have to see me again.'

'What is it?'

'You don't want to know, trust me.'

'Trust you? After you got Gary killed? After you nearly got Kat killed?'

She rubbed her hands on her thighs. 'I didn't have anything to do with Gary's death. I know you think I did, but I didn't.'

'And Kat? That wasn't your fault either? You gave her up to a fucking killer.'

'I was trying to protect you! And I killed a man to save you both, so maybe you should start fucking remembering that.'

'He broke her fingers. He just, he snapped them. And then he cut–' Caleb stopped. Losing it in front of Frankie, what the hell was he doing? 'There's nothing left,' he said. 'I threw your stuff out when I closed the office.'

Frankie clenched her hands to stop herself from fidgeting but didn't quite manage to still her jiggling foot. 'What about –?'

'Nothing. Now tell me about the photos. Who took them?'

She hesitated. 'No one. They're stills from the CCTV. I figured they'd get me a few minutes of your time.'

'Well done, go to the top of the class.' He stood, but Frankie stayed seated. God, she'd sit there all night if she needed to say something. 'Just say it and go,' he told her.

'Don't tell anyone we spoke. You don't want people thinking you're involved with me.'

'Not much fucking fear of that.'

'I mean it, Cal.' She leaned forward, speaking slowly. 'It's not over, none of it's over.'

'What do you mean?' He held up a hand to stop himself. 'No, forget it, I don't want to know. Just tell me one thing before you go, did you send Portia Hirst to me?'

'No.'

'So you know who I'm talking about?'

'Sure, I've been following you.'

Well that was honest, at least.

Frankie sat back, crossing her legs. 'You've got yourself a weird one there. Poor little rich girl driving around planting trees and getting shot at. I'd be checking that crash site again, if I were you. There's definitely something odd about her being out on that road. Have you thought about –?'

He went to the door.

Frankie followed him but stopped when she reached his side. 'I know I fucked up, Cal, but I tried, I really did.' She switched to sign. 'My heart big sorry. Forgive please.'

She looked too pale, too thin. For years, she'd been the perfect counterbalance to his skills and weaknesses. She'd understood his jokes and put up with his moods, seen him through all the times – good, bad and horrendous – with Kat.

He opened the door, looked away until she'd gone.

18.

The storage unit he'd sublet from a neighbour was a three-by-three metre cell in the basement carpark. For some lemon-juice-in-the-wound reason that he couldn't quite fathom, he'd shoved all of Frankie's stuff in there along with the excess office furniture.

He started with her desk, a chunky grey thing with steel legs and a single drawer. There was no space for a secret compartment, but he ran his hands over it anyway, knelt down and peered beneath it. Nothing but cobwebs. Nothing hidden in the padding of her chair or in its wheels; nothing taped to its underside. He checked everything again, then turned to the box of junk. A sad assortment. Gnawed pens, a desk phone, old notepads, half a dozen dead batteries. Waste management, Frankie-style. She couldn't be arsed recycling anything but couldn't quite bring herself to throw it in the bin. He flicked through the notepads, peering at her spider-scrawl handwriting, but they only contained notes on old cases. He swept everything back into the box. Enough of Frankie's intrigues, it was time to move on to more important things, like illegally obtaining information from a Myki card. He went to lock the door, then grabbed the box and carried it to the car. It might be petty, but if it did contain what Frankie was after, he didn't want to leave it lying around for her to find.

———

It wasn't until he got to the darkened café where Sammi Ng hung out that he realised it was almost midnight. Damn. Sammi might be a money-scamming computer-whisperer, but she was also a high school student with parents and a bedtime. Or so he assumed.

He stood back and looked up at the first-floor windows. Lights were on in Sammi's workshop. No intercom on the street, but the door was unlocked so he went up the narrow stairs. He knocked and waited. Always an awkward moment, wondering if someone had yelled for him to come in. Knock again or barge in? Teenage girl by herself – better knock again, keep knocking.

The door was flung open and Sammi's scowling face appeared.

'...you fricken deaf or someth– Oh, it's you. Just come in next time, will ya?'

If she was embarrassed, she hid it well. She was as bright-eyed as ever, looking like an ad for a children's health retreat instead of the foul-mouthed sixteen-year-old she really was.

'You need better security,' he said. 'Any lunatic could walk in off the street.'

'Apparently.' She turned away with a flip of her ponytail.

Her workshop was a wide room filled with gutted hard drives and dismantled motherboards. Keyboards and routers lay on every surface. The whizz-bang computer on the far side of the room looked like the only new thing in the place.

'Where are your parents?' he asked.

'Why? You wanna adopt me?' Sammi settled herself on a swivel chair in front of the new computer. 'No Frankie today?'

As though she'd seen Frankie recently. Which gave him a possible answer to the nagging question of how Frankie had timed her visit to his flat so perfectly.

'When did you last see her?' he asked.

'About a month ago.' She shot him a long look. 'Why? Have you guys split up or something?'

'Yes. Why was she here?'

'Mate, I can't go giving away client secrets. This room is a cone of silence.'

'Was it something to do with tracking people using their phones?'

Her eyes widened. 'Wow, mind-reading. That's impressive. Hey, test me – what am I thinking now?' She had the expression of bar-room storytellers the world over waiting for a reaction to their foulest joke. So very far out of his depth here.

'I need some information,' he said quickly, handing her the Myki card. 'Can you see who owns this?'

She turned it over. 'Interesting. Yeah, I've got a skimmer around here somewhere.' She hunted through the detritus on the desk and unearthed a small plastic tag, exactly the right size to slip into an ATM and skim the data from bank cards.

'What are you doing with something like that?'

She glanced at him. 'Well, right now I'm getting some dodgy info from a card you don't own.'

Fair point.

She swung around to face the computer, her fingers skipping over the keyboard. He nudged a monitor out of the way and leaned against the desk.

After a few minutes, she looked up at him. 'There isn't much info on the card, just the last few trips, that sort of thing. So I got into the actual system to see if it was registered.'

Of course she had.

'Any luck?'

'Yep, it belongs to some company.'

He straightened. 'Transis?'

'Nah, Hilvington Care.' She gestured at the screen like a game-show model. 'Got a bit of info on them for you.'

He peered over her shoulder. According to its website, Hilvington Care was a rehabilitation company specialising in medium and long-term care. Its home page showed gently smiling nurses in rooms with muted colours and large windows. Down the right-hand side of the page was a list of its centres: Redhill, Renmark, Resurrection Bay. The scent of the hunt – he was onto something. A scam, a money-laundering scheme, dirty books.

'What can you find on the place in Resurrection Bay?'

She frowned. 'What are you after?'

'Start with a list of current directors and staff. Patients, too, if you can find it.'

She nodded. 'Even-handed in your invasion of privacy, I like it. Make yourself comfortable – this might take a while.'

He removed a dismantled hard drive from a chair and pulled out his phone. If Frankie was using it to track him, he should get rid of it. But it'd be hard without it. No texts or instant emails, no easy communication between him and lots of people not called Kat. Maybe a compromise: turn off every app, GPS and location service on the thing. He unlocked it and set about making his smartphone into a dumb one.

How long had Frankie been following him? And how many lies had she spun him in their little chat? He'd caught two of them: that her 'misunderstanding' with the Baymar brothers was sorted, and that the warehouse photos had been taken from CCTV footage. No video footage in the world could have produced images of that quality – they'd been taken by someone with a top-of-the-range camera. Hard to know why she'd lie about it. Even harder to know why he hadn't pushed her for more information.

'It's not over, none of it's over.'

Probably just Frankie using all the weapons in her arsenal: pain, lies, friendship, whatever it took to survive. She'd struggle this time if she was up against the Baymar brothers, though. And she knew it.

Something hit him in the face. A heart-stuttering moment until he realised it was a small toy mouse. 'Jesus.' He flicked it onto a bench. 'Try waving next time.'

'Try fricken seeing me next time. D'you want this stuff or not? I found heaps.'

He crossed to the computer, but she waved him towards a nearby printer. 'I figured you'd cope better with analogue.'

She hadn't been exaggerating about finding 'heaps'.

He hefted the wedge of paper from the printer and leafed through it. Details on Hilvington Care's board of directors, staff, clients, all with the thoughtful addition of their home addresses and dates of birth. Jesus. Maybe he should pay Sammi a retainer not to dox him. He perched against the table and went through the company structure. Nothing obviously dodgy about it, but these things rarely jump out at you. On to the list of clients: one jumped out at him. Graeme Hirst, eighty-five years old. Hirst, that had to be Portia's grandfather. Damn it, no scent, no hunt, just a young woman borrowing a train card from her grandfather. Caleb lowered the pages.

Sammi was watching him. 'Thorough enough?'

'More than, thank you.'

'Would you like your fully itemised bill now, or can I be of further assistance?'

He thought it through. He was pretty adept at finding the right thread in the endlessly spooling internet, but he had a strong feeling that Sammi would be even better.

'What do you know about the dark web?'

———

After a solid hour's hunting, Sammi unearthed a mention of Transis in a chat room: a three-month-old conversation between two hackers.

—*transis fucked me up. Ds gone to ground*

—*lie low. cant win against them. yet*

'Any good?' Sammi asked.

Two hackers talking about their difficulties with

something called Transis; could he do anything with that? 'Can you trace the people talking?'

'Sure, I'll just click on their avatars and follow the links to their Wikipedia pages.'

A sneaking suspicion she was being sarcastic.

'What about leaving them a message? Asking them to contact me?'

'Yeah OK,' she said slowly. 'But you'll have to keep checking the site. You don't want to go giving out any personal details.'

'I'll use a fake email address.'

'Jesus, it's a fricken chat room for hackers. Do we need to have a grown-up talk about security? Don't leave breadcrumbs. And don't be a dickhead and log in using your own computer, either.'

'You did.'

She flicked her ponytail. 'Yeah, but I'm smarter than you.'

19.

He spent the next day appeasing his only current client, the owner of a chain of sadomasochistic clubs who wanted a due diligence report on a business she was buying. Surprisingly dull work, but it was quick, and it paid well. He declined Madame Douleur's offer of a 'dungeon experience' in lieu of payment, and drove back to the Bay.

He reached the outskirts of town just as the sun nudged the horizon. A red-gold light on the rooftops, long shadows stretching, the time of day when he most felt the pull of home. Hard to know where that was these days. Or what it was. It had once been here, and then in Melbourne with Kat. The little flat in Collingwood, then the ramshackle house in Preston with the leaking roof. Evenings spent on the couch with her; the comforting rhythms of Saturday shopping and Sunday walks. The ultrasound pictures stuck to the fridge, the list of names pinned to the wall.

She'd be sitting down to dinner at her parents' place about now. It was only a few blocks away, on a quiet back road on the edge of town. He could drive past, maybe catch a glimpse of her. Brush up on his stalking skills.

He headed for Hilvington Care; according to their website, he had half an hour before visiting hours ended.

———————

Hilvington Care was in a sleek concrete building near the train station. Its lush garden of ferns and grasses was discreetly spotlit, with a simple brass plaque directing visitors to the main entrance. Lavender oil wafted through the air as he walked inside, almost managing to mask the underlying scents of disease and disinfectant. The receptionist was a wisp of a thing around forty. She was on the phone, scribbling furiously on a notepad. A personal call – just a hunch, something to do with the way she'd written *fuck you Liam, fuck you Liam, fuck you Liam* down the page.

Caleb waited for her to look at him. Waited a long time. Her centre part was three shades lighter than the rest of her hair and flecked with grey. No dandruff.

She finally lowered the phone a few centimetres. 'Can I help you?' The words were like a dare.

'I'm looking for Mr Hirst.'

'Rude sex,' she said, raising the receiver to her mouth.

'Sorry, what?'

She didn't bother lowering the phone as she repeated herself. Places this slick usually hired staff with saccharine sweet manners – this was a woman having a very bad day. And he wasn't stupid enough to make it any worse. He made an educated guess that she hadn't actually said 'rude sex' and headed for Room 6, a small room in a corridor marked *Long-Term Care*. Its single occupant was a young man with greyish-brown skin and thin limbs, a slackness to his face that made him look empty. Fading photographs were stuck to the walls beside a curling banner that read *Get well soon, Pete.*

God. A feeling of having stumbled into some private sorrow.

He'd want the plug pulled. Better still, do it himself before he was that far gone. Not a gun or a hosepipe, but something that would look like an accident to those he left behind. The car, or a quick walk in front of a train. He shivered and backed away.

He finally found Mr Graeme Hirst in Room 16. These walls were bare of photos and banners, the only decoration the printed sign above the bed bearing his name. The carpet and wafting lavender had to come with a hefty price tag, but Mr Hirst didn't seem to be aware of his surroundings. Caleb called his name, then tried again a little louder.

'Mr Hirst, can you hear me?'

Graeme Hirst didn't stir. Caleb had a growing feeling that Portia's grandfather hadn't given her the train card. He touched the man's arm: soft and dry, no reflexive movement. He yelled Hirst's name a few more times, then left.

The receptionist was off the phone but looking no happier for it. He checked the nameplate on the desk: Joy McKay. Either he was right about her having a bad day, or her parents had got the whole naming thing terribly wrong.

'Hi, Joy, I –'

'It's Joy,' she said, her mouth snapping shut.

'Sorry, what?'

'It's not *Joy*, it's *Joy*.'

Right, he'd got some subtle emphasis wrong. Hard to see how with a one-syllable name. Was it Zhoy? Joey? Impossible to know, go to plan B: abort use of name and clutch desperately at straws. 'Sorry, I know that's annoying. People sometimes call me Culeb instead of Caleb.'

She stared at him.

It was a gift, this way he had with women. Had to be born with it, couldn't learn it.

'I was just visiting Mr Hirst and –'

Her eyelid twitched. 'What's wrong now?'

'Nothing. Nothing at all. I'm just after some information about his granddaughter, Portia. I'm looking into her death.'

'Oh.' Her hand touched her mouth. 'I hadn't realised she'd died. What happened?'

'A car accident.'

'Oh, that's terrible, she was so young.' Joy had the blank-eyed look of real shock with no tears; she'd known Portia and hadn't liked her.

He handed her a business card. 'As I said, I'm looking into her death, but I'm finding the Hirst family a bit difficult to deal with.'

'Difficult? That family's never happy.' Joy sighed, but she didn't seem to be fully invested in her crankiness anymore.

He rested an elbow on the counter. 'I guess you'd cop the worst of it, being on the front desk.'

'I'll say. Portia strode around here like she owned the place. Telling us how to do our jobs.' She pressed her lips together. 'God, I can't believe I'm talking that way with her dead.'

'It's the shock.'

'Shock. Yeah, that's it. And she was very dutiful towards her grandad, visited every week, even though he's not really with us anymore. That's a whole lot more than most her age would do.'

'I don't suppose you can remember if she was here last Friday?'

'Oh, sure. She ran straight past me like I was invisible.'

'She borrowed a Myki card from here. Do you know how she got it?'

'One of our cards? That's odd.'

'You've got more than one?'

'Sure. The staff use them for rehab, teaching our clients how to get around with walkers and things. We don't give them out to visitors.'

'Are they well secured?'

'They should be. Everything walks off from around here – staplers, stationery, chewing gum. I had a bag of groceries stolen from the staffroom last week.' She pulled a plastic container from an open shelf and dumped it on the desk: full of Myki cards. Damn.

He clutched at his last straw. 'I guess you'd see anyone taking one, though?'

'Sure. Unless I was on a toilet break, or at lunch, or showing a visitor around.'

He was back at the car before it twigged. He went inside again, catching Joy mid-yawn.

'That bag of groceries you had stolen, did it have a packet of black hair dye in it?'

A blush rose up her face to her greying roots. 'Jesus, do you want to know about my tampons, too?'

Excellent. Portia might have known where the train cards were kept, but only a staff member would have known the contents of a grocery bag in the staffroom.

'Can I have a look at the staff roster for last Friday?'

That raised a genuine smile. 'Oh, you're funny.'

OK, he'd work it out for himself. He had the list of Hilvington staff from Sammi – all he had to do was interview them and find out who'd been working last Friday. All twenty-one of them. And the cleaners. And the casual staff. Fuck.

'Yeah,' Joy said. 'I'm having one of those days, too.'

———

He drove back to the motel, slowing as he crested the hill that ran down to Red Water Creek. A police car was outside Dean Hirst's house, its red lights flashing. A small crowd had gathered in front of it. More trouble for the Hirst family? No, people had their backs to the mansion and were looking towards the old scar tree. Please don't let Rat-tail Luke and his mates have vandalised the tree, too. It would break so many hearts.

Caleb pulled over and made his way through the crowd, brushing against bodies stiff with shock. The tree loomed before him, a ghostly silhouette in the stuttering red lights. It had somehow grown an extra limb: a monstrous, weighted thing with limp brown arms and a lolling head, bloodied and unfathomable. A blade of light sliced the darkness as someone approached with a torch. It swept across the trunk and branches to the hard line of the noose, and finally came to rest on the battered figure of a young man. Jai Johnson.

20.

They gathered outside the tiny weatherboard church in the Mish. The hottest day of the year. The Aboriginal flag hung at half-mast, its colours echoed on T-shirts and wristbands, tattoos and hats. People raised their umbrellas against the late afternoon sun and tipped bottles of water over babies. No one glanced at the news vans on the road, or the two police cars idling by the gate, the cops' faces turned to the crowd as though the danger came from within instead of without. Five days since Jai's murder and no hint of an arrest, just fear and rumours, closed doors in the Mish and huddled groups in the town.

Caleb steered clear of the cop cars and headed for the shade of a peppercorn tree. He'd fronted up to the police station the day after the murder. A long chat with Sergeant Ramsden, then a longer one with two blank-faced homicide detectives from Melbourne. He'd told them about Jai's involvement in the attack on Snake Gully Road: the young man's description of the Harley-riding shooter, Portia's return fire. They hadn't seemed impressed. Difficult to know whether it was because he'd waited three days after his conversation with Jai to report it, or because they didn't believe him.

A flash of something pale caught his eye – a feather on

the grass up ahead. He detoured towards it. Long and grey: the wing feather of a white-bellied sea eagle, Kat's totem animal. Giving it to her would be a bit of an obvious move. More than obvious – tragic. She was standing over by the church with her parents and sisters, but hadn't looked his way yet. She'd finally texted yesterday – a short message, not a lot of encouragement to be gleaned from it – but a text nevertheless.

—*Still pretty busy. Talk soon x K*

A hand slapped his back. Kat's cousin, Mick, was grinning at him. He had a plump one-year-old slung under his arm, and a girl of around six clinging to his leg. His white shirt and black pants were a much smarter choice than the wide-lapelled blue suit Caleb had borrowed from Ant. It was one of their father's, last fashionable in the 1970s, if ever: too tight across the shoulders, too short in the leg and increasingly itchy as the day went on.

Mick nodded at the feather. 'It's not gunna bite, you know. You developing one of them weird phobias or something?'

'Yeah, fear of being a dickhead.'

'Some'd say too late.'

They hugged and thumped each other's backs, held on for a second longer than usual.

'I'm sorry about Jai,' Caleb said. 'I don't know what to say.'

'There's no words for it, mate.' Mick hoisted his youngest daughter a little higher and smoothed her dark curls.

A flash of Jai's bloodied head, the crust of red drying on his disfigured face. He'd been dead before he was strung from the tree.

'Thanks for comin', mate,' Mick said. 'People appreciate it.'

That wasn't the impression he'd been getting. He hadn't felt this subtle distancing since his early days of dating Kat: eyes flicking away, conversations halted. Not exactly being pushed outside, but definitely nudged towards the door. It hurt more than it should have.

Mick caught his expression and shook his head. 'A blackfella was lynched. You'd better believe this mob are taking note of who's here and who's not.'

Not, for the most part – his was one of the few white faces.

'What's the word?' he asked. 'Have people got any idea who did it?'

'Ideas is all they've got – the Ku Klux Klan opening a local chapter, Reclaim Australia getting their races mixed up. Plenty of fuckwits to choose from.' Mick winced and looked down at his eldest daughter. 'Don't tell Mummy I said the naughty word.'

'What about bikies?' Caleb asked.

A flash of something fierce in Mick's eyes. 'What the fuck would bikies want with Jai?'

Caleb kept his voice low. 'Nothing. Just wondering.'

'Well fucken wonder about something else, don't go spreading rumours Jai was connected to bikies. Family's got enough shit to deal with. Yeah, I know, sweetheart, I'm trying, only Caleb here is being a bit of a di– silly-billy.'

'No rumours,' Caleb said. 'I'm only saying it to you. What about Luke Blundon and his mates? Do you think they could've been involved?'

Mick's jaw loosened a little. 'Nah. They're brainless

little fu– people. I can see them bashing Jai, but they wouldn't have stuck around to string him up.'

An echo of Caleb's thoughts.

'I asked around about Luke for you,' Mick said. 'No one's seen him with Dave McGregor, but someone reckoned they saw him talking to some guy out on the jetty. About your age, bit of a limp.'

A guy with a limp. Did he know anyone with a limp?

'Anything else? Height? Build?'

Mick shrugged.

'Who told you about him?'

'Jeez, I dunno.'

'Someone in the Arms?'

'Probably. Spend half me life there.'

'A regular, you think?'

'I'm not a fucken secretary, I didn't take notes.' Mick nodded at his daughter. 'Yeah, you can tell Mummy. But maybe round it down to one or two, hey?' He glanced towards the church.

A minister was standing on the steps, a microphone in one hand, Bible in the other.

Mick settled the baby on his hip. 'I'd better go and find the wife before I fu– find myself in more trouble.' He clapped Caleb on the shoulder and left, his stiff-kneed gait made even slower by his eldest daughter hanging on to his pants leg.

Caleb waited until he was gone, then picked up the feather.

———

He imitated those around him, bowing his head when they bowed theirs, turning the pages of the photocopied order of service when they turned theirs. At the end, six men around Jai's age carried his coffin from the church, grim-faced and sweating. There was a burst of feedback loud enough for Caleb to catch, and a recorded song began. He didn't need to look at the sheet to know that it was 'The Old Rugged Cross', a country version of the old hymn that had been played at nearly every Koori funeral he'd been to.

On a hill far away, stood an old rugged Cross
The emblem of suffering and shame
And I love that old Cross where the dearest and best
For a world of lost sinners was slain

There had been enough funerals for him to know the hymn well enough to mouth along, but no one was singing it this time. People stood silently as Jai's coffin was carried to the hearse, tears running unchecked down their faces. A few of the younger men were shifting restlessly, jaws jutting, fire in their eyes. Caleb glanced towards the police cars and sent a fervent prayer that the aunties would have the strength to rein the young fellas in.

Kat came over as everyone headed for their cars. She wore a black sundress with a long strand of red and yellow beads looped around her neck. A hug and the brush of her lips, soft against his cheek. He made himself release her and step back.

She looked him up and down. 'Nice suit.'

Not everyone could convey dry humour in sign language, but Kat was a natural: her expression both genuine and arch, the flick of her wrist ever so slightly exaggerated as she gave him the universal 'thumbs up' sign.

He smiled blandly and passed her the feather. 'Found this.'

Kat turned it over in her hand and frowned. A creeping feeling that he'd really embarrassed himself this time.

'Sorry, chuck it. I know you've got thousands of them.'

She blinked and refocused, stuck the feather behind her ear. 'No, I was just thinking... No, this is good, thanks.' Her gaze went to something behind him.

Aunty Eileen was talking to two of the restless young men he'd noticed earlier. A lecture, not a conversation. She jabbed her finger as she spoke, her face full of warning. The men's mutiny showed in their wide-legged stances, but they both nodded when she'd finished and left without argument. Aunty Eileen lowered herself into a plastic lawn chair, her shoulders sagging. A group of women gathered quickly around her.

Caleb turned to Kat. 'Is she OK?'

Kat pressed a fist to her chest. 'I don't know how she's still upright. She's sick, her kids are gone, her grandson's gone, and now Jai's gone.'

'Jai isn't her grandson? She told me he was.'

She shrugged. 'Keeping it simple for the gubba.'

He had a flash of the diagram she'd once drawn to explain the complex relationships within the Bay's Koori community – a multicoloured web: blue for friends, green for outsiders, red for family. Red had been the dominant colour, an entangled whorl of lines that seemed to have no beginning or end.

'It was bad enough with the reporters,' Kat said. 'But now she's got cops going on the radio saying that Jai had associations with "known criminal elements".' Her fingers stabbed the quote marks.

He'd seen those words repeated endlessly around town this week. It had only taken two days for the displays of grief to stop in the wider community. No more candlelit vigils at the scar tree, no cards and garlands of flowers, just rapidly growing rumours about Jai's dubious associations. But nothing Caleb had discovered supported them. By all evidence, Jai had turned his life around pretty spectacularly. The 'bit of strife' Aunty Eileen had mentioned was a stint in jail for a near-fatal crash he'd had while driving high on ice. He'd got out, got clean and started his apprenticeship. Even his thin-lipped boss at the service station had nothing but praise for him. If the young man had been hanging around with crooks, he'd been pretty subtle about it.

'What criminal elements?' Caleb asked.

A look that could freeze blood; involuntary cryonics a sudden possibility.

'I'm not victim-blaming,' he said quickly. 'I think Jai's and Portia's deaths are connected, but I can't work out how.'

Her expression thawed a little. 'You know about the crash?'

'The one Jai did time for?'

'Yeah. It was bad and it was his fault, but if Aunty Eileen can forgive him, I reckon everyone else can. All the newspapers want to talk about is how he fucked up as an eighteen-year-old, not how someone crushed his skull and strung him up on a scar tree.' Her face was bleak.

He touched her arm. 'Are you OK?'

'Sure. It's not like I knew him that well.'

'That doesn't mean you can't be upset.'

'I'm not upset, I'm...' Her fists clenched. 'I'm angry. I'm so angry I could punch someone.'

'Yeah.'

'Why?' she said. 'That's not me. I'm not like that.'

She really seemed to want an answer.

'Because it's better than feeling helpless.'

Her face wiped blank. Endless seconds, wishing he could snatch the words from the air, knowing she was reliving those terrible moments in the warehouse.

The emblem of suffering and shame.

'Some emotional insight, there,' she eventually said. 'A little unexpected.'

'I'm trying.'

Her quick flickers of expressions were as easy to follow as if she'd signed them: confusion, hope, indecision. She glanced over her shoulder at her waiting family. 'I'd better go.' She kissed him again, this time on his lips.

The warmth of it lingered after she'd gone.

Back at the car, the suit was chafing at his neck and thighs. He threw the jacket onto the passenger seat, but resisted the temptation to rip off the pants. He joined the slow crawl of traffic and turned right towards town – the only vehicle not heading for the wake, including the two cop cars. Strange not to be going to it with Kat. The wake was where the real mourning would begin, sheltered from the gaze of the outside world. Hard to know what would happen with those restless young men, their anger turned inwards and fuelled by alcohol, but one thing was sure – there'd be two police cars waiting nearby, with cops primed for action, all of them white. His foot lifted from the accelerator. Would it be overstepping the boundaries to offer to go with Kat? Definitely. Probably. Definitely.

He suddenly realised that he'd slowed to a crawl on a road with double white lines and a speed limit of sixty. He checked the rear-view mirror, but the car behind him was hanging back, not flashing its lights or driving up his arse. Unusually polite for the Bay. Unprecedented.

The car was a boxy black SUV, too far away for him to catch the licence plate. Just paranoid, no reason to think it was following him. Then again, there was paranoia and there was reasonable fucking fear. He kept a steady speed into the town centre. At the first set of lights, he accelerated and did a right-hand turn on the orange. The SUV swung around on the red.

Not paranoid.

21.

He drove sedately down the hill towards the shops. Try and scare them off by driving to the police station? Or corner them and find out who the fuck they were and why they were following him? One against one were good odds. Unless they had a weapon. So go somewhere public, an enclosed space but not too noisy, light enough to lip-read. After five on a Monday – only the pubs and the supermarket would be open. Maybe not even the supermarket.

He signalled left and turned into Bay Road, pulled up in front of the IGA. It had front and rear exits – the driver would have to be tempted to follow him in. According to the sign on the door, he had ten minutes until closing time. He lingered outside until he saw the SUV park across the road, then headed inside and wandered slowly through the empty aisles to the back of the store. He spent a bit of time in front of the flavoured milks, and scratching at his pants watching the reflection in the cabinet doors but no one appeared.

And then he smelled it: a familiar floral scent. His mouth went dry – Jasmine was here. And close by, if he could smell her perfume. He sprinted to the end of the aisle and peered around the corner. A glimpse of her

139

turning into the frozen food section. No sign of Baggy-eyes. He checked behind him, then followed.

She was waiting for him; standing halfway down the aisle, her hands raised in the universal come-in-peace sign.

He glanced over his shoulder. 'Where's your mate?'

'Not here.'

She didn't have the intense focus most people get when they're trying not to look for someone. A fair chance she was telling the truth.

'Turn around slowly,' he said. 'Full circle.'

She heaved a little sigh but went through the motions. Nothing bulky in her pockets, nothing tucked into the waistband of her jeans.

He ventured closer and stood with his back to the glass cabinet. She was looking different from their last meeting, like an actor playing another role, in a neat blue T-shirt and un-scuffed shoes, her hair falling smoothly to her shoulders. A sudden realisation that he was scratching at his pants again. He lowered his hand.

'Why are you following me?'

'...need to talk to you... and the...'

'Slow down, I can't understand you.'

'...tell me where...'

Christ. It was bad enough that she'd seen him piss himself – now he had to admit that he couldn't understand a thing she was saying.

'For fuck's sake, slow down. I can't hear you. I'm deaf.'

'Yeah, I know that *now*.' Accusing, as though he'd been holding out on her.

'What do you mean you know it now?'

'...bloody intel... morons.'

Intel? As in, 'intelligence'? A word that belonged in spy films, not the frozen-food section of the Bay Road IGA.

'Who are you?' he said.

'Afpy.'

Was that her name? Her Myers-Briggs type?

'What?'

'Australian Federal Police,' she said slowly.

He checked her words for alternate meanings but couldn't find any. Was she really a cop? And not just any cop: a federal one?

'You're a cop and you stunned me? Stunned me and then stood there watching while your mate nearly drowned me. Is he a cop, too?'

'No. Which is why I had to go along with it. So let's hurry things up before I blow my cover. I –'

'What's your name?'

'Martha Simpson.' Fluently delivered; a well-memorised lie.

'Show me your ID,' he said.

'I'm undercover, I don't carry ID.'

'You've got a bit of a problem, then.'

She checked the exits and faced him. 'Look, I haven't got time for this. Just tell me where she is and I'll leave you alone.'

A moment to compute what she'd said. How could she not know Portia was dead?

'She's –' He shook his head. 'She's dead.'

'No one believes that. And that's a problem for you.'

'What are you talking about? I saw her die. Her photo was on the news.'

'...we seem... I'm talking about...'

'Slower.'

Her mouth tightened. 'Frankie Reynolds. I'm. Talking. About. Frankie. Reynolds.'

She kept speaking, the words tripping from her tongue.

'I just need to –' He held up a hand. 'Give me a minute.'

Frankie. She was after Frankie, not Portia. God, everything in this investigation was based on the assumption that Jasmine had been interrogating him about Portia. How could he have got it so wrong?

'What's your connection to Portia Hirst?' he asked.

'Who?'

'Portia Hirst. What's your connection to her?'

'I've got no idea what you're talking about.'

It was possible to fake the direct gaze and even breathing, much harder to manufacture that flash of anger; she was annoyed by her confusion and at him for causing it.

'So it's just a coincidence that you and your mate jumped me as soon as I came to the Bay?'

'Coincidence? You took off in the middle of the night, right after Frankie Reynolds visited you. It raised a few alarm bells.'

'What are you talking about? Frankie didn't visit me that day.'

And then it clicked. All those times he'd thought someone had been in his flat – not a delusion, but Frankie looking for her mystery belongings. Her lock-picking skills had obviously improved. But not her skills of evasion, if the federal cops had managed to track her to his place. Or whoever Jasmine really worked for.

'Look, Mr Zelic, I know you spoke to her a few days

ago, so tell me where I can find her and I'll leave you alone.'

He shook his head. 'I don't care if your cover's blown, so how about you tell me what's going on instead? Start with Transis. How's that connected to the feds?'

She paused. 'Transis?'

'Your car was registered to them.'

Her silence lasted a beat too long. 'I borrowed the car from a friend. I don't know who it's registered to.' She nodded at the ceiling. 'They're saying the store's closing. We need to get a move on.'

Convenient timing. Particularly as his aids hadn't picked up the usual muffled blur of the PA announcement.

'Why are you after Frankie?' he asked.

'She's a person of interest in an ongoing investigation.'

'And you've lost track of her?'

The slightest of winces. 'There have been developments which make finding her urgent. So tell me, where can I find her?'

'I don't know.'

'Does she have a favourite place? Somewhere she goes to get away from things?'

'The bottom of a bottle.'

'I'm quite serious, Mr Zelic.'

'So am I. Frankie doesn't travel for fun – she doesn't even drink for fun. Everything's about running away for her.'

Jasmine glanced towards the exits again. 'Any old lovers she'd stay with? Friends? Someone we might not know about?'

'No.'

'Did you give her anything?'

'No.'

'Anything at all, even something innocuous, like a book or a –'

'Nothing. I didn't keep anything of hers.' The words came straight from his mouth, bypassing his brain. Examine why he'd lied later, just stick with the story for now. 'Why are you after her?' he asked. 'What's she done?'

Jasmine pulled a slip of paper from her pocket. 'Ring me on this number if she approaches you again.'

He shoved it in his pocket without a glance, giving his thigh a quick scratch while he was at it. 'She won't.'

'I would like to emphasise the seriousness of the situation, Mr Zelic. I know you're friends with Frankie Reynolds, but it would be a serious mistake to help her.'

'You're right about your intel being shit.' He turned for the rear exit. 'I wouldn't piss on Frankie if she was on fire.'

22.

He waited until Jasmine's car had disappeared around the corner, then drove to Ant's place via a scenic route, keeping an eye out for tailing cars, an easy job on the quiet backstreets. What to make of that conversation? Were the feds really after Frankie, or was Jasmine just trying a different approach to shake information from him? Whatever the truth, Frankie was in deep shit.

The house was empty, so he went straight to Ant's bedroom and ripped off the suit. A moment for a vigorous full-body scratch, then he pulled on his shorts and T-shirt, and shoved the suit back in the wardrobe. Had a quick check while he was in there.

Etty caught him running his hand along the top shelf. He snatched it away. How much did she know about Ant's past? Town gossip and Ant's old track marks would have given her some of the story, but she might not know how far he'd fallen, or for how long.

'Hey,' he said, 'do you know where Ant keeps the spare, um, toilet paper?'

She gave him a long look. 'Doyouwantacupoftea?'

Etty made the worse tea he'd ever tasted. He'd had tea in polystyrene cups from hospital kiosks, enamel-stripping stuff from country cafés, but none of it came close to the tepid beige liquid that Etty produced. He took a second sip to be polite and lowered the cup. Hard to believe that she'd used the standard ingredients of water and a tea bag.

She left her own cup untouched on the kitchen table and perched on the edge of her chair, all energy and twitching limbs, looking as though she might take off for a quick sprint around the room at any minute. 'IknowallaboutAnt,' she said.

'Sorry, what?'

She grimaced. 'Sorry. Ant keeps telling me to slow down. Mum says I was born on fast forward. Is this OK?'

'Perfect.'

'I know all about Ant. The full catastrophe – the smack, the robbing, the conning, the jail sentence. Everything.'

'OK. Good.'

'We met at a support group, you know. A friends-and-family thing. My brother was a user. Incredible, really – I was only there because I was so angry at Noah, but then I turn around and pick up a boyfriend. Everyone said, "God, what are you doing, dating an addict after Noah?" but Ant smiled that smile of his and cracked one of his jokes, and I was just gone.'

A short lag while Caleb's brain caught up with her words. Even at half-speed, she was a challenge. So her brother had been a user; that put Ant in very capable hands.

'Your brother's clean now?'

'Dead,' she said. 'OD'ed when I was twenty.'

She spoke as though she was reading from a cue card, but the raw sorrow in her face made his gut clench.

'I'm really sorry,' he said. 'Me checking before, that was just me being paranoid. I don't think Ant's using.'

'I know he's not. Ant's an all-or-nothing guy – it'll be pretty obvious if he gets back on the gear. But he's not going to, because I'm the best fucking thing that's ever happened to him and I'm out that door if he touches the stuff. No excuses, no second chances. I'm not going through that shit again. Not just losing him, but all those years of hoping. Hoping is unbearable.' Her eyes watered. She grabbed her cup and gulped at the tea, gave a small shudder.

Why had she made tea if she didn't like it? Ah, a little slow on the uptake today.

'You don't have to drink that to win me over,' he said. 'I agree that you're the best fucking thing that's ever happened to him.'

She grinned. 'Thank God, because drinking tea could be a real deal-breaker. I'm a coffee girl.'

'It usually tastes better than this.'

'It'd want to.' She pushed the cup away. 'Anyway, Ant and I are moving in together.'

'Wow, that's great. Really great.'

Ant had been a root-rat since he was a teenager; strange to think of him settling down. Still, he was twenty-eight. By that age, Kat had lost two pregnancies, and Caleb was in the throes of fucking things up between them.

Etty jiggled on her chair. 'He was supposed to talk to you about the trust, but he keeps chickening out. He wants to sell this place so we can buy somewhere together. What do you reckon?'

He didn't answer for a moment. One of the last things their father had done before he died was put the house in a trust so Ant couldn't get his hands on the money. Dissolving it would be a big move. Enormous.

'OK,' he said. 'Let me think about it.'

Her eyes lit up. 'Thanks, that's great. He's been so nervous about bringing it up – thought you'd just say no.'

'Won't he be pissed off when he finds out that you've spoken to me about it?'

'Sure, but he's a big boy. He can suck it the fuck up.'

He smiled. It was going to be a joy watching her handle Ant.

He left Etty to bounce around waiting for Ant, and headed for the motel, caught sight of a familiar figure walking along the verge ahead of him. Kat. Why wasn't she at the wake? Her entire family would be there. Aunts, uncles, cousins from across the country, many of them seen only at funerals. She had duties to perform, consolation to give. It was inconceivable that she'd leave so soon.

She turned around as he pulled up alongside. Her face was tight with tension, her shoulders hunched.

'Want a lift?'

She hesitated, then touched her fingers to her chin in a 'thank you'.

'No Beetle?' he asked as she climbed in.

'It didn't seem the best choice for a funeral.'

'Good call.' He looked at her clenched hands. 'Everything OK at the wake?'

'Yeah. Just, you know, sorry business. I needed a break. You'd better drop me back there.'

He signed without thinking. 'Do you want to go to the beach first? Clear your head?'

She looked at him. A strong impression of decisions being made and discarded. 'Yeah, I would. Let's go to Lantern Cove.'

———

There was no carpark at the cove, just a long walk to the water and the promise of privacy. They'd come here a lot in their teen years. He parked on the shoulder and followed Kat through the trees; the scent of ti-tree mingled with seaweed. Kat hesitated at the top of the dune that led down to the sea. She glanced back at him, then headed away from the beach towards the broad expanse of white hillocks to their right. Layer upon layer of ancient shells that marked the place where Kat's people had gathered for millennia. Sixty thousand years by recent estimate. She stopped at the midden's edge and kicked off her sandals, raised her face to the sky.

He retreated and waited for her on the beach.

———

Kat joined him a long time later. Long enough for the day to have slipped into night and a crescent moon to rise. She touched the back of his neck to warn him of her presence.

Sand was clinging to her hand. Her right hand. A memory of a long-ago conversation.

'Left hand to give back to country, right hand to gain strength.'

'OK?' he said.

'Much better.'

She did look better: smiling now, a slight wildness to her expression.

'Do you want to go back to the wake?' he asked.

'God, no.' She laughed. 'This was a great idea. Thanks.'

'I have them sometimes.'

Having a few ideas right now – sudden insanity brought about by the heat, the glint in Kat's eye, the memory of what they usually ended up doing after fraught family occasions.

Her eyes held his. 'Nice night for a swim.'

Blood humming, a sudden weakness to his legs.

'Come on,' she said.

And she was running. Across the sand towards the water, pulling off her dress. It fluttered into the night, followed by her bra and underpants.

A moment for rudimentary thought to return, then he stripped and sprinted after her.

She was surfacing when he reached her. Waist-deep, with her back to the breaking waves, the moonlight folding shadows across her. She grasped his hand and drew him in. The shock of her body against his. The satin touch of her skin, the taste of salt and honey. Touching and stroking, grasping. The surge of each wave pushing them together. A building urgency. More. Now. And they were moving. Out of the water and onto the hard sand. Everything hard. Everything except Kat. She was soft and smooth and silken. On his back, grasping her tightly. She straddled him and lowered herself onto him. A velvet heat. She rocked urgently, her head thrown back. Darkness gathering behind his eyes, pressure building. Then she bucked and pulsed around him, and he let himself go.

———

Afterwards, she lay on him, her weight a blessing. He summoned the energy to raise a hand and stroked the nape of her neck. A growing appreciation for the short hair. He'd tell her once he could remember how to form words.

Something damp on his chest, Kat shaking. Oh God, she was crying.

'Sorry,' he said. 'I'm sorry.'

He wrapped his arms around her, murmuring meaning-less sounds. She clung to him for long minutes until a shudder ran through her and she stilled. She rolled off him and knelt in the sand.

He sat up. 'Are you OK?'

'Yeah, sorry – sex as a release.' She laughed. 'Thanks, I needed that.'

She wiped her eyes and gave him a little smile. Rare insight: this was where he always fucked up, some emo-tional need gone unanswered. Say something. Something true.

He touched her cheek. 'I've missed you so much.'

And there was her real smile, broad and blinding. Seven months since he'd seen it.

'I've missed you, too. I just –' Her hands dipped into shadow as a cloud moved across the moon.

Damn. 'I can't see,' he said.

She moved closer, her knees touching his: more a presence than a shape, only the flash of her eyes visible.

'It's still too dark,' he said, but she slipped her hands beneath his and lifted them.

She sketched the shapes, carrying his hands with her. A moment to realise that she was signing. Tactile signing. He'd read about it but never seen it done, never felt its intimacy. He closed his eyes and fell into her movements.

'Can you follow me like this?'

It was like being a part of her. 'Yes.'

'I feel wrong.'

'I know.'

'Really? Everyone else keeps telling me how well I'm doing, giving me little gold stars. What gave me away?'

Her separateness, her hair, her callus-free hands.

'You're not working.'

A tremor ran through her. 'I haven't done anything since it happened. Haven't even picked up a pencil. I can't.'

His breath caught. 'The doctors –'

'It's not my hand, it's me. There's nothing there. I can't concentrate, I can't think. I feel so weak.'

It took him a few seconds to find his voice. 'You're not weak, you're healing. And you're one of the strongest people I know. I'm in awe of you.'

Her hands faltered in midair. 'Thanks. That really helps.' She threaded her fingers through his and squeezed. *Right hand to gain strength.*

'Is it easier now you're home?' he asked.

'Harder. But better.' She touched his chest, a fleeting warmth. 'What about you? How are you going?'

'Great, now you're here.'

'No, I mean really. How are you, *really*?' She chopped the edge of her hand against her palm to form the sign. So emphatic – had he let something slip? Let her glimpse the grasping darkness inside?

'Pretty good. The business is going well now I've got it set up differently.'

A pause.

'That's great.' She pulled her hands from his, and he fell back to earth. He opened his eyes. Enough moonlight now to see the smooth blankness of her expression.

'We'd better wash off,' she said. 'Or we'll be finding sand for years.'

And she strode away.

23.

He drove out to Snake Gully Road the next afternoon, trying to convince himself that it was the next logical step in his investigation, but knowing it was because Frankie had told him to take another look at the place. It had been a morning of restless impatience – interviewing staff from Hilvington Care, organising his notes, trying to find information on Jasmine – his mind half on Kat and the beach. Things had been good there for a moment. More than good, perfect, but then he'd lost her again. She'd been unusually quiet during the car trip back to her parents' place. She'd given him a kiss on the lips, a touch to his hand, and left him with the vague promise of meeting up soon. Not together, not apart, still caught between breaths.

He passed Portia's crash site and reached for his sunglasses as the dark green pines gave way to semi-grazed bushland. Scattered gums and knee-high grass, no sign of any cattle. A gap in the undergrowth as he passed a winding driveway. He caught a flash of colour and stopped, put the car into reverse. A Coast Care poster was stapled to the gate.

He parked in the driveway and got out. According to a faded wooden sign, the driveway led to the Bay Creek

School camp. A row of saplings had been planted along the boundary fence, a wilting collection of gums. So Jai had told the truth about driving out to help Portia with Coast Care. Which was nice, but didn't get Caleb any closer to understanding why bikies had been shooting at them. He stepped off the road to piss while he thought. What was it about trees that made him want to urinate? Bladder of a dog.

Maybe Portia's environmental efforts had made her a target. Or the ingredients she'd needed for them. It was getting harder to make bombs from fertiliser these days – people tended to get antsy when motorbike-riding men strode into their stores wanting a metric tonne of the stuff. A bit excessive to open fire on someone because of their access to it, but bikies weren't always known for their subtlety. He zipped up and headed for the camp; if there was a caretaker, he might be able to get some information.

The gravel driveway wound a few hundred metres into the bush, speckled with rye grass and fallen leaves. It ended in a wide clearing with a cluster of buildings: cabins and sheds, a shipping container, a larger, barn-like structure, all painted a dull green that conjured visions of 'team building' games and obstacle courses. He checked one of the cabins first. Dirt and cobwebs, a startled blue-tongue lizard. A growing feeling he wasn't going to be finding a caretaker.

On to the larger building. Its tiled roof and wide wooden doors were familiar – an overlapping image of the place as a construction site. He'd been here as a child. A visit to see his father at work. Probably one of Ivan's attempts to re-socialise him after the meningitis. There'd been a lot of that during the early days: bewildering trips to shops and friends, tickets to incomprehensible movies. This excursion couldn't have been any more successful than those, because he'd never accompanied his father to a building site again. Unusual for Ivan to have admitted defeat, even when it hinged on another person's failings. It must have galled.

Caleb circled the building, trying the doors. There were locks on them, new and expensive, a little unexpected for an abandoned school camp. An increasing desire to get inside and snoop around. He tried to rattle the back door from its hinges, but it was a solid Ivan Zelic product: built to outlast its maker. He stood back and checked the windows – boarded shut and screwed from the inside. A solid-looking drainpipe, but good balance was something else he hadn't recovered after the meningitis. What were his chances of picking one of those locks? About zero. What he needed was a locksmith. Or a burglar.

Ant readily agreed to a trip out to Snake Gully Road but insisted on taking his air-conditioned car. Ten seconds into the journey, Caleb regretted asking for his help. His brother kept up a steady flow of Auslan as he drove, looking at Caleb instead of the road and rarely touching the wheel with anything as mundane as a hand.

Caleb was OK with the shit driving, but the conversation was killing him.

'…and then she said –' Ant nudged the wheel with

his elbow '– that we need to work on a few things if we're going to move in together.'

'Right.'

'Quite a few things, as it turns out. I thought she was going to bring out a spreadsheet at one stage.'

'Yeah.'

'But her main concern seems to be my "communication skills".' The car wandered into the next lane as Ant turned to see his response.

Caleb switched from sign to speech on the off-chance that it might stop them from dying in a fiery head-on collision. 'She wants you to talk less?'

'Fuck you, she wants me to talk more. She said that I don't express my emotional needs clearly and that great sex isn't enough to sustain a relationship.'

'Too much information.'

'And that I need to bring my oral skills out of the bedroom.'

'Still too much.'

Ant grinned and executed a zippy turn onto Snake Gully Road. A distinct possibility that two tyres left the asphalt at the same time both hands left the wheel.

'Did Kat ever say anything like that to you? About the emotional needs, I mean. I'm sure you two fu–'

'Yes,' Caleb said quickly. 'Often.'

So often that it was remarkable he hadn't actually learned anything at the time. Still, he was doing better now, some definite progress on that front. And some backwards steps. Maybe he wasn't doing as well as he'd thought. Perhaps a spreadsheet wasn't such a bad idea.

'So, any pointers?' Ant asked. 'How'd you go?'

'Well, she left me.'

'Good point. Guess I'll have to make something up. Half the time I'm just sitting there thinking, "I could really do with a pizza right now."'

Ant still hadn't mentioned the trust, or wanting to buy a place with Etty. Caleb decided to put him out of his misery. 'Etty spoke to me about the trust.'

A pause.

'Yeah,' Ant said. 'She told me.' His hands went to the wheel and gripped it in the recommended ten-to-two position.

'I emailed the solicitor this morning,' Caleb said. 'Asked him to dissolve it.'

Ant jerked around to look at him, and the car veered off the road towards the trees.

OK, now Caleb was worried about the driving. 'Trees,' he said.

Ant yanked the car back onto the road. 'OK. Thanks.'

Caleb waited for more, but Ant's hands stayed on the wheel. If he'd known that was all it took to shut Ant up, he would have dissolved the trust months ago.

He pointed out the windscreen. 'Pull in a bit past that driveway. Get right off the road into the trees.'

Ant drove slowly off the road, threading his way through the gum trees until they were far enough in to avoid casual observation. Out of the air-conditioned comfort of Ant's car, the air was like a wall.

Caleb hesitated, one hand still on the car door. With his record, Ant couldn't afford to be caught breaking in anywhere, abandoned or not.

'You sure you're OK to do this?' he asked.

Ant shrugged. 'An abandoned shed in the middle of nowhere, think I'm right.' He headed towards the camp. 'Just don't get your hopes up – I'm pretty shit at picking locks. I got caught, remember? Multiple times.'

'Yeah, but you were off your face. It's impressive you could even find the lock, really.'

'True.' Ant climbed the low wire fence that lay between them and the camp. 'This is odd, you know, you bolstering my confidence in my B and E abilities. I think it might be what my counsellor would call a new stage in our relationship.'

Counsellor? He wasn't going to ask.

'The rehab place recommended her,' Ant said. 'She's really good if you ever, you know, want to share the load a bit.'

Spilling secrets to a stranger; discussing things best left unthought, let alone unsaid. He ignored Ant's earnest expression and headed for the barn.

He'd seen a therapist last year, just before Kat left for Broome. It had gone against his every instinct, but it had seemed so important to Kat that he'd sat in a soothing blue room and spoken to a well-dressed woman about horror and death and despair. And then he'd forced himself to go back. Three sessions. One hundred and fifty minutes of stilted agony that had done nothing except stir the sludge in his mind, awakening things that had lain safely dormant. That was when the real nightmares had begun.

'This is the one,' he said, reaching the barn. 'There's a mortice on the front doors, but I thought the back one might be doable.'

Ant circled the building, examining the back door and then the front. He straightened, shaking his head. 'Yeah, nah, we'll have to get in some other way. Maybe try and get the boards off a window and smash the glass.'

'They're screwed from the inside. We'll have to climb onto the roof, lift a tile.'

'You've got Buckley's – your balance is shit.'

Caleb smiled. 'Yours isn't.'

———

After a few failed attempts and some skinned knuckles, Ant finally managed to shimmy up a drainpipe. He disappeared from view and reappeared a few minutes later at the front door. He had a netting of cobwebs on his hair and shoulders, a scratch down one cheek.

'You owe me big time,' he said.

'Yeah? Remind me again who totalled my first car?'

'Yeah, yeah.' Ant brushed at his hair, shaking his hand wildly when it came away covered in cobwebs. 'Just come in, will you? The sooner we get out of here, the better.'

The building turned out to be an open-plan recreation room with a high ceiling and exposed wooden walls, a kitchen to one side. Caleb opened both doors to get some light inside. Empty except for a few plastic trestle tables and rows of metal shelving down the back. Dust-free surfaces, the faint chemical smell of cleaning fluids.

'Check the kitchen,' he told Ant. 'Let me know if you find fertiliser or anything else weird.'

'Fertiliser?'

'From Portia's tree-planting scheme. I'm playing

around with the idea that bikies were stealing fertiliser for bombs.'

'You don't fertilise gums.'

'You don't?'

'Nah, burns their roots.'

He examined Ant. 'Since when did you become Mr Nature?'

'Basic knowledge, city boy. You've lost touch with *your* roots.'

Could be. Or maybe they'd always been shallow.

Caleb headed for the shelving at the back of the room. Eight rows of sturdy metal units, the kind found in hardware stores and nurseries, designed to support the weight of potting mix and paint tins. No bags of fertiliser, just half a dozen cardboard boxes.

He opened one and found blank address labels. On to the next box: more blank labels. He went through them all until he found a handful of discarded labels in the last box. Someone had had trouble with the printer: the addresses were smudged and off-centre. An old ink jet, judging by the blurred lines. He'd seen something similar recently. Where had he come across cheaply printed address labels in the past couple of weeks? On Dave McGregor's kitchen table. Printed labels in a house without a printer. Damn, he should have paid more attention to that. Was it a dodgy mailing scheme? Blackmail? Or just coincidence?

A vibration. Ant was in the kitchen doorway, stomping on the floor to get his attention. Even from this side of the room, he looked pale.

'There's a car coming,' he signed.

Shit.

'How close?'

'Coming up the driveway.'

Make a run for it? A vast stretch of cleared land around the building – they'd never make it. Shit, shit, shit.

'Bolt the front doors,' Caleb said calmly. 'I'll do the back.'

He slid the bolt into place just as Ant closed the front door. Darkness, no sense of shadow or shape. He fumbled for his phone and turned on the torch. A faint thrumming beneath his feet. He crouched down and pressed his hand to the floor. A car wouldn't make the floorboards hum like that; it had to be something bigger, like a ute or a van. The vibration stopped. A bobbing light appeared as Ant crossed the room. He reached Caleb's side and signed something about a door.

'It's too dark,' Caleb said.

Ant shone the light on his own mouth and enunciated very clearly, 'Whisper.'

Not one of his stronger talents.

'Sorry. How many people are there?'

'I don't know, they're not talking. They tried the front door and now they're at the back.' Ant screwed up his face. 'They're having a good go at it.'

Caleb could feel the percussive thuds; whoever it was had some heft behind them. Ant glanced towards the front of the hall, poised to run.

'It's a solid door,' Caleb said. 'Dad made it.'

That was enough to surprise Ant into immobility. The thuds slowed and then stopped. A long wait, then the rumble of the truck's engine. It idled for a moment, then faded away.

Ant let out a long breath. 'Debt now paid in full for trashing your car.'

'You think?'

'Yeah, and those aids you "lost" when you were ten.'

24.

They reached town just before sunset – unscathed and, as far as Caleb could tell, undetected. Ant suddenly pulled over and turned off the engine. They were parked outside the Queen's Hotel, a 1920s bluestone that had been efficiently gutted of all charm in a 1970s reno.

'What are we doing here?' Caleb asked.

'You're buying me a beer.'

'You don't drink anymore.'

Ant opened the door. 'Well, thanks, Mum, but I do. I drink two days a week and I've decided that this is going be one of them.' He got out of the car and headed inside.

The Queen's Hotel was as dead as you'd expect for a pretty average pub on a Tuesday evening. A beer-gutted businessman was sitting at the bar, along with a couple of fast-drinking women who looked as though they'd survived a tough first day back at the local high school. Caleb grabbed two beers and joined Ant at a table in the back corner. Ant took a long drink and kept hold of the glass when he'd finished. He caught Caleb's glance.

'Stop watching me, for fuck's sake. *I'm* fine. You're the one we're all worried about.'

We. Who the hell was we?

'He must have known we were in there,' Ant said. 'Both doors were bolted from the inside. Do you reckon he went looking for my car when he couldn't get in?'

That was exactly what Caleb would have done.

'Maybe,' Caleb said. 'But it was a fair way off the road. And it's not like it's got your name on it. People can't just rock up to VicRoads and ask for a car owner's details, you know.' You needed a Sammi for that.

'I'm not worried about some pissed-off groundskeeper, I'm worried about the cops.'

Caleb should have remembered that Ant couldn't handle stress. As a kid, he'd been set off by everything: scary movies, school bullies, their father. Any of the thousand things you had to face up to in day-to-day life.

'It doesn't matter if he goes to the cops,' Caleb said. 'I borrowed your car. You were at home watching TV, remember?'

'But what if –'

'Jesus, harden up, Ant.'

A flash of hurt on Ant's face, quickly hidden.

He'd spoken the words, not signed. Which wasn't surprising, seeing as he'd apparently turned into his father. He could still hear Ivan's voice sometimes, an auditory memory that had wedged in his brain. A little disconcerting to feel it coming from his own mouth.

'Sorry,' he signed. 'Arsehole thing to say.'

'Coming, as it does, from an arsehole.' Ant took

another drink, then made a show of pushing the glass away, half-empty.

Caleb pulled the address labels from his back pocket and examined them. There was no match for the name he'd seen at McGregor's house, the anonymous-sounding A. Anderson. The sheet was obviously the B section of an alphabetical mailing list: M. Bowen, J. Brown, A. Byron. No street addresses, just PO Boxes, none of them in the Bay.

He slid the page across the table. 'Know anyone on this list?'

The barest of glances. 'No.'

'You want to put a little more brainpower into it?'

Ant picked up the page. 'I can confirm that I do not know any of these people. Why do you think they're important, anyway? It's just a list of names you found in an empty shed.'

'There was a similar sheet at McGregor's house.'

'Same names?'

'Same type of printer.'

'Seriously? Someone's got a shit printer that a million other people own and you're ready to get the handcuffs out?'

Put like that, it did seem a bit of a tenuous link.

'You never know what's relevant,' he said.

Ant sighed and pulled out his phone.

'I'm sorry,' Caleb said, 'am I boring you?'

'Always, but I'm googling the names.' Ant managed to flip the two-fingered salute that was the sign for 'name' into a double-fingered 'fuck you'.

Good to see that things were returning to normal.

'You take the top six,' Caleb told him. 'I'll do the rest.'

Twenty minutes later, he was ready to bang his head against the table in frustration. He'd given up on Google after thirty seconds and used Pipl, a search engine that trawled through parts of the web unavailable to standard searches, and one that he'd previously found terrifyingly good at attaching people's names to their addresses. But the flood of possible hits was still overwhelming.

'You get anything?' he asked Ant.

'Depends on what you find interesting. Would you be enthralled by the knowledge that there are twenty thousand, six hundred and eighty-six J. Browns listed in the Australian telephone directory, none of whom seem to live anywhere near this PO address?'

Caleb scrubbed his face. He might have to get Sammi to do a little more hacking – they wouldn't be able to trace any of these names through his usual methods. It was hard to imagine a blander list outside of an all-white organisation. Which was an interesting idea.

'Maybe they're some kind of Anglo group,' he said.

Ant's eyes went to something behind him. 'What, like a tweed shopping network?'

'More along the lines of swastikas.'

'Oh, right.' Ant frowned, his eyes darting across the room again. 'Yeah, they are pretty white bread.'

Caleb turned to see what was happening. Nothing was out of place, but their fellow drinkers were glancing towards the windows.

'What's going on?' he asked.

'Bit of shouting outside. Think someone broke a bottle.

Or a couple of bottles.' Ant pushed back his chair. 'Let's go. I need to express my emotional needs to my woman with some hot and dirty sex.' He chose the most graphic signs possible, ones easily readable by a non-signing ten-year-old.

The high school teachers applauded and raised their glasses in salute. Ant bowed.

———

It was dark outside, with a stillness to the air that promised a night of suffocating heat and restless dreams. Tomorrow was going to be a shocker.

Ant stopped as they got to the car, his head angled to listen. 'Car alarms,' he told Caleb without being asked. 'Police sirens, too. Someone's having a big night.'

He could just hear them: a high-pitched whine right at the threshold of his hearing. Impossible to know how close they were.

'Close?'

'A few blocks away,' Ant said, unlocking the door.

Caleb switched on the internal light as Ant pulled away from the kerb. 'What would you use a mailing list for?'

'Um, a wine club?'

This was where he missed Frankie. She would have formed half a dozen theories before he'd finished the question, with the added bonus of some top-quality foul language.

'Illegal,' he said. 'But able to be mailed. I've drawn a blank after kiddie porn and Indigenous artefacts.'

'Endangered animals, maybe, snakes and things, or –

Shit.' Ant stopped signing and gripped the wheel. He pulled onto the side of the road.

A flash of red as two police cars sped past in quick succession. Two cars – that would have to be the Bay's entire pool of police vehicles.

Ant's shoulders released as he watched them disappear around the corner. 'Excited about something. Maybe they found the other pages of your mailing list.'

Up ahead there was a hint of movement, people running along the shadowed street. Caleb switched off the light. 'Hang on,' he said, as Ant went to pull out.

It was a group of teenagers wearing bandanas and carrying cricket bats and sticks. A loping wildness to their gait, as though they were out partying with their mates. They turned the corner and headed down towards the shops. A glimpse of fair skin above their bandanas. That had to be Rat-tail Luke and his band of thugs.

Caleb opened the car door. 'Meet you back at the house.'

Ant signed something, but it was impossible to follow him with the light off.

'Tell me later.' He closed the door and ran after the boys.

There was no sign of them by the time he reached the corner, so he ran down the hill and ducked into the carpark behind the supermarket. He made his way along the pedestrian walkway to the street and peered out. The boys were sweeping along the footpath away from him, barely stopping as they smashed windows and streetlights, upended bins. And there was Luke Blundon, bashing in a glass door with a cricket bat, his rat-tail hair hanging down his neck.

A tap on his shoulder.

He spun around: Ant.

A sudden realisation that rectal muscles could release involuntarily if you weren't careful.

'Christ.' He pressed a hand to his heart. 'Bit of warning next time.'

'How? Send up a flare?' Ant's face was ghostly in the green light of the supermarket exit sign. 'What the hell are you doing?'

'Trying to work out what they're up to. This is a lot worse than their previous shit.'

Ant peered at the street. 'More even-handed in their racism, though.'

True. There were only three Koori-run businesses in town, but the kids were wrecking shops indiscriminately. No, not indiscriminately – some discipline in their actions: waiting for the police to go past, then slipping out behind them; smashing streetlights so they couldn't be identified. And their tight formation. This wasn't a gang of hoodlums, it was an army.

'Car alarms are going off in the next street,' Ant said. 'Sounds like they're heading back towards the highway.'

Caleb checked the street. No sign of the gang, but he waited in the shadows, the reptilian part of his brain warning him not to move. A distant flicker of red as a police car sped through the intersection and disappeared. Two men stepped out of the shadows in its wake. They were coming up from the beach: grey against grey in the bruised light, wearing hoodies and tracksuit pants. One of their hoods had fallen back to reveal an oddly blank face; dark, with a pale gash for a mouth. A balaclava. Something familiar about both of them, particularly the shorter one: he had a thick neck and swinging arms, a slight catch to his stride, the barest of limps. They were heading closer.

Caleb stepped further back and held up his hand to warn Ant to be quiet. The men passed centimetres away, carrying with them a strong smell of alcohol. Another scent, too – something that didn't belong. Paint thinner? Glue? They weren't drunk, despite the smell of alcohol, walking properly, their feet lifting. A sense that the taller one was talking.

Caleb motioned for Ant to stay where he was and slipped out to follow them. He stopped as a lone teenager appeared around the corner ahead of him. He was wearing a blue bandana and clutching a half-brick, running down the middle of the road. The boy passed the two men with a brief glance, but slowed as he saw Caleb. He pulled back his arm and threw the brick. Caleb ducked. The window next to him exploded. Shards of glass flying, a sting across his back and neck.

A moment of stunned immobility, then Ant pulled him into the walkway. 'Jesus, are you OK?'

He made a quick assessment – a few cuts, normal vision, no gaping wounds.

'Yeah.'

The men had turned at the sound of the glass breaking. Had they seen him on the darkened street? Yes. The talking man had put his arm out, as though to stop his companion from coming back for Caleb. Shit. He peered around the corner, but they'd gone.

Ant tapped his shoulder. 'I vote we don't frig around getting back to the car. Let's go back via the beach.'

Good idea. He wanted to know what the men had been doing down there.

They ran across the road and over the bluestone retaining wall onto the sand. No one in sight: everyone barricaded in their homes, or out on the streets, smashing shop windows. They jogged along the beach, towards Ant's place.

'Were they talking when they passed us?' Caleb asked.

'Yeah. The guy furthest from us. He was pissed off about something, but speaking quietly, sort of whispering. He said something about doing it well or not.'

Doing it well or not? Obviously key details lost in translation there.

'What were his exact words?'

Ant went to sign again, but Caleb shook his head. 'Fingerspell the English.'

Ant stopped jogging and spelt out each word on his fingers. 'Do. It. Properly. Or. Don't. Do. It. At. All.'

Jesus, now their father's voice was coming from stranger's mouths. And he might just leave analysing that thought to a more appropriate time. Like on his deathbed.

'Do it properly.'

Do what properly? What would you need the cover of a riot to do? Because that was what those kids had been doing – creating maximum havoc with minimum effort in order to keep the police busy.

The beach track was up ahead, steep wooden stairs leading to the top of the dunes. Caleb started up them. Away from the salt-laden wind was the unmistakable smell of smoke. And Caleb suddenly realised what other scent the two men had carried with them: kerosene. Alcohol and kerosene. Oh, shit. He jogged the rest of the way up the stairs, Ant close behind him. Down the path and out onto the road. They were at the hilltop, looking across the houses towards the south.

Bright pyres lit the darkness. Four of them, five, six.

The Mish was burning.

25.

News vans had sprouted like toadstools overnight in the Mish, so Caleb ducked around the back road, keeping an eye out for Kat as he drove.

Her parents' house had been lit up like a landing strip when he'd got there last night. He'd arrived out of breath to find the front door wide open and the house crowded with friends and family, people fleeing the Mish. Kat had gripped him in a fierce hug, pointed him towards the coffee machine and gone back to answering the continually ringing phone. He'd stayed, making endless cups of tea and coffee, until the final report had come in: four homes destroyed, three people hospitalised, no fatalities. When the household had finally stumbled to bed, Kat had taken him by the hand and led him to her room. This morning she'd slipped from bed without waking him, leaving a cup of cooling tea and a note to say that she'd gone to the Mish.

He parked in the shade of a straggly wattle tree and went to find her. The Mish was only a few blocks wide, so it shouldn't take too long. He passed a couple of burnt-out cars and came to the first ruined house: a shell of blackened walls and twisted beams. A pall of smoke hung in the still air, the stench of wet ash and charcoal. People were milling on the street and in their yards, some wearing dressing-gowns and pyjamas, empty disbelief in their faces. The feeling of eyes on him as he passed. No burnt letterboxes or bus stops, no half-hearted scorch marks around the bases of trees: the two men had done a good job with their Molotov cocktails, lobbed each one with surgical accuracy.

Sergeant Ramsden stepped out of a house ahead of him. Caleb ducked into a side street. He needed to give Ramsden a description of the arsonists, but he'd have a lot more luck getting people to talk to him if he wasn't seen chatting to the cops beforehand. He turned the corner and came to an abrupt halt. There was a gap like a missing tooth where Aunty Eileen's house had stood. An ache in his heart. First Jai, now her home – it was too much for anyone to bear.

He turned away and saw a young man across the road staring at him. Around Jai's age, with long dark hair and a narrowed expression. He was standing in his front yard rolling a cigarette. Jai's dog by his side. Jaws obviously held as fond a memory of Caleb as Caleb did of it – the animal's ears were lying flat, tail down. Why the hell had Aunty Eileen allowed that beast into her home? An image of the dog's makeshift bed and bowl, the strong sense that Aunty Eileen had quickly cleared her house of children. The way she'd deflected Caleb when he'd mentioned the vandalism to her house. Aunty Eileen hadn't been worried about Jai getting into trouble with the police, she'd been fearful for his life.

Caleb went to talk to Jaws' new friend. The man lit his rollie as Caleb approached, and inhaled deeply. 'If you're a journo, no fucken comment.'

Jaws quivered at his tone. The fence was a scant fifty centimetres high, an easy lope for the beast.

'Not a journo,' Caleb said. 'I'm looking for Aunty Eileen. Do you know where she is?'

'Why?'

'I'm a bit worried about her. With the house and Jai and everything.'

'Yeah?' Another deep drag, but the man was looking at him with more interest. 'Seen you around a bit. Where you from?'

Damn, he was about to fail a test. He'd hung around Kat and her family long enough to know what that question meant: Are you one of us?

'The Bay,' he said without much hope.

The man exhaled a lungful of smoke and headed for the house.

'Married Kat Anderson,' Caleb called, but he didn't look back.

———

Caleb tracked Aunty Eileen down at the Boorai playgroup centre, a steepled weatherboard building that used to be a church hall. She was wearing new slippers and the clothes of a much larger woman, staring at a bundle of sewing that lay, untouched, in her lap. It was a sunny room with shelves of well-loved books and toys, and a hand-woven rug of red, black and yellow. Bright posters lined the walls: *Koori Kids Are Great Kids*; *Nothing About Us, Without Us*; *Immunise Now*. A handful of preschool kids were involved in a complex game involving saucepans and wooden blocks.

Aunty Eileen looked up as Caleb pulled a plastic chair around to face her. Her skin was yellow-tinged and tufts of her grey-white hair were standing on end. A local newspaper was folded by her chair, a photo of the scar tree on its front page, its trunk garlanded with flowers.

'I'm so sorry about everything,' Caleb said. 'About Jai, and your house. It must be hard.'

She nodded and found new interest in her sewing.

'Aunty Eileen.' He hesitated, then ploughed on. 'Who was Jai scared of?'

She seemed to give the question some thought. 'No one now.'

'It's not just teenagers mucking about. Not any more. Someone's targeting your mob.'

'No prizes for workin' that one out, love.' She turned her sewing over, and he realised that it was a doll; blank-faced and limp, the size of newborn baby.

He dragged his eyes from it. 'Do you know what's behind all the violence?'

'Terra fucken nullius, love.' She pushed the needle into the doll's dark scalp and yanked it out. 'Gubbas can't stand that us blackfellas were here first.'

He chose his words carefully. 'Some of us can.'

She stabbed the needle into the doll. 'You want a round of applause? Bring me back my kids. Bring me back my aunties and uncles, my grandsons. I'll give you a standing fucken ovation.' Another stab of the needle.

God. Give it two more questions, then slink away. Make them count – what would bikies be interested in? Money, prostitution, arms, drugs. Drugs. Jai's history with ice. The spark of an idea: violence as a sales technique. It wouldn't be the first time a bikie gang had used fear to push ice in a small community.

'Did Jai say anything about the Copperheads pressuring people? Forcing them to buy ice?'

Her head jerked up. 'Jai was clean. You can ask the coroner. They opened him right up, had a good poke around. He learned his lesson after Pete, never touched the stuff.'

'No, I didn't mean – I think Jai witnessed something the night Portia died. I think he was killed because he knew something. What did he tell you about that day?'

'That he wanted to go away. I told him that he'd lose his apprenticeship, lose all that hard work. So he stayed. I should've told him to go. Shouldn't have held on so tight.' She smoothed the doll's back, a gesture of self-comfort she'd obviously done a thousand times before. She'd spoken about children a moment ago.

'Bring me back my kids.'

A terrible realisation crept into his heart – Aunty Eileen's children were part of the Stolen Generations. Taken away under the guise of assimilation. Taken to foster homes or servitude, orphanages, the unknown. How to convince her to put her trust in the same system that had ripped her children from her? How to convince himself?

'Aunty Eileen,' he said slowly, 'these people aren't going to stop. If you know something about Jai's death, you have to tell the cops.'

Her face hardened. 'Don't you go bringing any gunyan around here.'

'OK. It doesn't have to be the police. Tell me, tell Maria.'

'Leave me alone now, love. I'm tired.'

She looked more than tired, she looked frail and ill, and much older than her seventy-odd years. A sudden, terrifying thought at the chaos that would follow if she died now. Those young men at the funeral, with their clenched fists and boiling fury – another generation would be lost if they gave vent to that anger.

'Aunty Eileen, you need help. Please let me help you.'

She shook her head with weary patience; a teacher who'd been lumbered with an endlessly stupid child. 'You gubbas. Always thinking you've got the answer to everything. I don't want your help, love, so piss off now, leave me alone.'

Sergeant Ramsden caught him coming out of the centre. There was a sheen of sweat on the policeman's broad face, damp patches staining the armpits of his shirt.

'Mr Zelic. What are you doing here?'

Caleb moved onto the footpath to draw the man's attention away from the building. 'Just helping out. I'm glad I found you – I've got a bit of information about last night.' He went through the events of the riot, describing Rat-tail's gang and the two balaclava-clad men, his vague theories about the Copperheads. Left out any mention of Jai and Aunty Eileen.

By the time he'd finished, Ramsden looked more exhausted than enthusiastic, but he pulled out his notebook and pen. 'How...?' he asked as he flipped through the pages.

'Sorry, what?'

Ramsden looked up. 'How. Well. Do. You. Know. Luke. Blundon?'

'I don't.'

'And. Yet. You. Managed. To...'

God, they'd be here all day at this rate.

'You can talk normally,' Caleb said. 'I just couldn't see your mouth.'

A slow-burn blush crept up Ramsden's face. 'And yet you managed to identify Luke Blundon from a distance? In the dark?'

'Yes. He's got a pretty distinctive haircut. Talk to him. It's more than just the riots – it's ongoing. Someone paid those kids to wreck the business in Bay Road, too.'

'That someone being the Copperheads?'

Caleb would have caught the man's disbelief even without the help of his aids; it was in the lift of Ramsden's eyebrows, the downwards pull of his mouth. This was hopeless: the cop didn't want more information, he wanted less. He wanted a straightforward case of racial violence, not some complicated theory about bikie gangs and diversions. He was just an average man, trying to do an average job. Not bad, not evil, just a little bit stupid and completely overwhelmed. And he was the most senior policeman in town.

'I don't know,' Caleb said. 'Maybe.'

'Right.' Ramsden tucked his notebook in his pocket. 'Well, I've got your number. I'll give you a call if I need anything.'

'Text,' Caleb said automatically.

The cop nodded and headed down the footpath towards the next house.

Kat was sorting tinned food into boxes behind the Mish's community centre. She was flushed and dusty, the eagle feather threaded through the top buttonhole of her sleeveless orange shirt. She smiled as she saw him, and his heart gave a little kick. 'Hey there,' she said.

He kissed her, the salt taste of her lips raising memories of her sweat-slicked skin against his last night.

'You should have got me up,' he said. 'I could have helped.'

Her eyes flicked across his face. 'I thought you could do with the sleep. Are you OK?'

'Me? Sure. What about you?'

'Fine. You know, considering.' She gave him another look, one that had him wanting to check the mirror for food stains.

He gave his face a quick scrub and thought about the best way of broaching what was going to be a touchy subject. 'Maybe you should –'

'Don't even suggest it,' she said. 'This is my mob and I'm not going anywhere.'

'I'm just –' He searched the air for the right words. 'I'm worried about you. Scared.'

Her expression softened. 'I know. I'm scared, too. I'm scared for Mum and Dad, and all my 'lations. But we can't all leave town.' She laid a hand against his cheek. 'And I reckon I'm OK. The fires were only in the Mish, and I don't live here. I'm bourgeois black, remember?'

He couldn't raise a smile at the insult one of her cousins had lobbed years ago; she'd turned it into a running joke, but he'd seen her stricken face as the words landed. She made a good point about the fires, though. Less than a third of the town's Koori population lived on the Mish, but only homes inside its borders had been torched. The knowledge didn't ease the pressure in his chest or wipe away the image of Kat's family home going up in flames.

'What if –?'

She shoved a tin of no-name baked beans into his hand, stopping him mid-sign. 'Two to a box.'

Conversation over, no debate to be entered into. For now.

They worked without speaking, brushing past each other, guiding with the touch of a hand, the nudge of a hip, a little dance of lifting, sorting and stacking. In the spirit of his new glasnost policy, he'd told her everything last night – about seeing the arsonists and the rioters, his theories on Jai and Portia. She'd listened with a fierce focus, asking a string of questions that had shown him exactly how little he knew. How had Jai and Portia met? Why would the Copperheads use teenagers to do their work? Why would they escalate from vandalism to arson?

But now she was looking distracted, as though she was working through a tricky problem. One that drew her eyebrows together and tightened the muscles around her eyes. She didn't seem ready to talk about it yet.

He grabbed another box and ripped it open. The shops had obviously donated all their off-brand tinned food: this one was Grandma Eileen's Minestrone with 'real' ham. What to make of the quotation marks – an unschooled copywriter, or an honest one?

'Have you tried this stuff?' he asked.

'I live on it.'

That was worryingly believable. Kat had a cast-iron stomach and little patience for cooking.

'You're not troubled by the quotation marks?'

She shrugged. 'I'm an equal opportunity lazy eater. Who am I to judge if Grandma Eileen likes to flirt with non-standard food products?'

The grin faded from his face as he thought of the other Eileen sitting a few streets away in new slippers and borrowed clothes. She'd lost everything dear to her. How did she not just get in her car and drive into a tree?

Kat touched his hand. 'Are you OK?'

'Yeah, sure. I was just thinking about Aunty Eileen. At the funeral, what exactly did you mean about her forgiving Jai?'

'Her grandson was the one Jai hurt when he smashed the car.'

No one he'd spoken to after Jai's death had mentioned that little fact; if people in the Koori community hadn't trusted him enough to tell him that, it was going to be an uphill battle trying to get any information about the Copperheads from them.

'God. And she took him in afterwards?'

'Before. Jai's parents are gone, so Aunty Eileen grew him up. Pete and Jai were best mates, pretty much brothers. But now Pete's... Well, I guess he's in what you'd call a vegetative state.'

Pete. He'd seen that name recently. On Aunty Eileen's lips, and written somewhere.

Kat wrote a name on the top of a box and tucked the

pen behind her ear. 'It nearly killed Aunty Eileen when Pete was hurt, but she took Jai back in when he got out of jail. She helped him get clean and get his apprenticeship. She copped a fair bit of flack for it, too.'

'Why?'

'I guess people thought Jai hadn't suffered enough.'

Best mate as good as dead, two years in jail, guilt staining your soul.

He spoke without thinking. 'God, how much is enough?'

'Yeah, I know, but he ended someone's life. That's unforgiveable to some people.'

He stared at her. She didn't know, she couldn't. She was going on with her story as though nothing had happened, not looking at him with fear and revulsion. He forced himself to concentrate on her words.

'... Jai never forgave himself. I used to see him going into that care place all the time, visiting Pete. Break your heart.'

He let go of the breath he'd been holding. So that was where he'd seen the name – the slack figure in the tiny room at Hilvington; the curling banner that read, *Get well soon, Pete.*

So Jai and Portia both had family members at Hilvington. And both visited regularly. They'd known each other a lot better than the just-helping-out line Jai had strung him. Had possibly used the visits as an excuse to meet up. But why? A woman with a sense of social justice and a young man trying to make amends, both dead. What had they been doing?

Kat wrote on the last box and put the pen down. 'That's it for now, thank God. I'm pooped.'

'Maybe you should go back to bed. I'd be happy to join you.'

'Did you get back to sleep OK last night?' she asked.

'After you had your way with me for the second time? Yes, but I'm flagging now, so you'll have to be gentle.'

The frown had returned, pinching her forehead. 'I meant after the nightmare.'

Shit, he'd thought she'd slept through that. It had been one of the bad ones. The really bad ones. Caught between dream and reality; trembling in sweat-soaked sheets, but somehow on the beach, facedown in the sand. The touch of the gun beneath him. Grabbing it, turning, squeezing the trigger. The bright spray of blood. The warmth of it on his skin, in his mouth.

Stop.

He wiped his damp palms on his shorts. 'Sorry, did I disturb you?'

'Jesus, Cal, don't apologise. It's a sign of stress, not bad manners.' She hesitated. 'Was it the warehouse again?'

'No.'

'Gary?'

'No. A dream, that's all.'

Her gaze had a strange intensity. 'A bad one.'

'Sure, it was a nightmare.'

'Babe, it was pretty bad. When I touched your shoulder, you were out of bed and across the room so fast I didn't know what had happened. You didn't seem to know I was there. You were –'

'Kat, seriously. It was just a dream. Leave it alone.'

Her blue eyes held his, unblinking. 'OK,' she finally said, and turned back to the boxes.

26.

He left Kat to do an apparently urgent and just-thought-of job – listing the contents of each box – and drove to Bay Road for a badly needed coffee. Why her obsession with a dream? It wasn't as though he could control the fucking things. If he could, he wouldn't wake each morning with an aching jaw and the lingering taste of blood.

He parked outside the supermarket and headed for Joe's Café. Paused a few metres from its door. What was that noise? Oh God, his old next-door neighbour, Mrs Naylor, was shuffling down the footpath, yelling some-thing at him. She was white-haired and tiny, looking like a biscuit-baking grandmother in a television ad. No amount of explaining could convince her that loudness didn't equal clarity, or deafness, stupidity. She was pretty slow; he could probably make it back to the car if he ran.

He went to meet her. 'Hi, Mrs Naylor. How are you?'

'Oh, I can't complain. My hips are terrible. I said, THEY'RE TERRIBLE.'

His hand twitched towards his hearing aids. It was always a delicate balancing act with Mrs Naylor: turn down the volume and risk missing everything, turn it up and risk bleeding eardrums.

'...your brother?'

'Sorry, what?'

'Oh dear,' she said. 'Is your hearing getting worse? I said, IS IT GETTING WORSE? Such a shame after all the hard work your father did with you. I said, IT'S A SHAME. My doctor says I've got the hearing of a young girl, you know. A YOUNG GIRL.'

A brief moment to ponder the fate of the girl. Had Mrs Naylor eaten her brains?

'...and apple cider vinegar in the morning. HAVE YOU TRIED THAT?'

'No, but I'll be sure to. What was that about Ant?'

'A woman was looking for you at his house. DID SHE FIND YOU?'

Fucking Jasmine, what did she want now?

'Brown hair, mid-thirties?' he asked.

'Oh no... and hair...'

'Sorry, what was that?'

Her face crumpled. 'Oh, you are getting worse. It's terrible. I said, IT'S TERRIBLE. But I suppose God never gives us more than we can bear.'

He wasn't too sure about that right now.

'Could you say that again?' he asked. 'Slowly.'

'SHE. WAS. TALL. WITH. SILLY. HAIR. FAR TOO OLD TO HAVE SILLY HAIR LIKE THAT.'

A slipknot tightened in his stomach – Frankie.

'Purple tips in her hair?'

'Yes. It's ridiculous at her age. I said, RIDICULOUS. I told her you weren't there, and she was quite rude to me. I said, SHE WAS VERY RUDE.'

Points for Frankie.

He went straight to the car. Frankie's box was still lying in the boot, seemingly undisturbed. A little pang at the sight of Portia's handbag next to it, the shoulder strap standing up like a broken wing. He should take it to her father, or maybe post it to her mother. He went to close the boot, then stopped.

Why was the bag's strap standing up like that? He felt along the material: there was something hard near the base of the strap. The length of his hand and a few millimetres thick. It had been inserted through a small hole in the lining.

He tore the material apart, and a piece of folded paper fell out. A plain white envelope. Sealed and stamped, addressed to a William Walker in Essendon, Melbourne. He tried to ease the seal open, then gave up and ripped it.

A short letter was inside, typed and unsigned.

Dear William,

The goods as promised. This is C.

Goods, what goods? He peered into the envelope – nothing in it, no sign that there ever had been. Maybe something else was hidden inside the handbag. He pulled the lining apart and examined each piece. Nothing. Whatever 'the goods' were, they were gone. Mr William Walker would presumably know what they were. Another seven-hour round trip to Melbourne in a car without air-conditioning. Was it worth it with no guarantee that William Walker would be home or even agree to speak to him?

He checked the address. A thrill of recognition: the label had been printed on a cheap ink jet.

27.

William Walker didn't encourage visitors. His house was set well back from the street and protected by a high fence topped with hacienda-style terracotta tiles and prison-style razor wire. An intercom by the gate – the damn things were haunting Caleb.

He parked on the street and walked back to the gate. A camera mounted on the fence swung around to track his movements. He pressed the buzzer and pretended to speak into the microphone. The gate didn't open. He waved at the camera and went through the pantomime a few more times, but no one came to rescue him. Shit, shit, shit. No way around it, he was going to have to ask for help.

He chose a restaurant around the corner from his flat, but realised as soon as he arrived that he'd made a mistake. The place had changed hands since his last visit, and what had once been a failing business with the hushed ambience of a library was now a bistro with a liquor licence and actual customers. Thursday seemed to be jackaroo night. At least, he hoped that was why most people were wearing akubras and cut-off jeans. He grabbed a couple of beers at the bar and found a table as far away as possible from the three-piece bush band setting up in the corner.

He checked his emails while he waited: one from Sammi, a reply to his request for information about the registered owners of the PO Boxes. A short message, along with a couple of attachments.

Took forever. System's a fricken mess. Want me to keep going?

He made the mistake of opening the invoice first – closed it again, wincing.

Her report didn't bring any more joy. The boxes were all rented by companies, none of which seemed to employ anyone whose name matched the addressee. Shit. Unless he was involved in an Australia-wide conspiracy involving everything from an abattoir to a car-cleaning company, the recipients weren't just using false names but company mailboxes, too. Very smart. It was pointless asking Sammi to keep digging, not to mention expensive; he'd have to come at it from a different angle. Just as soon as he thought of one.

He sent a quick email telling her to hold off doing any more work, then looked up in time to see Tedesco's hulking figure appear in the doorway.

Tedesco gave the room the cop once-over before crossing to him. 'Didn't realise there was a dress code.'

Caleb slid a beer across the table. 'This might help ease the embarrassment.'

Tedesco sat, angling his chair a little towards the wall. The only person Caleb knew who hated sitting with his back to the room more than him. A nicer person would offer to change places.

'Bit cryptic in your text,' Tedesco said, his eyes landing on a particularly short pair of cut-offs. 'I take it this wasn't just an invitation to view the sweating arse cheeks of Melbourne.'

'No. I need some help. I've been looking into that woman's death.'

A little sigh. 'Of course you have.'

He began to give Tedesco a rundown of the investigation, but the detective was less focused than usual, gazing at his beer instead of Caleb, nodding a beat too late at each point.

Caleb stopped halfway through his explanation. 'What's up?'

'Up?'

'You're distracted.'

Tedesco nodded. 'That business with the Baymar brothers. Didn't want to break it to you in here, but it's pretty much confirmed that the woman they took was Frankie. Her body –' He coughed. 'She hasn't turned up yet.'

Should he tell Tedesco that Frankie had resurfaced?

Don't tell anyone we spoke.

Unusually sound advice for Frankie, but Tedesco might be able to find out what she was up to. More than that – Caleb owed the man his honesty. He'd dragged Tedesco into the whole mess with Frankie last year, and not only had the detective saved his life, but he'd also killed a bent cop in the process.

It hadn't made Tedesco's life easy. Although he'd been cleared of any wrongdoing, killing a colleague hadn't endeared him to his fellow cops. It was impressive, how well Tedesco had coped with it all. He'd gone straight back to work, hadn't applied for stress leave. Didn't jump at sudden movements or avoid dark rooms, didn't have to leave butcher shops because panic gripped his throat, squeezing it shut. Was it just willpower, or some innate strength of character?

'Frankie's OK,' Caleb said. 'She came to see me a couple of days ago.'

The detective's dark eyebrows rose a few millimetres: the Tedesco equivalent of a double take. 'Right. Bit of a surprise. How'd she get away from the Baymars?'

'I think she did a deal with them. She's looking for something they want.'

'She'd better find it, then.'

'Yeah. I think the feds are after her, too.' He sketched a colourless version of Jasmine's visits, but Tedesco just nodded when he'd finished.

'What do you think?' Caleb prompted.

'That you should avoid anyone and anything to do with Frankie Reynolds.'

'Agreed. I meant about Jasmine being AFP or not. She says she doesn't carry ID when she's undercover. That sound right?'

Tedesco inclined his head. 'Sounds essential. Not to say it's true, though.'

'Can you find out if she is?'

'No. She's a fed or someone Frankie's crossed. Either way, you need to stay clear.'

Said with the downwards inflection of a non-negotiable topic. Still, it wouldn't hurt to ask about Transis. Caleb opened his mouth just as the band started up: bass-heavy, with a beat that travelled up through his body into his throat.

'What about Transis?' he said. 'Do you know anything about them?'

Tedesco shook his head. 'What?'

It wasn't just him, then – that band was really loud. He turned off his aids, the silence like a caress.

'Transis,' he yelled – hoped he yelled. 'Do you know anything about them?'

'No… and you…'

This was hopeless. 'Sorry, what?'

Tedesco lifted his big hands and laboriously signed, 'Loud. Go us somewhere to fuck.'

Caleb took a moment. 'You've got to stop listening to Ant.'

'Why, what did I say?'

'You don't want to know.' Caleb stood. 'Come on, I've got beer at home.'

———————

Caleb headed around the corner towards his flat, but Tedesco stopped by the window of a lighting store, his face illuminated by a thousand tonnes of greenhouse gases. Was he looking a bit pale, or was that just a trick of the light?

'What did those signs mean?' Tedesco asked.

Tougher men than Caleb had crumbled under that steely glare.

'That we should go somewhere to fuck.'

Tedesco was definitely pale. And getting paler. A man

who'd faced down an armed murderer without flinching, turning grey-green at the thought of swearing in sign language.

'You've used that phrase on someone who signs,' Caleb guessed.

Tedesco gave the slightest of nods.

'Someone you'd, ah, like to know better?'

Tedesco nodded again.

Caleb choked back a laugh. 'What was the response?'

'Looked blank. I thought I'd done it wrong.' Tedesco brightened. 'It was pretty messy, yeah? Hard to follow?'

'Mate, it was perfect, couldn't fault you.'

———

Back in the flat, Caleb opened the windows to let in the stale-piss smell of the city. He wasn't sure it was cooler outside than in, but at least he felt as though he was doing something. He grabbed a couple of beers and brought them back to the living room.

Tedesco was sitting on the edge of the couch, still looking a little washed out. Caleb handed him William Walker's letter and a beer.

Tedesco stared at the envelope. 'What's this?'

'It was hidden in Portia's handbag.'

'A letter to William Walker?' The detective's eyebrows rose again, higher than before.

'You know him?'

'Billy Walker? I should think so.'

Billy Walker, that rang a bell. 'Shit, Billy Walker the strip club guy?'

'If it's the Billy Walker I know, he also runs illegal betting and collection agencies. Allegedly.'

'Lives in Essendon? Big house with a high white fence?'

Tedesco sat back. 'You've been casing Billy Walker's house?'

'Didn't know it was his.'

'Christ.' Tedesco ran a hand over his bristled hair. 'You're not going back there.'

'Not now I know who he is.'

'Good.' Tedesco took a long swig of his beer and settled on the couch, looking a lot more relaxed now they were back in cop-talk territory. 'So you think Portia intercepted "the goods" intended for Walker?' An actual question, a tiny nibble on the hook.

'That's the theory I'm going with at the moment.'

'Any idea what they are?'

'No.' But he might know who had them – Portia's attacker. The big blond man who'd dragged her from the alleyway. If Portia had hidden the goods nearby, he could easily have doubled back to look for them after she died.

A flash of Blondie writhing on the cobblestones, clutching the knee Caleb had kicked. And a series of thoughts fell into place. A man with a limp had been seen talking to Rat-tail Luke. And a man with a limp had walked past him in the middle of a riot, wearing a balaclava and stinking of kerosene. Blondie from the alleyway. Blondie with his muscled body and tattooed arms and neck. Was he a bikie? Everyone had tatts these days, but his had seemed a little rawer than the usual High Street hipster designs.

Tedesco was watching him, amused. 'Ideas?'

'Occasionally. Does Billy Walker have any connection to the Copperheads?'

'The Copperheads?' Tedesco's grin faded. 'What have they got to do with it?'

'Nothing solid, just a few things adding up. I think they were responsible for the arson in town. And Jai Johnson's death.'

Tedesco stilled. 'The Indigenous man who was hanged? That's connected to your case?'

'Maybe. Probably. But I haven't got any evidence yet. Can you find out if Walker's connected to the Copperheads?'

'Mate, you need to drop this now. The Copperheads aren't a bunch of country hicks – they run most of the drugs and sex trade from Geelong to Adelaide. If you keep wandering around your hometown asking questions about them, they're going to hear about it. And when they do, they're going to stomp on you. Do you know what they did to the last guy who got in their way? They tortured him to death with a blowtorch. And he was a cop.' Tedesco leaned forward, his grey eyes fixed on Caleb's. 'If they did that to a cop, imagine what they'd do to you.'

28.

He hit the road early and was back in the Bay by mid-morning, fuelled by a bowl of dry cereal and a watery coffee made from the last of his beans; at some stage he'd have to stop and do some shopping. He couldn't quite face Vicky Graham's brand of smiling racism at the EezyWay, so he filled up at the tiny service station where he'd dumped McGregor's ute, a single-bowser place with a shop that stocked dead flies along with its dubious-looking chocolate bars. Common sense told him not to consume anything from the place, but there was a coffee machine, and he was in desperate need of caffeine. He ordered a long black and checked his phone while he waited. His heart gave a little loop of joy: a message from Kat. He'd sent her a short text late last night, an I'm-thinking-of-you message that had taken him an embarrassingly long time to compose. It didn't look as though Kat had had the same concerns in crafting her reply.

—*all good prob good to see you pm xx*

The Rosetta Stone of a long relationship was needed to translate that one: she was busy but hadn't wanted to ignore his text; probably free to see him this afternoon. God, he hoped so. Less than twenty-four hours away from her, and his arms felt empty.

He put his phone away and realised that the barista-cum-petrol-station-attendant was glaring at him. A thin-faced man in his sixties, with plenty of wrinkles and very few smile lines.

'Sorry, what?' Caleb said.

The man scowled at the takeaway cup sitting on the flyspecked counter. 'You want hot water with that? It's strong.'

Caleb looked at the coffee without much hope. It was thick and black, and topped by a layer of perfect golden crema. Like finding the Holy Grail in a public toilet.

'Jesus,' Caleb said.

The bloke sniffed. 'So you want water?'

'God, no. It'd be sacrilege.'

He got a sudden, gap-toothed smile for that. 'New machine. Never used to touch the stuff, but the girlfriend put me onto it. They take it pretty seriously where she's from.'

'Italy?'

'Nah, Coburg.'

———

He made sure no Harley-riding men were lurking around the bowsers, then returned to the car, turning off his phone and removing the SIM: nothing like a cautionary chat with a homicide detective to make you up your security game. He savoured the remaining drops of coffee and started the car. Time to hunt down Rat-tail Luke. No guarantee that the boy would lead him to Blondie, but he was feeling confident of his chances. Or caffeinated, at least, which was almost the same thing.

There was no sign of Luke anywhere, but Caleb eventually caught sight of a familiar figure hanging around the foreshore toilets: a dark-haired teenager about sixteen years old. No court of law would accept the ID, but it was Blue Bandana Boy, the one who'd chucked the half-brick at him. The kid he was talking to had been in the riots, too, carrying a cricket bat and running down the middle of Bay Road.

Caleb parked under the Norfolk Island pines that lined the foreshore and directed the fan towards his face. He calculated that he had five minutes before he either died from heat exhaustion or fused with the seat. Five minutes was probably the cut-off time for grown men to hang around watching teenage boys outside public toilets, anyway.

The two boys were popular, with a constant trickle of people stopping by for a chat. A couple of words, a shake of the hand, and the customers left happy. Enterprising. Back in his day, the favoured pastime for teenage gangs had been throwing stones and thumping the shit out of people like him. The dark-haired kid was obviously the minder, the smaller one doing the selling. A little bit of genius to the set-up. People barely saw teenage boys, couldn't tell them apart, expected them to be hanging around public places. And if they got caught smashing windows or selling a few grams, they'd probably get off with a bit of community service.

A flash of blue to the right – Rat-tail Luke riding up on his BMX, the black backpack swinging from his handlebars.

He skidded to a dusty stop beside the two boys and jumped off. A cursory check to ensure no one was watching, then he opened the backpack. The smaller boy grabbed handfuls of cash from his pockets and dropped them inside. So Rat-tail was the money man. He was leaning against the toilet wall now, looking as though he was up for a leisurely chat.

Caleb pulled onto the road and drove around the corner. He doubled back on foot, keeping the toilet block between him and the boys. The building was made from grey Besser blocks, with a high band of latticework that was a bad choice for the Bay's frigid winter winds but a great opportunity to spy on nearby teenagers. Caleb slipped around the back to the entrance closest to the boys, then stopped. There weren't too many places in this world where a white man couldn't confidently venture, but the women's toilets was one of them. Then again, only the bladder-challenged and tourists were brave enough to use these toilets; he'd probably be able to get in and out without being seen.

He ducked into the cubicle by the wall and stood on the toilet so he could peer through the latticework. The tops of three floppy-haired heads came into view. He was still trying to make himself comfortable when the cubicle door swung open. A woman and a six-year-old girl stared up at him, their mouths open.

Shit: Milly Howard, one of Kat's old high school friends – loud, opinionated, not a huge fan of his.

'Hey, Milly, how's it going?'

She gripped her daughter's hand and bustled away.

Well, that had gone pretty much as he'd expected it to, minus the yelling.

He turned back to the boys. They obviously had a lot to say to each other, jostling and gesticulating, but none of them was thoughtful enough to turn his head towards Caleb.

A man in his forties approached them, rubbing at his arms, raising red welts on already scabbed skin. 'You got me?' he asked.

The smaller kid shook his head and said something.

The man's face crumpled. 'No, I don't want that.'

The boy stepped forward, waving his arms in a clear 'fuck off'.

'C'mon,' the man said. 'I've gotta get off this. I want me. I've got the money.'

Caleb craned his neck to try and get a better view. He'd obviously got a word wrong there, possibly more than one. He'd have to ask Ant for a translation. Ask him who he should be talking to about the drug trade while he was at it. Maybe –

A tap on his leg.

He lurched backwards and stepped into the toilet bowl.

Kat was looking up at him, a shopping bag over her shoulder. She made the OK sign, her single raised eyebrow making it both a question about his wellbeing and a comment on his lack of judgement.

'What are you doing here?' he asked.

'What are you doing here, is what Milly Howard would like to know. She came running up to me in the supermarket, shouting at the top of her voice that you were lurking inside the women's loos. She's probably round at the police station by now.' Kat examined his dripping foot. 'Would you like to dry off in Joe's while you avoid them?'

The yellow walls and lace curtains were a little faded, but not much else had changed in the fourteen years since he'd first taken Kat to Joe's Café. There were only a few other customers: an elderly couple lingering over their cappuccinos, and Bert Manningham, the owner of the EezyWay. Bert was a man with a worrying fondness for khaki and the thick-headed ability to unintentionally turn any conversation into a racist slur. Caleb steered Kat to a table on the furthest side of the room.

A waitress slumped towards them with a fuck-you air that promised unintelligible speech. Caleb straightened. Excellent. The last time he'd been in here with Kat, they'd had a massive argument over his unwillingness to reveal his deafness when faced with an incomprehensible waitress. This time he'd be ready to admit defeat at the first muttered word.

The waitress drooped to a halt in front of their table and pulled out her notepad. 'What can I get you?'

Damn. Perfect enunciation, her voice neither too high nor too low but just right – the Goldilocks of elocution. Kat would never believe he couldn't understand her. He gave his order, then watched as Kat set about ordering the entire dessert menu. Something was different about her: eyes shining, a zing of energy to her movements.

She grinned at him as Goldilocks left. 'You had a whole victory-in-defeat speech planned, didn't you?'

'Yeah.'

'I'm sorry, babe, I'm sure someone will come along and mutter at you soon.' She patted his arm.

Her hand – there was ink on her fingers.

An easing in his chest, like breath returning after a bad fall. 'You've been drawing.'

'Yeah.' She smiled and he caught a glimpse of the old Kat, the Kat who'd taken all the sorrow in her life and wrought something beautiful from it. 'I started last night. It was incredible. This idea just appeared in my brain, and I had to get it down. It flowed onto the page like it had been waiting for the right moment. God, I'm so relieved. I could just cry, you know.'

He did know. Might do it himself right here in the café. He took her smudged hand and kissed it, then pressed her palm to his face.

She rubbed her thumb across his cheek. 'You look tired. Bad night again?'

'No.'

A frown crept onto her face.

'Really,' he said. 'I was up early. I popped back to Melbourne yesterday.'

'That's quite a pop. Is this still about Portia Hirst?'

'Yeah.'

'And your public toilet stakeout too?'

'No, that's just a hobby.'

Her smile didn't quite reach her eyes. She hesitated, then asked, 'Why are you so obsessed with her?'

'I'm not obsessed, I'm focused.'

'Do you think you might be –?' She broke off, scowling at something behind him.

Damn, Bert Manningham was swaggering over for a chat. When he reached their table, he stopped and hooked his thumbs through the belt loops of his excess-stock army pants. He was pink and fleshless like a skinned rabbit.

'Nice to see you two getting along.'

'Hi Bert,' Caleb said, through gritted teeth. 'On a short break, are you?'

'Yeah, just a quick one. No rest for the wicked, hey? I'm a bit surprised to see you in here, Kathryn. I thought you'd be helping your lot clean up.'

'My lot?' Kat echoed, her face impassive.

'Yeah, after the –'

'How's business, Bert?' Caleb asked.

'Oh well, could always be better.' Bert turned back to Kat. 'Hear your mum had a bit of trouble at that place of hers, too. Terrible stuff. But only a matter of time, I suppose.'

Caleb jumped in again. 'That CCTV you put in at the EezyWay must've cost a bit.'

That got Bert's full attention. 'Spent a bloody fortune on it. Though maybe I can sell it now Jai's gone. Gave the boy a chance, but he brought enough trouble with him.'

Kat became very still. 'Jai caused the trouble?'

Anyone with a scrap of sense would have backed away. Bert doubled down. 'Oh yeah. We had a fair bit of vandalism while he was around.'

'So it was Jai's fault that he was targeted? That he was killed?'

'Well, if he was mixed up in something stupid...' Bert shrugged.

'Time to stop talking now, Bert,' Caleb said. He put a bit of diaphragm support behind the words to make them carry.

Kat kept her eyes on Bert. 'And my mother? Did she bring it on herself, too?'

'Oh well, I dunno what happened there. Maybe one of her patients, hey?'

'One of her Abo patients?' Kat asked.

Bert's rabbit face twitched. 'Yeah, well, anyway. Best be off to work.' He gave a nod and scurried away.

'Racist shit,' Kat said, watching him go. 'And as for you –' She jabbed a finger at his chest.

Caleb sat up. 'Me? What about me?'

'Don't do that. I can fight my own battles.'

'It's my battle too.'

'No, it's not. Your role is supportive bystander.'

'Jesus, Kat. I'm not going to sit there and let some prick insult you. Are you a bystander when people are arseholes to me?'

'That's different.'

'How? You once stood in this very room and ripped shreds off Howard Green for saying that I was a menace to society for driving while deaf.'

Her jaw jutted. 'I don't want you getting involved.'

'And if we have kids? Will I be allowed to get involved then?'

She jerked back.

Fuck. What was it about him that made him say such monumentally stupid things? Kat had lost two babies in late pregnancy, and he threw imaginary children into the fight.

'I'm sorry,' he said. 'That was a really stupid thing to say.'

'Cal.' Her eyes were too bright. 'I don't even know if I…'

He waited, but she didn't finish the sentence. Didn't know what? If she could bear the pain of losing another pregnancy? If she still wanted to have children? If she wanted to have them with him?

Goldilocks appeared with their coffees and a platter of cakes. She took her time laying out the food, Kat seemingly fascinated by the process.

'I'm really sorry,' he said when the waitress had finally left. 'Can we start over? How about I take you out to dinner tonight? I can practise eating without putting my foot in my mouth.'

Kat finally met his eyes; her face was tight. 'Do you think we've maybe rushed into things a bit?'

He'd caught a fish hook in his calf once. Eleven years old and fishing alone by the creek. A similar feeling – the sharp bite of pain, wanting to yank out the barb, but knowing he had to push it deeper into his flesh.

'What do you mean?' he asked.

'I'm only just back and we're both still dealing with a lot of stuff. You in particular. It's probably not a good idea to go rushing into things.'

'Is this about me butting in with Bert?'

'God, Cal, of course not. I just think we should slow things down a bit.'

'Slow things down? You were gone for four months.'

'Yeah.' She pushed back an imaginary strand of hair. 'So let's just slow it down, see how we go.'

29.

Ant wasn't home from work yet, so Caleb spent a bit of time pacing the kitchen, then retrieved Frankie's box of junk from the car. If she'd gone to the trouble of following him back to the Bay, there was a good chance her mystery object was actually in there. And God knows, he needed something to distract him.

'Slow it down.'

There was no need to panic. If Kat wanted to end it, she'd end it. He'd just made a few assumptions, thought they were further along the road than they were. 'Slow it down' just meant an easing on the accelerator.

Probably.

He emptied the box onto the coffee table. The contents didn't look any more promising than last time: notepads and batteries, a stapler, a desk phone, glue sticks, pens. He leafed through the notebooks again – nothing, unless Frankie had managed to incorporate code into legitimate case notes. Not impossible but unlikely. Whatever she'd hidden had to be small, maybe even a microdot. Which would make it almost impossible to find.

'Slow it down.'

What did that mean? Not sleeping together? Not seeing each other as often? At all?

Focus: Frankie. Get inside her head.

She's got something important; she's nervous about carrying it but wants to keep it close. So she hides it in the office. Somewhere it will be safe from casual discovery, not just by strangers but by him.

The phone. It was the only thing Frankie could guarantee he wouldn't touch. A voice message? A secret compartment? He examined it. No loose panels or buttons, nothing taped to the underside, but one of the screws on the casing was slightly burred. He got up and grabbed the old screwdriver set from the kitchen junk drawer, set to work on the screws. The overhead lights flicked on and off as he started on the last of them – Ant warning him that he was home. Caleb raised a hand in greeting and pulled the back off the phone – nothing but wiring. Damn.

Ant sprawled on an armchair. He made a lazy circle in the air with one finger, shorthand for, 'What the hell are you doing?'

'Looking for something Frankie left behind.'

Ant stared at him. 'You're talking to Frankie? She's OK?'

'Talked. Once. She wants –' He broke off, almost smiled: he knew where Frankie had hidden her treasure. He grabbed a screwdriver and pried apart the casing on the receiver, and there, nestled in the wiring, was a silver key. Stubby, with a square head and a cap of yellow plastic. He slipped it onto his keyring and shoved it in his back pocket.

'What's it for?' Ant asked.

'No idea, but Frankie wants it pretty badly.'

Ant nodded, less engaged than Caleb would have

expected for the level of intrigue. He was looking tired and cranky, tapping his fingers on the arm of the couch. Caleb hesitated. Of the long list of topics they avoided, Ant's addiction was right up there. But questioning him about the local drug trade would be difficult without mentioning drugs.

'Just say it,' Ant told him.

'Who should I talk to about the drug trade in the Bay?'

Ant stilled. 'What? Why?'

'I want some information. Who should I talk to?'

'What information?'

Damn, Ant could do this all day if he was trying to avoid something – bounce question off question, never answering any of them. Childhood experience had taught Caleb that the only ways to end the cycle were either to involve Ant or to give him a cripple nipple. He should probably start by involving him.

'It looks like the blond guy who attacked Portia is connected to some kids who are dealing. So who should I be talking to about it?'

'No idea.'

'The Copperheads?'

'Yeah, you should definitely front up to a bikie gang and ask about their drug-dealing connections. Why don't you ask to see their stash of weaponry while you're at it?'

Fair point. 'What about your old dealer? Think he'd know?'

Ant shrugged.

'What's his address?' Caleb asked.

'He won't speak to you without an intro.'

'So give me an intro.'

Ant didn't answer.

Last try, then it was time for the cripple nipple.

'I don't want to drag you into it – I just want to know who I should be talking to.'

'Mate, it's not me I'm worried about. If you go stumbling around asking questions, you're going to get yourself squashed.'

Stumbling. Acid soured his stomach.

'Guess I'll have a chat with the Copperheads, then.'

He was halfway to the door when something flew past his head and landed on the floor: a cushion.

'You're an arsehole,' Ant said. 'You know that, don't you?'

'Yeah, but at least I can throw.'

30.

Ant's old dealer lived in a concrete-grey unit on the out-skirts of town. It had net curtains on the windows and a basket of geraniums hanging by the front door. A tricycle lay on the front path.

Ant parked outside but kept the engine running. 'Squirrel's a bit of a mumbler, but he's jumpy. Don't ask him to repeat himself – he's paranoid about being taped. If you don't get something, ask me about it afterwards.'

Ant chatting with his old dealer? Not a good idea.

'You're not getting out of the car.'

Ant shrugged. 'Have fun talking to yourself, then.'

'You don't think he'll talk to me?'

'I know he won't.'

'He's a dealer, how does he get new business?'

Ant's dark eyes didn't blink. 'I told you – referrals.' He got out and headed to the front door.

Caleb followed him. Which bottom-feeding arsehole had been Ant's referral? Someone with an eye for easy money. Smoking pot passed as a hobby around here, but Ant had shown a natural flair for it; could have gone pro, smoked for Australia. After their mother's death, he'd started getting stoned after breakfast. Easy to see him jumping at the offer of a free taste of smack. Not so easy to understand how Caleb hadn't noticed in time to stop him.

Ant hesitated at the door. 'Squirrel's pretty jumpy.'

'So you said.'

'Yeah so, um, I might have to say some stuff to get you inside. Stuff you're not going to like. If you want to get through that door, you're going to have to suck it up and go with it, OK?'

'What kind of stuff?'

Ant's gaze wandered over Caleb's right shoulder. 'Stuff you're not going to like.'

There couldn't be many of Ant's past transgressions he didn't know about, could there? Ant had ripped off their parents, sold half the furniture in the house, done time and totalled Caleb's car. What else could there be?

'Yeah, sure,' he said. 'Let's go.'

A thin guy with greasy, shoulder-length hair opened the door to Ant's knock. His cut-off black T-shirt showed wiry muscles and a few good tattoos mixed in with some truly bad ones.

'Ant, the man. Long time, no see.' A mouth full of teeth, but no consonants. He eyed Caleb. 'Who's this?'

'...brother... help... come in?'

'One of youse. You know the rules.'

Caleb shrugged his apologies to Ant, but his brother was focused on Squirrel.

'He needs me to translate,' Ant said.

Heat flushed Caleb's face. Be fucked if he was going to stand here like some kid who needed his arse wiped. 'Bullshit, I do.'

Ant stepped in front of him, his head and hands moving as he spoke rapidly.

Squirrel's eyes darted to Caleb and an oily grin slid across face. 'Yeah, you're right. Fucken hilarious. Go on, then.' He swung the door open.

Ant went inside without looking at Caleb. Squirrel gestured for him to follow, the smirk still firmly in place. A strong desire to punch him in the face. Him, or someone else.

The door opened onto a small living room dominated by a black faux-leather lounge suite. A young woman in tracksuit pants and a T-shirt was watching a game show on an enormous TV, a pink-cheeked baby sitting on the floor by her feet. Caleb stopped just inside the door. Shit – all he could hear was the muffled roar of the TV. This was going to be a disaster. Squirrel made a shooing motion, and the woman slung the baby onto her hip and wandered slowly from the room. Squirrel took the chair she'd vacated and waved for them to sit. Ant casually picked up the TV remote and muted the sound.

'So whatcha after?' Squirrel said. 'I've got some great smack.'

Ant opened his hands, palms outwards. 'Nah, I'm off it. Almost two years.'

'Mate, that's the best time to do it – the tiniest taste'll send you flying. It'd be like doin' it for the first time. Like a fucken virgin.'

The hair stood up along Caleb's arms. 'We're not after smack,' he said quickly. 'I need –'

'You understood that?' Squirrel glared at Ant. 'You said he wouldn't understand.'

Ant kept his eyes on Squirrel. 'No. I said he *might* not understand.'

'Yeah, whatever. So whatcha after? I've got uppers if you don't want downers. Great ice, speed, eccies.'

Caleb thought of the man he'd seen pleading with the teenage dealers by the public toilets.

'What about me? Have you got me?'

'Me?' A look of blank confusion, then Squirrel laughed. 'Oh, fuck mate, you wanna watch how ya go round saying stuff. Get you into all sorts of trouble.' He sniggered. 'It's bee, mate, beeee.'

Caleb dug his nails into his palms. 'You got any?'

'Nah, you don't want bee, mate. I've got the blue stuff if you wanna party.'

'You know where I can get it?'

'Not a fucken information service.'

'For a fee.'

'Still can't help ya.'

'What about other information? About people?'

Squirrel's eyes hardened. 'What the fuck's this? You a fucken dog or somethin'?'

Ant stirred, but Caleb held up a hand to stop him speaking. 'I'm just after information. Business information, nothing to do with the cops. You know where we live, right? I'm not stupid enough to cross you.'

Squirrel sat back and eyed him. 'Fifty bucks a question.'

'Twenty.'

'Fifty or fuck off.'

He had two hundred dollars in his wallet.

'Who's Luke Blundon and his gang working for?'

'No idea.' A blatant lie, but Squirrel had the tightly pressed lips of a man unwilling to say more on a subject.

Caleb laid fifty dollars on the table. 'What about Dave McGregor? Is he in the business?'

A shrug. 'Amateur stuff.'

Another fifty. Two more questions; make them count.

'I'm looking for a big blond man, lot of tatts. Might be limping at the moment. Do you know where I can find him?'

A flicker in Squirrel's eyes. 'No.' Fear, and a definite yes.

Caleb held up the last of his fifty-dollar notes. 'If I wanted to find someone like that, who would I ask?'

Squirrel's eyes darted from Caleb to the cash. 'Maybe Johnno.'

'Johnno who?'

'Drinks at the Arms. And if you tell him I sent you, I'll fucken gut ya.' Squirrel stood. 'Right, youse can piss off if you're not buying.' He eyed Ant. 'Although I could give you a little taste for free. Favour to an old friend, hey?'

Ant shook his head.

Squirrel hustled them to the door and looked through the spy-hole before opening it.

'You know where to find me,' he told Ant as he started to close the door.

Caleb put his foot out to stop it.

Squirrel stared at his foot. 'Move it or lose it.'

Caleb moved it. 'Did the Copperheads torch the Mish?'

Squirrel laughed. 'Why don't you ask' em?' He closed the door.

Ant was halfway through his excuses before they were off the front step. '...one-person policy. He's paranoid about getting jumped. You can't –'

Caleb headed for the road.

Ant started up again when they got to the car. 'I know you –'

'Drop me at my car,' Caleb said.

'I didn't mean that –'

'Are you going to drive, or should I walk?'

Ant gave a theatrical sigh and pulled out his keys. A tiny Ziploc bag of white powder came with them. Ant stared at it, then stuffed it back in his pocket and got in the car.

A chill ran down the back of Caleb's neck. OK, don't panic. There was no doubting the surprise on Ant's face, the shock. Squirrel had obviously slipped the bag into his pocket. Just shut up and let Ant deal with it. He got in the car.

Ant drove a few blocks without speaking, then pulled over without warning outside the foreshore toilets; no sign of Rat-tail Luke or his mates. Ant left the engine running and strode across the grass. Caleb was out of the car and halfway to the toilets before he stopped to think: Ant was clean, he wouldn't be carrying his kit on him.

He walked slowly back to the car and waited for his pulse to settle. Fucking Squirrel, the evil bastard. Should have punched the guy as soon as he'd offered Ant a free taste. Should have punched him again when he'd laughed about bee.

Bee. A memory stirred – in the alleyway, trying to catch Portia's words. He'd thought she'd said something about bees. And then later, as she'd lain on the road, her mouth bloodied and broken. '…the be… got the be…'

Not nonsense words: she'd been talking about bee. Ice seemed to get rebranded every few months. New recipe, new colour, new name. If 'the goods' mentioned in the letter to William Walker had been a couple of kilos of the latest popular hit, it would go a long way to explaining the violence. Particularly if Blondie hadn't managed to recover it – his teenager dealers hadn't been selling bee, so they'd been losing customers. Had Portia and Jai stolen it? That seemed less likely. Unless they'd been trying to get rid of it.

Sweat trickled down his face and splashed onto his T-shirt. He wiped his forehead. It was getting pretty unbearable in here, even with Ant's air-con going full blast. What the hell was taking him so long, anyway? Ten seconds to flush the drugs, thirty if he took a piss. The needle disposal bin. You could break one of those open if you were desperate enough. Caleb had the door open, one foot on the road, when a figure appeared in the toilet doorway.

Ant walked straight to the car and got in, but didn't speak. His breathing was normal, his muscles tight. A wave of dizzying relief.

'Flushed it,' Ant finally said.

'Never doubted it.'

Ant laughed, but his eyes were blank. He pulled onto the road without checking for traffic.

31.

He woke clawing at the air, the iron tang of blood in his mouth. Onto the floor, scrambling away from the body.

No body. No sand. Just carpet and a bed, yellow walls. He dropped his head into his hands and tried to slow his breathing. OK. OK, he was in a motel room, not on the beach. Not covered in blood. So get it the fuck together and go for a run. He stumbled into the bathroom for a piss and a mouthful of water, then pulled on his clothes. Out the door, eyes still bleary, joints clicking. He ran up the hill towards the highway, the dream snapping at his heels.

The day was already limp with heat. It was later than he usually ran, but sleep had been so slow to come that he'd worked until the early hours of the morning.

Tedesco's email had arrived around midnight. The subject line: One Time Only Offer; the sender: dont. think.this.makes.me.your.bitch@hotmail.com. Tedesco's sense of humour seeping through his propriety. And the level of his concern – the detective had never given Caleb confidential information before. The email itself was pure Tedesco, a study in clarity and grammar.

Reliable sources have informed me that Walker has no known associates in Resurrection Bay or the surrounding areas. There is no known connection between William Walker and the Copperheads; however, caution is strongly advised. Do NOT pursue this line of enquiry.

If Walker wasn't running the show, who was? The Copperheads, or someone else? Someone capable of killing Jai and setting a thug onto Portia. It wasn't that easy to kill another human being, harder still to live with it afterwards. You had to be either ruthless, or desperate.

He'd been desperate.

Facedown in the sand, struggling to get up. The flurry of punches, then the slam of the boot in his ribs. Trying to breathe, to escape, knowing it was almost over. Pain pinning him to the ground. Then the hardness of the gun beneath him. Grasping it, turning, squeezing the trigger. The hot spray of blood on his face, the salt taste of it. The bright arc pumping from the ruin of the man's throat. Petronin's throat. Michael Petronin, thirty-seven years old, father of one. Petronin's eyes had held his as he'd bled out. Fear in them, terror. Their light flickering and dulling, fading to nothing.

Stop.

Push it away. And run. One foot and then the other. Pain hammering in his chest. Couldn't breathe. He stumbled and fell to one knee. Up, get up. A car was pulling in ahead of him. Go. Move. He staggered to his feet and kept going. The driver climbed out and stood in front of him. Kat's mother, Maria.

'Sorry,' he said as he reached her. An automatic response, no idea why she was glaring at him.

Maria swayed. Or the world did.

'Get in the car,' she said.

He opened his mouth to protest, and vomited on her shoes.

———

Maria drove to her house without speaking and marched him inside. Down the cool white hallway, bumping into walls. Incapable of protest or speech, limbs not quite where they should be. No sign of Kat, thank God. Into the bathroom.

Maria shoved him into the shower and turned on the cold water. 'Fifteen minutes.' She stabbed a finger at the timer suctioned to the glass and left.

He slid down the tiles and expelled the lining of his stomach.

———

He got out after the allotted time and found dry clothes on the edge of the bath. He hadn't noticed Maria come back in, but she'd probably popped in a few times to make sure that he hadn't messed up her bathroom by drowning in it. Three roads out of town and he'd had to choose the one Maria was driving down. Maria and half the town. Should have headed towards the plantations and taken his chances with the logging trucks instead. He dressed and considered taking a nap on the tiles. Strangely tired now he'd finished vomiting. A squeezing headache to accompany the exhaustion, with flickering lights at the edges of his vision. He hitched up the waistband of the too-large jeans Maria had left for him, and went to face her.

No one in the hallway, but the house felt full of people; air moving, doors opening and closing, the thump of footsteps. He checked Kat's old room but it was empty. Disappointment mixed with a hefty dose of relief. The living room next. The chairs and couch had been rearranged along the walls, a pile of dog-eared magazines stacked on the coffee table. Three strangers stared back at him: slings and bandages, a walking frame. A moment of blankness until he remembered that Maria was using her home as a temporary workspace.

He found her in the kitchen, a bright room with a wall of family photos that stretched from benchtop to ceiling. His eye went straight to the blank space where his and Kat's wedding photo had once been. Stupid to have hoped that Kat had reinstated it in the four months since he'd last been here. She'd probably stashed it in a drawer somewhere, along with her wedding ring and unsigned divorce papers. He had a drawer like that in the flat: a dark limbo of half-finished tasks and relationships.

Maria was working at the table on her laptop, stacks of files and papers to one side of her, paperclips and pens to the other. She could have written a book on how to incorporate a makeshift office into a living space, using his flat as an example of 'what not to do'. She looked up as he stood, hesitating, in the doorway.

'Thanks for the lift,' he said. 'I'll get out of your way.'

She pointed to a large tumbler of water on the table. 'Sit down and drink that.'

He looked at her expression and obeyed. It took him both hands to lift the tumbler.

Maria crossed to him, impatience in the clipped strut

of her walk. She was holding a digital thermometer and wearing a clean pair of shoes. 'Running in 38-degree heat,' she said. 'No hat, in full sun.' She broke off, frowning. 'You don't wear your aids when you run, do you? Can you follow me?'

'Yes.'

'So there won't be any misunderstandings when I tell you that that was ridiculous behaviour, even for you?'

'No.'

'People die from heatstroke. Usually the frail or the elderly, but occasionally fit young men with a lack of self-preservation and an excess of stupidity.' She shoved the thermometer into his ear with all the gentleness of a plumber. 'Still too high. Have a cold bath when you get home and stay in air-conditioning for the rest of the day. And don't even think about running for the next few days.'

'OK.' He got to his feet. 'Thanks, I'll –'

'Sit down and finish the water. Your brother's on his way to pick you up.'

Oh good, because what this day needed was a little more humiliation.

Maria sat and waited for his attention. God, she couldn't have too much more to say, could she?

He took a breath and faced her.

'You've had some traumatic experiences in the past year,' she said. 'How are you coping generally?'

Heat crept up his face. 'Fine.'

'By "fine" you mean that you're eating well and sleeping well, interested in new and existing pursuits?'

'Yes.'

She gazed at him without speaking. The only hearie in

the world who could outlast him in a silence-off, and he'd married her daughter. Where the hell was Ant? Was he enjoying a leisurely Saturday brunch? Exacting revenge for some act of fraternal arseholery?

Caleb cast desperately for a new topic of conversation. 'What do you know about the drug situation in the Bay?'

Maria's eyes narrowed. A familiar look, one inherited by Kat – a look that said very plainly: There is only so much of your idiocy that I will take.

'That was a lot less subtle than your usual diversionary tactics,' she said.

'But did it work?'

A fleeting smile, gone before he was sure he'd seen it.

'Are you genuinely interested in the answer?' she asked.

'Yes.'

'Well, there's obviously widespread use of alcohol and marijuana in town, but the main issue is methamphetamine or ice. Ice use has risen approximately thirty per cent per annum over the past four years, peaking last year, with a marked decrease in some areas in the past few months.'

He closed his mouth, opened it again. 'That's... How do you know all that?'

'I had assumed you asked because you thought I'd know.'

'Um, yes. But I wasn't expecting statistics.' Although of course she'd have statistics – Maria never said anything without cause or evidence.

'I'm part of a taskforce looking into ways of curbing drug use in regional areas. We test the wastewater in order to identify patterns of drug abuse.'

'And ice use is down?'

'Significantly down in some areas, stable in others.'

'Where's it down?'

Maria paused. 'There are some privacy issues. We get quite comprehensive data.'

'Broad brushstrokes.'

She thought it through, then said slowly, 'Use has somewhat decreased in the town centre and southern side of town, and greatly decreased in the Mish.'

'How bad was it in the Mish?'

The lines around her eyes deepened. 'It's a small community, Caleb, I don't feel comfortable discussing it.'

Bad. But something was obviously working if ice use was down there. And a lack of sales meant a serious dent in someone's profits. Which made his theory about the Copperheads being behind the violence even more likely.

'Have the Copperheads been hassling people?'

'I don't know.'

'There's a history of bikie gangs strong-arming Koori communities to buy ice.'

'Yes,' Maria said. 'I am aware of that.'

A definite smile this time, one that brought the heat back to his cheeks.

'Of course. Sorry.'

He pressed his fingers to his temples as his headache ratcheted up a notch. He was pretty sure there were some obvious questions he should be asking right now, but this thumping pain made thinking difficult.

Maria stood and refilled his empty glass, placed it in front of him. 'Drink,' she said.

'Thanks,' he said, not touching it: he wasn't entirely sure whether the first glass of water was going to stay down. 'Your clinic being destroyed – do you think that's connected to the fires in the Mish?'

'I don't know. Drink the water.'

'But you suspect something. Kat said that you were at odds with the police about it. That you didn't agree with them that one of your patients was responsible.'

She sat back. 'That isn't your fight, Caleb. Please don't get involved.'

Fight. An interesting choice of words for a woman who rarely misspoke.

'Do you know who did it?'

'No.'

'Would you tell the police if you did?'

'Oh yes.' A flash of raw anger in her eyes; a stomach-turning moment before he realised it wasn't directed at him.

'I think Jai's death is linked to the fires,' he said. 'And to Portia Hirst's death.'

'Do you need to urinate?'

He stopped to check her words, decided that he'd misunderstood. 'Sorry, what?'

'I asked if you need to urinate. You're dehydrated. For the next few hours, if you don't feel the urge to urinate, drink water. Keep drinking until your urine runs clear.'

He gulped at the water – anything to not have to watch his mother-in-law say the word 'urinate' again. There was a glint in Maria's eye as he placed the empty glass on the table.

'I spoke to Aunty Eileen the day after the fires,' he said. 'I think she might know who killed Jai, but she's too scared to go to the police and she doesn't trust me enough to talk to me. Will you talk to her? She respects you. If you ask, she'll tell you.'

Maria shook her head. 'She might respect me, but she doesn't trust me.'

'But you're –'

'Black? Not quite black enough for Aunty Eileen, I'm afraid. You've heard the term "coconut"?'

He winced, tried to hide it.

'Indeed,' Maria said. 'Well, that's how Aunty Eileen sees me – brown on the outside, white in the middle. She'd no sooner talk to me than she would the police.' She glanced towards the door. 'That will be your brother.'

Caleb got to his feet, suddenly reluctant to go. 'Thanks for everything. I'm sorry about your shoes.'

'They've had worse.'

He could imagine – blood, tears, urine, faeces. How did she keep doing it, year after year? Striding on despite the crushing weight of everyone's expectations, including her own.

'Don't you get tired of it all?' The words left his mouth before he could stop himself.

She considered the question. 'Yes, but I could ask the same of you. I'm helping people I care about. What's driving you?'

32.

Ant was waiting for him on the front doorstep, red-faced and sweating. He was wearing his CFA uniform.

'Shit,' Caleb said. 'You should have told her you were busy. I could've caught a taxi.'

Ant gave him a quick up-and-down. 'The CFA is dedicated to risk management in all its forms, no matter its level of stupidity.'

Caleb followed him across the circular driveway to the car, squinting as the sunlight drilled holes through the back of his eyeballs and into his brain. He paused as a dusty blue Datsun drove in and parked beside Ant's car. Oh, for fuck's sake, not Honey Kovac again. It wasn't that surprising she was here – she was a nurse, and one of Maria's protégées – but it really did feel like the universe was fucking with him today. No doubt Honey would feel the same way: if she'd been pissed off seeing him at her mechanics', she was going to be overjoyed seeing him at her workplace.

She got out of the car looking hot and irritable, wearing a flowing red dress, and carrying her nurse's uniform over one arm. She scowled at him and strode towards the house.

Ant watched her go. 'I see she got the memo about you being a dickhead.'

Something was flashing at the back of his brain, a little warning light telling him that he'd just missed something important.

Red dress. Honey was wearing a loose-weave red cotton dress. A sudden, clear knowledge that Honey was the owner of the dress that Portia had been wearing.

He went after her and caught her by the front door. 'I need to talk to you about Portia.'

She spun around. 'What?'

'Why did you send her to me?'

'I don't know what you're talking about.' The words tumbled from her mouth.

'I don't want to cause trouble, I just want to know why you sent her to me.'

'Why the fuck would I send anyone to you?' Said with the vehemence of truth.

'OK,' he said, 'maybe you didn't send her to me, but you helped her. You lent her a red dress. And now she's dead, and Jai is, too. What happened?'

'Jesus, I don't know, all right? I barely knew her, she just came into the centre freaking out, saying some guy was after her. I gave her a dress and some stuff, that's all.'

'You work at the rehab centre, too?' He hadn't seen her name on the list of Hilvington employees.

'I temp there. Some of us have got kids to feed, you know.'

Something about the way she said that made him pause. 'Have you and Vince split?'

'What the fuck's that got to do with you?'

Excellent point. He was badly off course here – how had that happened?

'Sorry. Can you just tell me what went on that night and I'll leave you alone?'

'She said that some guy was after her, so I helped her get away.'

'A big blond guy riding a motorbike? Tatts on his neck and arms?'

Her mouth hung open. 'How'd you know that?'

'A wild guess. Do you know why he was after her?'

'No.'

Too quick with that answer, she definitely knew more. 'Did Portia ever mention a mailing list to you?'

'A what?'

'A list of names and addresses.'

'No. Look, I've gotta go. My shift starts in five minutes and Aunty Maria's really strict about time.' She was looking towards the front door.

Shit, she wouldn't give him another chance to talk to her.

'Portia was scared,' he said quickly. 'Scared before that night. And you know why. You knew her well enough to lend her clothes, to steal a packet of hair dye for her. So what did she tell you?'

'How the hell do you know about the hair dye?'

'I talked to people. And I'm going to keep talking to people. But this can be our last conversation if you want. Just tell me what you know and I'll leave you alone.'

Her eyes flicked around the driveway and back to him. 'She'd been worried about some guy for a couple of weeks. Said to tell her if I saw him hanging around.'

'Someone else? Not the blond guy on the motorbike?'

'Yeah.'

'So she described him?'

'No, but he was older, or maybe overweight. She said she could outrun him if she had to. I think –' Honey pressed a hand to her mouth.

'What's wrong?' he asked.

Tears started in her eyes; she shook her head.

'What have you remembered?' he asked.

A tap on his shoulder: Ant.

'Look,' Ant said. 'If you're going to be a dickhead and stand around interrogating people in the sun, can you at least not do it on my watch? Maria's glaring at us through the window and I'm pretty fond of all the layers of my skin.'

Sure enough, Maria was standing at the front window, her hands on her hips. Shit. Double shit – Maria had warned him off hassling Honey last year when he'd been investigating Gary's death. One more question, then he'd better go.

He turned back in time to see Honey slip inside the house.

―――――――――

Ant came with him into the motel room and stood just inside the door. He looked around its yellow walls and closed curtains, the bedclothes in a twisted knot on the floor.

'Last year,' Ant said, and then hesitated. 'It's fucking awful, what you've been through. Your best mate killed, Kat hurt, Frankie…'

'Way to go, Ant. Why don't you remind me of a few

more fucking horrors in my life?'

Ant sat on the bed and rubbed a hand across his face. 'Just go and have a cold shower, will you? I promised Maria that I'd sit with you for a while, make sure you didn't do anything stupid like go for a run. Or drop dead.'

Fucking fantastic.

He stayed in the shower until his skin began to prune, then wrapped a towel around his waist and went into the bedroom, still dripping. Ant had stripped down to his shorts and T-shirt and was reclined on the freshly made bed, watching cartoons on television. He'd raided the minibar for its entire supply of chips and chocolates.

'Your phone rang before,' Ant said. 'Unknown number. Want me to answer it next time?'

Shit, he'd forgotten to take the SIM out last night. Straight to the top of the class for that little act of genius. Still, the phone had been on for nearly twelve hours without anyone hunting him down – maybe he was being overly cautious.

'There's a message telling people to text,' he told Ant.

'Or I could answer it.'

A passing thought that Maria was punishing him by getting Ant to babysit him.

'Or you could piss off.'

Ant shrugged and opened a pack of salted peanuts. Caleb hunted through his bag for a clean T-shirt and shorts, thinking about the man Portia had been worried about. Not Blondie, but someone older or overweight.

'She said she could outrun him if she had to.'

Blondie's Molotov cocktail-making mate? He seemed the most likely candidate. He had an average build, but Honey could have got the details wrong. Second-hand knowledge was always a dangerous thing to trust.

Ant was fidgeting.

'Need me to worm you?' Caleb asked.

'Your phone's ringing again.'

Oh for fuck's sake. 'Answer the damn thing.'

Ant grabbed it. 'It's stopped, but you've got… Jesus, six missed calls.'

'Most of them are old.'

'Yeah? Tell me again how well it's going for you working without a partner. OK, only the last three are from today, all from an unknown number. One voice message, two hang-ups.' Ant smirked. 'Three hang-ups if you count your inability to accept help.' He jabbed at the screen and listened to the message. Listened to it a couple more times – not looking worried, just milking the situation.

Caleb cleared a junk food-free space on the bed and sat down to wait.

Ant finally lowered the phone. 'A woman about Portia.'

'You're kidding me?' He'd passed his business card around like confetti when he'd first got into town – but that had been two weeks ago. Why was someone ringing him about Portia now? 'What did she say?'

'That you should talk to Portia's mother.'

'Her mother?'

'Yep.'

Portia's mother: a woman who'd factored so little into the investigation that he didn't even know her name.

He grabbed his notebook and pen from the bedside table. 'What exactly did she say?'

Ant smiled. 'You see, I listened to it a few times because I knew you'd interrogate me like this.'

'Well done. And what did she say?'

Ant switched to English. '"If you want to know more about Portia, you should talk to her mum."'

Caleb lowered the pen. 'That's it?'

'Word for word.'

OK, it was a short message but to the point. So, either a legitimate tip or an attempt to get him out of town for a few days while he followed a dead end to Adelaide. Tricky to know which, without knowing who.

'What could you tell about the speaker?'

Ant paused with a handful of peanuts halfway to his mouth. He shoved them in so he could sign. 'It was a woman.'

'Yeah, I got that. What else? Accent?'

'Aussie.'

'Education?'

'I'd say a leaning towards the humanities, with some interest in particle physics.' Ant stuffed another handful of peanuts in his mouth.

'Fuck off, you know what I mean.'

'She didn't sound thick, didn't sound posh.'

'Did she have those broader vowels, like she was a country girl?'

Ant's eyes widened in surprise. 'Yeah. Now you mention it, she did. Oh.' His face brightened. 'And she sounded young. Probably twenties, maybe early thirties.' He scavenged in the packet for the last few nuts and tipped them into his mouth.

A young woman calling with anonymous information weeks after he'd handed out his card. But half an hour after he'd talked to Honey Kovac. Honey had been awfully keen to get away from him. And she'd been even keener to get away from him two weeks ago at the EezyWay, spinning the line that she was worried about her marriage if her husband caught her talking to him. Her apparently ex-husband.

A growing feeling that Honey knew a lot more than she'd let on.

'Could it have been Honey Kovac?'

'Nah. Anyway, Honey knows you're deaf – she wouldn't be stupid enough to leave you a voicemail.'

'Not stupid enough, smart enough. Honey's pretty sharp. Leaving a voice message is a great way of putting me off her scent. Gets a friend to ring in case it's you or Kat listening to the message, and she's all set.'

Ant took that in. 'Yeah, I can see that. Or it could be a stranger. Or someone yanking your chain. Or someone else trying to cover their tracks.' He lobbed the phone back to Caleb. 'Guess we'll never know.'

'Thanks for the encouragement.'

Caleb checked his texts, felt the heart-slide of disappointment that there was nothing from Kat. At least she hadn't been there to witness his humiliation today. He was pretty sure Maria wouldn't say anything to her, either – members of the Mafia had looser mouths than Maria. He turned off the phone and pulled out the SIM.

'Taking sensible precautions,' Ant said. 'Good to see. Maybe you'll remember not to get heatstroke next time.'

'And maybe I'll shove this phone up your arse.' He put it on the bedside table and grabbed his car keys.

Ant plucked a bag of potato chips from the bed. 'Where are you going?'

'To talk to Honey.'

'At the clinic? Brave move. Some would say foolhardy.'

Damn.

Ant shoved a handful of chips into his mouth and patted the bed. 'Come and watch TV. I'll interpret for you. It's Greek myths for kids. I think you'll like this one – it's about some dickhead called Icarus.'

He went straight to bed when Ant left and woke at some stage in the darkness, the urgent pressure of gallons of water pressing against his bladder. Into the bathroom, limbs heavy with sleep.

Something in the corner of his eye – a square of deeper shadow on the bathroom mirror. He peered at it, then switched on the light. A newspaper article: photos of Jai's smiling face, the festooned scar tree.

Someone had broken into his room while he slept.

33.

Caleb went for a leisurely drive the next morning, making sudden stops and abrupt U-turns, his eyes more on the rear-view mirror than the road. Vicky had sorted out a short-term hire on an ancient Mini for him when the EezyWay had opened at 8 a.m. He'd moved to another motel in the middle of the night, leaving behind his car and a hefty dose of his courage. People sneaking around his room while he slept – the stuff of childhood nightmares.

At least he knew that he was getting close to the truth. Close enough to make someone worried. Not the Copperheads. A drive-by shooting was more their style, a cricket bat to the back of the head, a sawn-off shotgun in the face. Either the bikies weren't involved, or someone with a cooler head was running the show.

He did another loop of the town – hunting in vain for an air conditioner switch and missing his Commodore's legroom, headroom and suspension – then headed for Honey's place.

A jolt at the sight of the vacant block opposite her house. Bare earth and bulldozed emptiness where Maria's clinic had stood for twenty years. She hadn't wasted any time mourning its loss, just moved on. Probably had new plans drawn up already, the builders standing by.

'*I'm helping people I care about. What's driving you?*'

He turned for Honey's bluestone cottage. A *Forthcoming Auction* sign was stapled to her front fence. No car in the driveway or pram on the front porch, no answer to his knock. Maybe she'd gone to drop the kids at day care. On a Sunday. Caleb pressed his hands to the front window and peered inside. A neatly made double bed and a cot, a library book and a glass of water on the bedside table. The dressing table was clutter-free, but two of its drawers were half open – a jarring sight in the rigidly neat room. He went to the next window. A pair of bunk beds, their covers smoothed, children's books perfectly aligned on the shelves. The wardrobe doors were flung open; empty. Honey had done a runner.

———

He had to try a few of the neighbouring houses until he found someone home. Sighed when he saw that it was Mr Henderson, a man full of excess information and phlegm. Mr Henderson had been ancient for as long as Caleb could remember, slowly shrinking inside his wardrobe of brown clothing. A brown flannelette shirt today, along with brown trousers, brown socks and, for some colour relief, a beige cardigan.

'Young Caleb. It is Caleb, isn't it? Not the other one? Bug?'

'Ant. But I'm Caleb. I'm looking for Honey. Do you know where she's gone? I think she's moved out.'

Mr Henderson pulled out a grim-looking hanky and hawked up a clot: brown. 'Really? She wasn't due to go for another few weeks. Couldn't wait to get to the Gold Coast, I suppose.'

'The Gold Coast?' Caleb struggled to picture the frowning Honey on the glitzy Gold Coast.

'Or maybe the Sunshine Coast. A coast, anyway. Got plenty of 'em in Australia, hey? Shame to see her go. She always took me bins out for me, brought the paper in, too. Bit of a shock when she told me she was off.' His throat made a convulsive motion, and Caleb swiftly averted his eyes. A quick hawk and a spit, and they were good to go again. 'But I guess she needs a bit of help from her sister now she's a single mum.'

'She's separated?'

'Oh yes. Months ago now. Terrible shouting matches. Poor girl, don't know what she did to deserve that.'

'Did she leave a forwarding number?'

'She was going to, but I guess she didn't get around to it. Busy woman with those three little ones.'

Maybe Maria would know. And maybe he'd gather the courage to ask her one day.

'OK,' he said. 'Thanks for your help.' He was at the gate before the question occurred to him.

Mr Henderson answered the door midway through lighting a cigarette. 'Taken a shine to me?' He exhaled on a cough and pressed his handkerchief to his mouth.

Caleb focused on his right ear until he'd stopped spitting.

'One more question,' he said. 'Do you know when Honey put the house on the market?'

'Coupla weeks.'

'Do you remember exactly when?'

Mr Henderson took a deep drag on the cigarette while he thought about it. 'Told me when she was bringin' me paper in. Only get it on a Saturday now, so I guess it must've been a Saturday. Total rubbish the other days, not worth me money.' Another hawk and spit.

Damn, too slow to avoid that one.

———————

Caleb headed for the motel, thinking through the timing. So Honey had been involved in Portia and Jai's scheme. Not a major player, but definitely a collaborator: she'd put her house on the market the day after Portia's death and left town hours after speaking to him. Grabbed her three children, left a house full of belongings, and fled.

'She said she could outrun him if she had to.'

That was the moment she'd decided to run. Tears welling in her eyes, her hand pressed to her mouth: raw fear as she'd realised who Portia had been describing. Did she know who'd broken into Caleb's motel room, too? Someone in town would have her new address – he could track her down. Or he could do the right thing and let her go. He couldn't live with any more blood on his hands.

He slowed as he passed a familiar iridescent-green ute parked by the side of the road. A slope-shouldered man was sitting in the driver's seat, his head turned towards the house he was parked outside. Dave McGregor, up and about on a Sunday morning. Dave McGregor, owner of address labels that matched the mailing list; possible friend of Rat-tail Luke.

'She said she could outrun him if she had to.'

McGregor was only thirty-two, but unfit, with a paunchy gut. Could he be the man Portia had been worried about? Whatever the case, it would be very interesting to know why he was watching that house.

Caleb parked around the corner and walked back to the wide drain that ran behind the house McGregor was casing, an old creek that had been concreted into submission years ago. It was littered with plastic bags and bottles, and a surprising number of shopping trolleys. Caleb hopped the low fence and walked through the weeds along the edge of the drain. He counted the houses and stopped at the back of a small blond-brick house. No curtains on the windows and an overgrown lawn, no sign of any movement inside.

He was halfway over the back fence when he saw the dark shadow of a dog kennel down the side of the house. A big one. Shit. He retreated to safety and banged on the fence, but no dog appeared. No dog bowl in the yard, no toys – it was probably safe. Come on, do it. Get it over with quickly. He scrambled over the fence and ran through the knee-high grass to the rear window. A clear view through an empty kitchen up the central hallway. McGregor's brown sports bag was lying by the front door.

The back door was locked, but an oversized dog door was set into it. He eyed its dimensions, then poked his head through. A moment caught halfway – aware that his shorts were too thin for this kind of manoeuvre, that he was fucked if there really was a dog, that his life hadn't exactly panned out the way he'd thought it would – and he was inside.

He froze on his hands and knees: someone was in the house. A rhythmic thumping ran through the floorboards up his arms. A consistent beat, not growing any stronger or weaker. Music? Someone running on the spot? He stood and peered around the kitchen door into the hallway. Empty. He made his way slowly down the hallway towards the sports bag, glancing in each room before he passed. Bare floorboards and stained walls; no furniture, no people. He stopped before the last room and squatted to press his hand to the floor. The thumping was stronger. They were making a lot of noise. Maybe he could creep past without them noticing.

He edged towards the door and looked in.

A bare mattress on the floor, a pale and scrawny arse working between two jiggling white thighs. The woman's mouth opened in an 'o' as she saw Caleb. 'Cops!' Her companion launched himself off her and onto the floor, scrambling to get clear.

Christ, he could never unsee that.

Scrawny-bum snatched up his jeans, hopping on one leg as he tried to simultaneously walk and get dressed. '…fuck… I didn't know… I thought she was…'

The girl thrust her head through a T-shirt that was two sizes too small for her, and Caleb got a good look at her face. Their frantic uncoupling suddenly made sense – she was underage. Scrawny-bum was still babbling about not knowing things, his eyes wet with tears. It seemed a pity to disabuse him of the notion that Caleb was a cop.

'ID,' he said.

'…didn't know… thought she was eighteen.'

'Keep the explanations for the station, please, Mr…?'

'Harolds.'

Caleb clicked his fingers, and Scrawny-bum handed

him his wallet. That was easier than he'd expected. He glanced at the man's driver's licence.

'OK, Paul Harolds of 3 Waterdale Street. What do you know about Dave McGregor?'

'What?'

Scrawny-bum looked blank, but Caleb had caught the girl's flinch.

'OK,' he told Scrawny, 'you can piss off.'

'My wallet.'

The girl was fully dressed now and edging towards the door. Caleb moved between her and the exit. 'I'll give it to you later,' he told Scrawny. 'When I pop around to have a chat to your wife and your…' He flipped over the wallet's photo sleeve. 'Four kids.' He shoved it in his back pocket.

Scrawny eyed Caleb as though considering tackling him, but his shoulders soon slumped, and he stumbled to the front door, clutching his half-done-up jeans.

'Out the back way,' Caleb called to him. 'Over the fence.'

'What? Why?'

'My colleagues are out the front. They'll shoot you.'

Scrawny took off without a backwards glance.

The girl had collapsed onto the mattress, covering her face with her hands. She was genuinely crying but peeking between her fingers to gauge his reaction to her tears.

He grabbed the sports bag from the hallway and knelt in front of her. 'What's your name?'

She lowered her hands. 'Beck.'

'Beck, I'm Caleb. Do you need help? Can I take you home?'

She reared back. 'Don't tell Mum! She'll fucken kill me after last time.'

'OK. I can take you somewhere else. Where do you want to go?'

'I have to ask Dave if you want a home visit.'

'What? No. I mean, can I take you somewhere safe? We can go out the back way so Dave doesn't see you.'

'I'm not going anywhere without Dave, you fucking perve. Dave! Dave!' She yelled so loudly his hearing aids buzzed.

'OK.' Caleb held up a hand, glancing at the front door. 'We don't have to go anywhere, just tell me what you're doing for Dave.'

Her head lifted. 'You won't tell Mum?'

Maybe not her mother, but definitely the cops, along with a few details about Scrawny-bum and McGregor.

'No, I won't tell your mum. What are you doing for Dave?'

She wiped her nose on the back of her hand. 'Just this. It's all clean. We use condoms – most of the time, anyway.'

'What else are you selling?'

'What?' She bit her lip, a child asked to complete a maths test she hadn't studied for.

'Are you selling ice?'

'No! You can't charge me for that. I don't do ice – it fucks you up, makes you ugly.'

'And Dave?'

'Not anymore.'

'Open the bag and take everything out.'

She unzipped the bag and began laying its contents on the mattress. No sachets of white crystals, no money, just condoms and sex toys, a pair of handcuffs, a tube of lubricant. She laid a sheet of paper on top of the pile – address labels.

'Hand me the labels,' he said.

'What?'

'The labels, give them to me.'

She handed them over. Most had been used, but the remaining names matched the mailing list from the school camp.

Beck was edging away on the mattress, getting ready to run.

'Where did you get these?' he asked.

'Dave.'

'Where did he get them?'

She shrugged. No guile in her face, just confusion.

'Do you know Jai Johnson?'

'Who?'

'Jai, the young bloke who was hanged.'

'The boong? Nah, never did him. I would've, though. He was cute, yeah? I saw his photo.'

'What about Portia Hirst?'

'I don't do girls.' She thought about it. 'Guess I could.' Her gaze flicked behind him, and the corners of her mouth lifted.

He spun around, his arm raising. Something hard slammed against his temple.

On the floor, McGregor's forearm against his throat. Ten years old and lying winded in the middle of the playground; McGregor's slit-eyed face looming above him, his arm pulling back for the final blow.

Not this time. Caleb formed a fist.

McGregor shoved down on his neck. 'Stay still, fuckhead. What the fuck are you doing with my girl?'

Pressure building, blood thumping in his head.

Caleb scrabbled at the arm. 'Can't. Breathe.'

McGregor eased the pressure but didn't release him. 'Go on, retard boy. What. Are. You. Doing. Here?'

Think quickly – make his answers work for him. 'Looking for a big blond guy with a limp.'

Open bewilderment on McGregor's face. 'What?'

'Might work for the Copperheads.'

'What?'

Shit, McGregor had no ability to obfuscate – he didn't know who Blondie was.

'Are the Copperheads involved?'

McGregor's face was growing steadily redder. 'What the fuck are you talking about? Involved in what?'

'The mailing list.'

'What mailing list?'

'The labels in your bag and –' No, bad idea to let McGregor know it was him who'd broken into his house.

But McGregor was smiling. He plucked the labels off the floor and grinned at Beck. '...fucken retard... mailing list...'

She laughed.

McGregor shoved the labels in his back pocket and leaned his weight against Caleb's throat. 'Stay away from me and my girl. You understand?'

'Yes.'

Another shove. 'You sure? I'll say it nice and slow for you. Stay. The. Fuck. Away. From. Me.'

Caleb clawed at his arm. The room's edges were slipping away.

Beck was by McGregor's side, pulling ineffectually at his shoulder. '…police… c'mon…'

'If I see you around, I'll rip your fucking arms off so you can't flap 'em anymore.'

And his throat was released. Gasping, dragging in air. Get up, hit the bastard. He managed a glancing blow before McGregor's punch landed. Pain. In his stomach, up his back, into his throat. Curled on the floor, trying not to moan. The thump of footsteps against his cheek, the slam of the door. Stillness.

34.

He went back to the one-bowser petrol station for another miraculous coffee. It wouldn't wash the taste of humiliation from his mouth, but it might come close. The same unsmiling man was behind the counter. He greeted Caleb with a slight raise of his chin and nodded towards the coffee machine. Caleb nodded back and leaned against a shelf of out-of-date biscuits to wait. This had been a good idea, this was his sort of place. A place of silent communication and really good coffee. Where he could do very little to fuck things up.

He'd done everything wrong. Stood with his back to the door, not got Beck on his side, let McGregor get in the first punch. And every punch after that. It shouldn't have gone that way; he was stronger than McGregor, fitter. But apparently a lot stupider.

'Retard boy.'

Move on. At least he'd discovered that McGregor didn't have any connection to Blondie or the Copperheads. The man was a minor player at most, not worth his time. Put the whole thing down to some hard-won information and be thankful that there'd only been one witness to his humiliation. And no involuntary pissing of his pants. God.

He pulled his phone from his pocket and tried to refit

the SIM. The fifth time today, but it probably couldn't be counted as obsessive until it reached double figures. He finally slotted the card into place and switched on the phone. A few seconds later it buzzed: a message from Kat, sent thirty minutes ago.

—*You around? I need to see you x K*

Oh thank God. Don't gush, but make it clear how welcome her message is.

He typed a reply then deleted it, wrote another one, deleted it. A sudden realisation that Kat's iPhone would be showing her exactly how long it was taking him to type a reply.

—*Yes. Where?*

Only a short wait before the phone vibrated.

—*I'm sketching out on coast rd. meet you at Ant's*

Ant's place was out of the question, ditto the motel, but a quiet moment alone with Kat on a clifftop would be safe. And perfect.

—*No. Stay there. I'll find you*

He went to the counter to pay. His coffee was waiting for him like an offering.

'Happy?' the old bloke asked.

He thought about it. 'Yes.'

He did a long and circuitous loop of the town, then drove along the coast road until he caught sight of Kat's Beetle, recognisable from a great distance. He parked behind it and winced. He hadn't viewed the X-rated mural from this angle before. The 'artist' had incorporated the exhaust pipe into a coupling that was both alarming and anatomically dubious. How was this car still on the road? Where were the outraged citizens when you needed them?

He followed a faint path through the scrub to a sandy clearing at the edge of the cliff. The sea stretched below him, silver in the midday sun, its salt smell lifting on the breeze. Kat was sitting on a beach towel in the shade of a banksia, the eagle feather tucked behind her ear. She was sketching, her shorn head bent in concentration, her hand moving freely as something looping and wild formed beneath it. He stood watching for a moment; Kat was drawing, and all was right in the world.

She gave a little start as he walked towards her. 'That was quick.'

He smiled. She really was getting back into her work – he'd driven around town for twenty minutes before heading here.

He kissed her forehead and sat in front of her, nodded at the sketchbook. 'Can I look?'

She closed it and tucked it away. 'When it's finished.'

'A new sculpture?'

'Tattoo.'

A tattoo? She didn't even have her ears pierced.

'You hate tattoos.'

'No I don't, I've just never felt the need for one before.'

A need for a tattoo. What sort of need was that?

'Are you OK?' he asked.

Something crossed her face, quickly gone. Worry? Fear?

His mouth was suddenly dry. 'What's wrong?'

'I'm fine. But half my 'lations have been on the phone

complaining about you. They say you're trying to connect Jai to bikies.'

'Not connect. But I think the Copperheads might have had something to do with his death.'

'Well, back off a bit, will you? If the cops agree, they'll never stop hassling Aunty Eileen. Mick said that you'd already had a go at her about it.'

'How does Mick know that? Not that I had a go at her.'

'Mick knows everything. Everybody knows everything, you know how it is. You've got to stop hassling her. She's old and she's sick and she's lost just about all she had.'

'I wasn't hassling her.'

It was impressive, really, how expressive her face was. A clear declaration of the exact level of his stupidity without her resorting to speech or sign.

'I won't speak to her again,' he said. 'Or anyone else you'd care to name. Make me a list.'

'Great. Thanks.' But she didn't look relieved. She turned the sketchbook over in her hands and flicked its edges. Kat fidgeting was not a good sign; whatever she was worried about, it wasn't her relatives getting snippy with her.

'What's wrong?' he asked.

She looked up at him, her eyes shadowed. 'You didn't even know Portia. Why are you still going with this?'

'Because she came to me for help.'

'And you did what you could. Did more than most people would. So, why?'

'Her eyes –'

No, not here. Not with Kat. Once open, those sluice gates might never close. He couldn't pour his vile sludge onto her happiness, not when he could barely keep himself from drowning in it.

'Working this case makes me feel better,' he said. 'Think of it as my version of sketching.'

She looked down at the sketchbook and ran her fingers across the cover.

'I want to ask you something,' she said. 'But I don't want to upset you.'

Oh God.

'Of course. Anything.'

'Are you getting any help? Seeing a counsellor again?'

A wave of heat rose up his neck and into his scalp. Only one thing could have prompted her to ask that. 'Maria told you what happened.'

'No, Mum knows how to keep a secret. But you had a panic attack in the middle of the highway. You think half the town hasn't told me?'

'It wasn't a panic attack.'

She slipped into speech. 'Oh, babe.'

'I just... It was hot.'

'Cal.' Tears welled in her eyes. 'I can't do this.'

'Do what?'

'Us.'

The ground slid away beneath him.

'I'm so sorry,' she said. 'I know I haven't been fair to you. I haven't been fair to either of us. I should have put an end to it months ago, instead of dragging it out. But we need to stop now, before it gets any harder.'

He managed to lift his hands. 'I know I fucked up before. With the miscarriages, and before that. But I've changed – I'm talking, *we're* talking. Look at us now, talking.'

She blinked rapidly. 'I know. I know how hard you've tried, and I love you for it, I really do. But I have to find a way of dealing with my own pain. I can't fix yours too.'

The weight lifted from his chest. Was that all she was worried about?

'You don't have to fix anything. I'm fine.'

'No, you're not. You are a very, very long way from fine, and you're not doing anything to get better.' She was signing too fast, her hands barely finishing each shape before flying to the next. 'I wish, I really wish I could help you, but I can't. Do you know why I went away? Because you were trying so hard to prove that you were all right, it was killing us both. I thought that if I gave you a bit of space, you'd work at getting better. But you haven't. You're even worse than before. You're not eating, you're not sleeping, you're just running around trying to save a woman who's already dead. And I can't handle that. I can't let that be my life.'

'I'll drop the case. It's not that important.'

'Cal.' She swiped at her eyes. 'The case isn't the problem. I'm trying to tell you that I don't think I'm good for you anymore. And I *know* you're not good for me.'

His hands were raised, gripping empty air. He let them fall.

Kat inhaled shakily. 'I want to finalise the divorce.'

Like a punch to the throat.

'OK. OK, I'll... OK.'

He stood, tried to remember how to walk. To breathe. To exist.

35.

He went to the Trawler's Arms. No thought behind the decision, just that it was the first pub he came to. Alcohol had never helped him much before, but millions swore by it, so maybe he just hadn't tried hard enough.

A dozen or so men were sitting at the tables, a couple of lone drinkers at the bar. Mick was behind the bar again, serving a red-faced man in a 'Keep Australia White' T-shirt. That had to hurt, but there probably wasn't much choice when you were a middle-aged man with a prison record and a family to feed.

Mick came over to Caleb as he sat. 'Becomin' a regular.'

Caleb tried to think of the correct response, then just nodded.

'What'll you have?' Mick prompted.

'Um, a beer.'

A frown for that, but Mick pulled him a pint of VB and placed it on the bar.

'Enjoy,' he said and went to serve another customer who'd decided that drinking in a pub at one o'clock on a Sunday afternoon was a good life decision.

Caleb downed most of the beer in one go but didn't hold out much hope. He needed something stronger to sear this ooze from his brain. Whisky, bleach, acid – just saw open his skull and pour the stuff in.

'*I know you're not good for me.*'

Smart woman. Very smart. She'd even known how pointless this case was. Because it was pointless. He'd known from the start exactly how pointless it was. It wasn't going to bring Portia back; it wasn't going to change what he'd done, or ease the tightness in his chest. But sometimes there wasn't any choice. Sometimes you had to stand behind a bar and serve racist arseholes so you could feed your family, and sometimes you had to investigate a pointless fucking case so you could just. Keep. Moving.

Mick was back, polishing an already clean glass. 'You right there, mate?'

'Sure.'

'While I've got you here. About Aunty Eileen. Don't go getting the gunyan riled up about Jai and the Copperheads – it's bad enough for her as it is.'

'Don't worry, Kat's already read me the riot act. Just look out for Aunty Eileen, will you? If she knows what happened to Jai, she might be in danger.'

Mick squinted at him. "Course I'll fucken look out for her – she's family.'

Family.

An uncomfortable thought wormed its way into his brain. Seven months ago, this man had clasped his shoulder and called him cuz, told him that he'd always be family.

'That woman I asked you about,' Caleb said. 'Portia Hirst. You sure you didn't know her?'

'Yeah. Why?'

'So you didn't send her to me?'

'No. D'you need it in writing?' Mick was looking around for someone else to serve. It wouldn't take him long.

Quick, the conversation with Ant's dealer – the name of the man who knew Blondie and drank in the Arms.

'Do you know a guy called Johnno?'

Mick was good. He didn't blink, didn't look away, but his posture had an exaggerated stillness. 'Know a few Johnnos. All of them shy.'

'This Johnno drinks here regularly.'

'Mate, go home. You are seriously out of your league with these guys.'

'Yeah? In what way?'

Mick heaved a sigh and wandered to the other end of the bar. Got busy rearranging the three clean glasses on the sink.

Caleb scanned the room. Judging by Mick's reaction, either Johnno or one of his mates was currently in the pub. Old bloke at the bar, two lone drinkers, three tables of men. The old bloke would be the best bet for information. Caleb crossed to him and put a ten-dollar note on the bar, kept his finger on it. 'Beer's on Johnno. You know him?'

The man's lips barely moved. 'Window.'

The table at the window was occupied by a scrawny man with a large bushy beard. He was wearing baggy jeans and a too-big black T-shirt, as though he'd once been much larger. A leather jacket was hanging over the back of his chair. Caleb didn't need to check to know that it had the image of a large yellow snake on it.

That beard was going to make things difficult. More than difficult – impossible. So drop it, drop everything.

Just get in the car and go back to Melbourne. Try not to drive into a tree on the way there. Plenty of places to do it: that first bend out of the Bay, or that long stretch of road before Geelong. Foot hard on the accelerator, the wheel firm in his hands, a moment of fear and then nothing.

Breathless. Icy arms gripping his chest and squeezing his lungs.

He crossed to the table. 'Johnno?'

The man raised his head, peering at Caleb as though looking into a bright light. Bloodshot eyes and pasty skin, the smell of ammonia and ancient sweat. His beard moved, exposing tombstone teeth. A short sentence, two words. Go on? Piss off?

Mick moved into Caleb's line of sight, putting a good shine on a bar that had never been clean.

'I'm looking for a blond guy,' Caleb said. 'Big bloke, has a bit of a sore knee.'

Johnno's mouth opened like a bear's maw, then closed again. Fuck, not a single word.

'I didn't catch that. Can y–'

Johnno stood, toppling his chair to the floor.

Scurrying movement: men leaving, men coming closer. Noise blared as someone turned up the music.

Johnno pulled out a flick-knife.

36.

It was a small knife, but small knives could cut as easily as large ones. They could slice through skin and tendons, sever veins. The blood spurting and flowing, pooling on the dusty warehouse floor.

Caleb showed his opened hands and backed away.

Thump. Into something solid behind him. Someone solid.

Johnno stepped in close. He was twitching and talking rapidly, jabbing the knife. Shit, the man was more than agitated, he was fried.

Caleb kept his eyes on the knife and calculated his moves. The pub door was behind him, one of Johnno's mates at his back, a few more close by. He wouldn't make it if he ran; he'd have to try and disarm Johnno.

Bare skin against blade.

A blast of hot air as the pub door opened. And Ant was beside him, drenched in sweat and breathing hard. A chill of fear: Jesus Christ, what was Ant doing here? He was going to get himself killed.

'Get out,' Caleb signed quickly. 'This guy's a lunatic.'

Ant ignored him and turned to Johnno, a string of words falling from his lips. '...brother... fuckwit... stupid...'

Johnno answered, gesticulating with the knife.

'I can't understand him,' Caleb signed. 'Tell him –'

Johnno grabbed the front of his T-shirt and jammed the knife under his Adam's apple. The sharp sting of the blade. The acrid stench of meth and rotting flesh. Ant tapped his shoulder, but he couldn't look away from Johnno's wild eyes. Another tap. He slowly turned his head.

Ant was blinking rapidly. 'Don't sign,' he said through tight lips. 'Johnno doesn't like it. English only, OK?'

'OK.'

'I told him that you're not interested in him. You're not, are you?'

'No.'

'And you're not interested in the Copperheads.'

'No.'

'You're going to leave now and never come back.'

'Yes.'

Johnno let out a string of guttural sounds, and the blade jabbed into Caleb's neck. He inhaled sharply – audibly, judging by Johnno's grin. A warm trickle of blood ran down his neck.

Ant swallowed. 'Tell him why you're here.'

He found some saliva and got his tongue to work. 'I want to know why Portia Hirst was killed.'

Johnno grunted something, then stabbed his knife towards the exit. No need to ask Ant to translate the gesture.

Quick, one question. 'Who's running the ice trade in the Bay?'

Ant's shoulders slumped.

The beard parted and closed. Hands clamped down on his shoulders and turned him around, shoved him towards the door. He stumbled, then righted himself, covering the distance at a near run, Ant by his side.

A glimpse of Mick standing rigid behind the bar as they left.

———

Ant drove without speaking, his body vibrating with tension, hands tight on the wheel. He kept going until they were a few kilometres out of town, then suddenly pulled over and yanked on the handbrake.

'You stupid fucking fucktard! What the hell were you trying to prove? That you're tougher than the rest of us? Jesus fucking Christ, you could've got us both killed!' He was flipping between speech and sign, almost impossible to follow.

'Stay home next time. I didn't ask you to come.'

'No, because you're too stupid! Lucky for you, Mick rang and said that you were about to get your head stomped in.'

'Well, fuck you both, I would've sorted it out.'

Ant yelled something wordless, the tendons in his neck standing out like tree roots. 'No, you wouldn't have. And do you know why? Because, despite what Dad kept telling you, there are some things you can't do. And hassling a bar full of bikies when you can't understand a fucking word they're saying is one of them!'

A wave of acid heat flowed through him. He got out of the car and slammed the door, started walking. After a few seconds, Ant's car sped past in a spray of gravel.

The wind was coming from the north, carrying with it the smell of burnt eucalypt and the promise of dust storms. His anger drained away within minutes, leaving a dull patina of embarrassment. Ant was right – all he'd proved in that bar was exactly how stupid he was. No great loss that he'd never be able to show his face in the Arms again, but avoiding Mick for the rest of his life was going to be a little tricky seeing as he lived across the road from Ant. And was Kat's favourite cousin.

'I know *you're not good for me.*'

What now? It'd take him about an hour to walk back into town, one and a half if he really dragged it out. Either way, he'd be at the motel well before dark. And then…
And then he'd go back to the beginning of the case. Start with Portia, talk to her father and try to find everyone who'd volunteered for Coast Care. That would keep him busy for a day or two. Another couple of days, if he added Portia's mother to the list and drove to Adelaide. And then… And then…

'I know *you're not good for me.*'

He'd always been aware of Kat, but they'd moved in parallel worlds until that first day by the river. One of those end-of-school-year piss-ups that happened without being organised. He'd swum for hours, pretending not to watch the long-legged Koori girl jumping from the rope swing into the water. Seventeen years old, and full of lust and longing. There'd been twenty or so kids, but she'd somehow ended up sitting next to him when they'd finally hauled themselves out of the water.

God, he'd been lucky. Lucky that she'd spoken to him that day. Lucky that she'd built a life with him. That she'd made him laugh. That she'd loved him.

There'd be no more luck now. Just a registered letter, the scrawl of a pen, and it would all be over. And then, one day in the not-too-distant future, he'd see her down the street and she'd be with someone else.

Unbearable.

A car was heading towards him, Ant's battered Toyota. Shit. He wiped his eyes and kept walking. Ant did a U-turn and pulled onto the verge in front of him, stuck his head out the window. 'Get in.'

Caleb ignored him.

Ant got out of the car and blocked his way. 'It's hot and I'm scared of your mother-in-law, so you can either get in *my* car, or I'll ring Maria and you can get in *hers*.'

———

'Drop me at the pub,' Caleb said when they were a little way down the road. 'The car's there.'

Ant wedged his knees under the wheel and signed, 'You do know that you're a dickhead, don't you? I mean, it hasn't just escaped your attention?'

'No, I'm fully aware of it.'

'That's something, I guess.' Ant frowned. 'You look like shit. You're not going to pass out or something, are you?'

Unfortunately not.

'No.'

He rested his head against the seat. Tired now. Deep weariness, like the aftermath of his session with Jasmine and her stun gun. A little over two weeks since that had happened. A lifetime. He was strongly tempted to close his eyes and sleep, but Ant was shooting him little glances, his expression earnest – always a precursor to him asking uncomfortable questions. Questions that would lead to answers like, 'I tried my hardest, but it wasn't enough.'

He roused himself and turned to Ant. 'What did Johnno say when I told him I was looking into Portia's death?'

'You mean apart from, "fuck off before I fucken fuck ya"? He said, "The stupid bitch should have asked us. We would've done it right."'

Done what right?

'You sure that's what he said?'

'Strangely enough, I was paying attention.'

'What about when I asked him who was running the ice trade?'

'Oh yeah,' Ant nudged the wheel with an elbow. 'Thanks for that, you nearly gave me a heart attack. Lucky for you, Johnno seemed to think it was funny.'

'How could you tell?'

'He said, "That's funny."'

'So, it's the Copperheads?'

'Of course. Everyone knows that. Why the hell were you talking to him if you didn't know that?'

Because assumptions got you into trouble. Got your heart shredded. Got you killed. And the Copperheads hadn't crept into his motel room while he slept, and stuck a newspaper photo to the bathroom mirror.

'I just wanted to confirm it.'

Ant closed his eyes for longer than was sensible for

a man driving at eighty kilometres an hour. They were on the outskirts of town, the strip of concrete-sheet buildings shimmering in the hard light. A lone car was parked outside Alaskan Rooster.

Ant smacked his arm to get his attention. 'Why were you asking about ice? I thought you were looking into the mailing list?'

'They might be the same thing. The camp where we found the list would be a good place to cook meth. All those shelves in the place – maybe we just missed a big cook-up.'

Ant shook his head. 'No, we would've smelled it. That stuff stinks forever.'

'You know what a meth lab smells like?'

'Yeah, there was one on Sanction Street a while back. Idiots set it up near the hospital, so it got shut down pretty quickly. Smelled like a meth user, only worse.'

Worse than Johnno's breath? He definitely would have noticed that.

Ant pulled up at the Arms. No sign of Johnno or his mates, no Harleys parked outside.

'Where's your car?' Ant asked.

'It's the Mini. I hired it.'

Ant gave him a long look. 'Why?'

'Air-conditioning,' he lied. He opened the door, then paused. 'Thanks for, you know, everything.'

Ant nodded but didn't quite meet his eyes. 'What I said before, that came out wrong. I just meant that you should play to your strengths. It's what the rest of us mere mortals do.'

Caleb considered that. 'You've got strengths?'

'Sexual prowess.'

'Is that what Etty says?'

'If I prompt her enough.' Ant's head bobbed to some internal dialogue.

Caleb waited; no synapse fired in Ant's brain without him expressing it within seconds.

Ant's head bobbed again. 'Johnno said something else as we were going.'

'What?'

'That you'd be easy to surprise on a dark night.'

37.

The shaft of sunlight had reached his foot. He'd got up and got dressed, but somewhere along the way he'd ended up sitting back on the bed. A while ago now: that blade of light had started over by the wall.

He'd known as soon as he'd woken that he wasn't going on with the case. He wasn't going to find out why Portia had come to him. He wasn't going to find out why Jai had died. He wasn't going to hammer on Kat's door and beg her to give him one last chance. He was going to put on his shoes, pack his bag and go back to Melbourne. Any minute now.

Something moved in the corner of his eye. The door was shivering, as though someone was hammering on it. He heaved himself to his feet. Realised halfway through opening the door that he probably should have checked the spy-hole, but there were no hyped-up bikies waiting for him, just the man from reception. Tall and wiry, with an air of eye-rolling boredom he should have outgrown twenty years ago.

He was halfway through a sentence before Caleb realised. '...right now.'

'Sorry, what?'

EMMA VISKIC

The man sighed. 'Your brother rang. He says you need to go to the house right now.'

An ambulance was parked outside the house, a police car behind it, neighbours gathered on the footpath.

Out of the car, running. Etty was sitting in the back of the ambulance, holding a compress to her head and talking to the ambos. Ant – where was Ant? His brother couldn't bear to be ten centimetres away from Etty when they were in the same room, so what would it take for him to stay away when she was hurt?

Up the front path and into the house. Down the hall, past a trail of broken plaster and hacked banisters. And into the kitchen. Ant was sitting with his back to the door, Sergeant Ramsden and a young constable facing him across the kitchen table. No pool of blood; no blank, staring eyes. Caleb gripped the doorframe to steady himself.

Sergeant Ramsden looked over at him and said something, made an obvious 'go away' gesture. Fuck that for a joke.

'Ant,' he said aloud, and went around the table to his brother.

Blood on Ant's mouth, the dark shadow of a bruise forming on one cheek. He was dragging on a cigarette with long, urgent inhalations, a packet of Winfield Blues by his hand. Not his usual brand, something cadged in desperation.

'Jesus, what happened?' Caleb asked. 'Are you OK?'

'Have you seen Etty?' Ant managed to keep hold of the cigarette as he signed, but it trembled.

'She's outside with the ambos. Sitting up, talking. What happened?'

'We went out for breakfast, came back and found one of the guys from the riot wrecking the place.'

Ramsden was trying to catch Caleb's attention, but he kept his eyes on Ant. 'You're sure it was the same guy?'

'No, but he was wearing a balaclava.'

'Limping?'

'Um, yeah. Can you check on Etty? He, um...' Ant touched his head, looked as though he was going to throw up. 'He punched her. They're checking for concussion.'

Ramsden stood and placed a heavy hand on Caleb's shoulder.

'Hang on,' Caleb told him, and faced Ant again. 'She looked OK, but come and talk to her, reassure yourself. You can deal with the cops later.'

'She doesn't want to see me. Can you go and check on her?' Ant's eyes welled with tears. 'Please.'

Ramsden moved in front of Caleb, blocking Ant from his view. 'Move away now, or we can move this to the station and add a charge of obstruction for you.'

Obstruction?

Then he noticed what was lying by the constable's hand: a tiny Ziploc bag of something crystalline and white. A weight dropped into his stomach.

He moved around Ramsden so he could see Ant. 'Where'd that come from?'

'It isn't mine. It really isn't. I know I've said that before, but it isn't this time.'

'Where's it from?'

Ant sucked on his cigarette. 'A fucking tip-off. Someone rang the cops saying that the balaclava guy and I were fighting over a stash and that the drugs were in the house. Ramsden showed up and went straight to my wardrobe, found it taped under my fucking sock draw.' Ash fell from Ant's shaking cigarette onto the table. 'The way Etty looked at me. God.'

Ramsden gripped Caleb's upper arm with pincer-like fingers. 'Move. Now.'

'It's not his,' Caleb told him. 'Someone planted it to get at me.'

Ramsden's broad face settled into loose-jawed exhaustion: the look of a man who's heard all the excuses and pleas in the world. 'Mr Zelic, we have found what we suspect is a drug of dependence in your brother's bedroom. Your brother is a known drug addict with a criminal record. You may not like those facts, but I suggest that you let us get on with our job before you end up in trouble yourself.' He guided Caleb towards the hallway.

'Don't say anything,' Caleb called over his shoulder to Ant. 'Nothing at all. Call Dad's old lawyer, Mr Wayward, then don't say anything until he comes.'

Etty was gone by the time he got outside, but according to Mrs Naylor she'd left with 'A WOMAN IN A CAR'. A car was good. A car meant no concussion or fractured cheekbones. He paced the dusty lawn, praying that Ant had pulled himself together, shut up and called the solicitor.

It was strange to actually believe his brother's protestations of innocence, but he'd discovered enough of Ant's stashes over the years to know that heroin didn't come in shard-like crystals: ice did. Ant didn't use stimulants. The only thing he'd been consistent in, over the years, was his love of downers. Grass, Valium, Oxy, Special K, heroin – Ant had used them all to soften life's edges.

Blondie had planted the ice, then stuck around to thump Ant and Etty around. A helpful little call to Ramsden and his job was done. What had prompted it? Caleb's chat with Johnno? Or the fact that he'd been too stupid to heed the warning taped to his motel mirror? It didn't matter: he should have been prepared for it. If Blondie and his mate had seen him on the night of the riots, they'd seen Ant pulling him back into the walkway, too.

An old Audi puttered to a stop outside the house. Caleb ran to the kerb as Mr Wayward climbed out slowly. Seventy years old, wearing shorts and long socks.

'The ice isn't Ant's,' Caleb told him. 'Someone planted it to get at me.'

'Goodness.' Mr Wayward hitched the waistband of his shorts a bit higher. 'Well, let's just have a little chat to the police and work out what's happening, shall we?'

A little chat? Caleb had a sick feeling that he'd told Ant to call the wrong person. Ant needed a criminal lawyer, not an ageing solicitor whose main income came from writing wills. 'Are you...? Do you know what to do?'

Wayward smiled. 'I'm not dead yet, Caleb. Let's just find out what the police want before we go into a full-scale panic, shall we?' He gave Caleb another genial smile, then wandered up the path and into the house.

Caleb followed him, but Ramsden barred his way.

'Etty's fine,' Caleb yelled as the cop closed the door. 'I think she's with her mum.'

———————

He was dumping broken glass in the outside bin when he saw Ramsden and the silent constable walking down the front path. Wayward's car was already gone. That was quick. A good or a bad sign? He ran inside.

Ant was still in the kitchen, lighting a cigarette from the butt of his old one.

'What happened?' Caleb asked.

Ant didn't answer, his focus somewhere internal.

'Ant?' Caleb said out loud. 'What happened?'

Ant pushed a piece of paper across the table to him; a handwritten note with a date and an address. A printed title: *Notice to Appear*.

The blood drained from Caleb's head. 'They're charging you with possession?'

Ant shook his head, taking desperate drags of his cigarette. 'Found three more packets. Over four grams.'

Oh fuck. Four grams meant a trafficking charge. A maximum sentence of fifteen years.

Be calm, think it through. 'OK,' Caleb said. 'OK, we've got twelve days before you have to appear. We'll get a criminal lawyer and –'

'Stay out of it.'

'I'll ask Tedesco who to get. He'll know the best ones.'

Ant held up a hand. 'Fuck off. Seriously. Just get the fuck out of here.'

'It's my fault. So let me fix it.'

Ant laughed. 'Fix it? Jesus. Do you ever look at your life? It's a wasteland of shattered people. You ruin everything you touch. Well, your job's done here, so you can just fuck off.'

38.

Dean Hirst's car was parked outside his house, but he didn't respond to Caleb's usual trick with the intercom. Caleb kept ringing the bell; he was prepared to ring it all day if he had to. It wasn't a great way of starting a conversation with a grieving father, but he couldn't afford to be delicate.

'Do you ever look at your life? It's a wasteland of shattered people. You ruin everything you touch.'

He held his finger on the buzzer and the gate finally swung open. He pushed through and crossed to the house. The front door opened as he reached it, and Dean Hirst stared out at him. He had the familiar hollow-cheeked look of someone who hasn't eaten or slept properly for weeks, but he was neatly dressed in his beige slacks and white shirt, his spine unbowed by grief.

'I'm sorry to disturb you,' Caleb said, 'but I need some information.'

'Yes?'

'I think Portia's death is connected to the violence that's been happening in town. I need to know more about what she was doing before she died.'

Hirst paused, then led him to the study without speaking. He let Caleb choose the chairs by the window, but made it obvious that he was allowing the choice. The study was as uncluttered and impersonal as before. No open books or newspapers, no letters, just sombre furniture and that cheerless portrait of a fractured family.

'I looked into you,' Hirst said when they were seated. 'You run a small business, dealing with other small businesses. Apparently you've got a knack for knowing how people think, but not enough to know that your business partner was a fuck-up. You've got no real qualifications, just a few TAFE certificates and some on-the-job training at a couple of the larger insurance companies. Oh, and a major chip on your shoulder. Don't get me wrong, in my opinion talent and real-life experience beat a university degree any day, but you're not exactly top-drawer stuff, are you? Not going to be knocking on ASIO's door anytime soon. Though I guess your disability would get in the way there, anyway. So tell me – why is a small-time investigator sniffing around my daughter's death? Did she owe you money? Or are you just trying to get up the guts to blackmail me over something she did?'

Caleb sat still for a moment. Be thankful for small mercies: at least Hirst hadn't got into his bank account and found out exactly how small-time he was.

Interesting that the man had spent time and money looking into him, but it was Hirst's speech, rather than his words, that was most revealing. Its blunt consistency made him a lot easier to lip-read than during their last conversation. The man's bones stripped bare: left school early, never travelled, seldom read. Always in charge. The question was whether to match his attitude or back away. Match – bullies never forgive weakness.

Caleb met the man's level gaze. 'Portia was involved in something dangerous, and people I know are caught up in it. So what do you know about it?'

'Nothing. Portia moved here as an independent adult. I didn't oversee her day-to-day activities.' He examined Caleb's face. 'They told me you were there when she died. What happened?'

They. Who were 'they'? It had to be the police. Another adjective to add to his growing description of Hirst: connected.

'A man tried to take her,' Caleb said. He went through the chaotic minutes in the alleyway as quickly and blood-lessly as possible, stopping short of Portia's terrified stumble onto the road, her last desperate moments. Hirst listened without comment.

'So you've got no idea why she came to you?' he said when Caleb had finished.

'No.'

The man's lack of emotion was reptilian. No despair or waver in his gaze, not even stoic resolve, just intense focus. Caleb had a strong temptation to poke him just to see how he responded. He gave in to it. 'I'm very sorry, I know this must be hard for you. Were you close to Portia?'

'Not particularly. She was a difficult child. Her mother blames me, of course, says I didn't love her enough.'

'I'm sure you did.'

'Why? Because that's what parents are supposed to do?'

The truth showed in the cracks between his words – Hirst had no strong feelings about his daughter, or her death. Then why the sleep-deprived eyes and sunken cheeks? Was Hirst worried about something else? In the alleyway, Portia had signed 'family' with the stiff-handed clumsiness of a non-signer: two fingers against two fingers, a flip of the wrist. Had she meant to tap her fingers instead? That small difference would have changed the meaning from 'family' to 'father'.

Caleb held Hirst's gaze. 'An organised group is terrorising the local Koori community. I think it's about ice, and I think Portia teamed up with a couple of the locals to try and stop it.'

A flicker of surprise on Hirst's face. 'Why would she do that?'

'Because she had a strong social conscience.'

Hirst's lips curled. '"Social conscience", what a ridiculous phrase.'

And one not used often in this house. Time to poke a bit harder.

'What do you know about Jai Johnson?'

Hirst's direct gaze faltered briefly. 'Who?'

'The young man who was hanged from the scar tree thirty metres from this room.'

'Nothing. I never met him.'

'Do you know a big blond guy with a limp?'

'No.' Hirst stood. 'Now, if you don't mind, I'm busy.'

Caleb stayed seated. 'Who killed Portia?'

'No one, by all accounts – she ran onto the road.'

'You don't care that someone was chasing her?'

Hirst gave him an expressionless look; Caleb almost expected to see his third eyelid slide into place. 'She should have come to me.'

———

Caleb stopped by the scar tree on the way back to the car. A need to pay his respects, to try and wipe the memory of Jai hanging from its branches. The tree looked unchanged. Its dappled bark was smooth and pale, its canopy spreading across the bank towards the water. Someone had cleared away all the floral tributes and photos, but ashes were scattered near the base of the tree. The elders had done a smoking ceremony to cleanse the area.

He put his palm against the trunk. It felt warm. The day after his father's funeral, Kat had brought him back here and pressed his fingers to the curved line of the scar. She'd told him that even though the wound would always be there, the bark would keep growing to soften its edges. That all wounds healed this way. That the scar usually became stronger than the original tree.

He'd believed her back then.

———

He resisted the urge to check on Ant, and returned to the motel.

Hirst hadn't asked about Portia's attacker: what he'd looked like, what he'd done to her, whether he'd spoken. Either Hirst knew who'd sent Blondie, or he'd sent the man himself.

'She should have come to me.'

A look of irritation as he'd said the words, and an echo of Johnno's words at the pub.

'The stupid bitch should have asked us. We would've done it right.'

Caleb grabbed a packet of stale biscuits and a cup of instant coffee from the 'complimentary beverage tray' and got to work. Dean Hirst kept a low online profile. He had no social media accounts or website. He'd never been arrested or caught drunk in public, never made a large donation to a political party or hit the newspapers because of a business venture. There were a couple of unsmiling photos of him at charity events, and a brief mention in the local paper when he'd purchased the mansion five years ago. The reporter had described him as a 'retired businessman'. Retired from what, was the question. He could get Sammi to hack into Hirst's bank records, but the personal touch usually elicited more information than dry numbers. Frankie's first rule of investigating dodgy businessmen: speak to the ex-wife.

Maybe it was time to take that anonymous phone message seriously.

'If you want to know more about Portia, you should talk to her mum.'

It was a six-hour trip to Adelaide. If he pushed it, he could make it there before dark.

39.

Portia's mother lived in a large sandstone house in a street devoid of people. It was fronted by a garden of rigid lines and topiary, with a lawn that was a deep, emerald green despite the gasping heat. A steady wind blew in from the west, dry air that had travelled across the Nullarbor Plain for days, gathering heat from the endless expanse of bare rock and earth. It would reach the Bay sometime late tomorrow; hopefully he'd be with it, holding all the answers he needed to fix everything.

'You ruin everything you touch.'

No answer to his first couple of knocks, but the door finally swung open and a woman looked out at him. Portia's eyes. Portia's eyes staring back at him. Sweat turned to ice on his forehead.

'Yes?' she said.

Not Portia, of course. Her mother was much older, with hair a shade of ash that hovered discreetly between grey and blonde. And her eyes were dull, with an unfocused quality that spoke of a packet of Valium close to hand.

'Yes,' she said again. 'Can I help you?'

He cleared his throat. 'Susan Hirst?'

'Yes.'

'My name's Caleb Zelic. I'm an investigator. I need to speak to you about Portia.'

'Oh. No, I don't think so.'

'It won't take long.' He handed her his business card and stepped forward, making her move automatically back into the house.

'Oh, well...' She gazed at the card, then wandered down the hallway, leaving him to close the front door.

Well done, gatecrashing the house of a medicated, grieving mother. Some days he found it difficult to feel enthusiastic about his life skills.

————

They sat in a large living room furnished with cream chairs and delicate glass-topped side tables. Susan Hirst had roused herself enough to make bad coffee, but hadn't lifted her own cup. Caleb drank his perched on the edge of his armchair, wishing that he'd stopped to wash away the fug that accompanied a six-and-a-half-hour car trip without air-conditioning. He was simultaneously hyped up on caffeine and exhausted from the supreme effort of spending the day not thinking about the many ways he'd fucked things up so badly.

'Mrs Hirst –'

'Susan.'

'Susan, why did Portia leave Adelaide?'

'She said she wanted a change.'

An upwards inflection at the end of the sentence. If Portia had used those words, her mother hadn't believed them. Boyfriend trouble, her father had said.

'Did she have problems with a boyfriend?'

'Boyfriend?' Susan blinked slowly. 'No. She dated, of course, but there was nothing serious.'

So Hirst had made up the story about the boyfriend. Why?

Caleb thought through his words and chose a lie smooth enough to cover most possibilities. 'Portia's father told me about the trouble she had. Was that why she moved?'

Susan sat up. 'How on Earth did he –' She composed her expression. 'No. That was just a misunderstanding. They reinstated her at the university.'

'What exactly happened?'

She pressed her lips together and began twisting the hem of her blouse: if he wasn't careful, she'd kick him out. No matter, he could learn about the 'misunderstanding' from the university itself. He had that old article about her prize-winning ceremony; it shouldn't be too hard to track down a couple of teachers and quiz them about her history.

'What was Portia like?'

'Oh.' Susan smoothed her blouse. 'She was such a blessing. So attentive to me.'

'In what way?'

'In every way. She always took care of me.' Her gaze wandered to the window.

'Your ex-husband said she was flighty. That she changed jobs, homes, university courses.'

This got through the fog. 'That man,' she spat. 'Portia got a better job and she changed from an Arts to a Science degree. Which she finished with honours, I might add. But Dean could never see the good in her.'

'Why not?'

'Because he can only see faults. Mr Driven, Mr Perfect. Well, he destroyed his son, and then he set about destroying Portia. I couldn't have left him soon enough.'

'His son,' he said. 'That was from your husband's first marriage?'

'Yes.'

'And your stepson... ?'

'Committed suicide. My poor baby never got over it. She blamed her father, and rightly so. Dean pushed and pushed and pushed that boy. "Do it properly or not at all," he told him. Well, Christopher did it properly. He took a bottle of sleeping pills and hanged himself in the shed.'

Like a cold wind across Caleb's skin.

Do it properly, or don't do it at all.

The words of the balaclava-clad man on the night of the fires.

Dean Hirst had burned down the Mish.

Caleb scrambled for ideas, trying to make sense of the connections. Why would Hirst burn down the Mish? Send a man to hurt his own daughter? Pay kids to vandalise property? Hirst, with his cold eyes and empty house – Power.

'How did your ex-husband make his money?'

Susan's gaze slipped away. 'Oh, his family had money.'

Had Caleb got Hirst's background wrong? Mistaken a dumbed-down rich-boy elocution for working class? No. Hirst wasn't interested in faking the common touch, he'd grown up poor. So how had he made his money?

'Where did the family money come from?'

Susan's face smoothed of all expression. 'Property.'

She began twisting her blouse again, pulling the material across her tight knuckles.

Ask the next question or not? It would be a good way of getting kicked out, but he was only a couple of questions shy of that, anyway. 'Susan.' He waited until she'd met his gaze. 'When did your husband start working with the Copperheads?'

'I don't know what you're talking about.' She stood. 'I'm tired now. I'll show you out.'

He let her escort him from the house, then walked slowly back to his car, testing the idea for holes and finding none.

Dean Hirst was running the ice trade in the Bay.

40.

Caleb went to Portia's old university early the next morning, armed with a notebook and a print-out of the article about her prize ceremony. He hadn't got much sleep, but he was feeling strangely energised. The end was almost in sight. He just needed a few more pieces of the puzzle, and he'd be able to explain everything to Sergeant Ramsden in simple words.

He waited for the receptionist in the admin office to deal with a couple of students, trying to watch her without being too obvious. Her name was Bethany and she was going to be a hard read: she had skin of botoxed smoothness and lips so artificially plumped that they bounced whenever she pursed her mouth. Which was often.

The students finally left, and Bethany turned her expressionless face towards him. 'Can I help you?'

He started on his spiel about writing an article on high-achieving students and fraud, but Bethany began shaking her head when he was halfway through it.

'I can't.' Bounce. 'Give information…' Bounce. '…students…' Bounce.

It was like trying to read a duck. How did she eat? Kiss?

'My newspaper is offering the university the right

of reply as a courtesy, but we will print what we have without it.'

'As I said...' Bounce. '...request... Miss Hirst... in writing.'

Time for a rethink – back off and try for general chitchat. He looked around the office for something to bond over. It had decades-old furniture, but a new computer and laser printer.

Printer. He hadn't really thought enough about the ink jet used for the mailing list. Why would someone use an old printer when laser printers were so cheap these days? Particularly for a big job like a mail-out. Unless he'd got it wrong and it wasn't a big job, but some kind of exclusive list.

He was suddenly aware that Bethany was bouncing her lips at him. Probably telling him to piss off.

'OK,' he said. 'Sorry to have wasted your time.'

'Not at all.' There was no expression to accompany her words, but she sat back. Was she irritated or bored? A fifty-fifty chance of getting it right – go for bored.

'Bit of a dull day, really, chasing this. I guess you'd know what it's like, working here.'

She sat bolt upright. 'I... and... important...' Her lips ricocheted off each other.

Fucking botox, should be banned.

It took an hour, but he managed to track down the staff member featured in the newspaper article with Portia. Gerald Sorenson was in his open-plan office, stacking books under his arm, keys in hand. He was in his late twenties, with a lean build and a glowing complexion that spoke of long bike rides and bracing showers.

Caleb tapped on the open door and launched into his speech. 'Hi, I'm Caleb Zelic from the *Advertiser*. Bethany from admin said that I'd catch you here.'

Sorenson rubbed his forehead. 'Bethany? Goodness, why?'

'I'm writing an article as part of the *Advertiser*'s series on student success. I'm after a couple of quick quotes from you about Portia Hirst.'

'I'm sorry, but I've got a class in five minutes. Summer school. You'll have to come back next week.'

Teaching summer school, a shared office, late twenties: no way did this man have tenure.

'We go to print tonight,' Caleb said. 'And the university is very keen for the article. It's great publicity.' He paused to let his words sink in. 'As I said, the admin office sent me.'

Sorenson glanced at his watch. 'Right. OK, but we'll have to walk and talk.' He headed for the door.

Caleb stood still. Damn. 'I, ah – I can't.'

'Oh well, sorry but I can't help you then.'

Suck it up and say the words. Do it.

'I have to face you when you're speaking. I'm lip-reading.'

'Really?' Sorenson's eyes lit up like those of a young child receiving an unexpected gift. 'How fascinating. How deaf are you?'

'Deaf enough.'

'Oh. Right. I suppose that's a personal question?'

'A bit.'

Sorenson nodded, as though satisfied with the answer. 'What's your success rate?'

'I'm sorry?'

'I assume you wouldn't get one hundred percent of spoken words? So how many do you get?'

'Enough. Most of the time.'

'Context would matter, I'd imagine. And background noise.' Sorenson glanced at the door and closed it.

Caleb pulled out his notebook and pen. 'If you could just give me a couple of quotes about Portia? How would you describe her?'

'Very bright. I guess it'd be easier reading people you know?'

'Yes. What else can you tell me about Portia?'

'She's, um, very innovative. And me? How easy am I to read?'

'Very.' Not so good at keeping focused, though.

'I had elocution lessons as a child – terrible stutter – that must help.'

'Mm. Can you tell me a little more about Portia's time here?'

A tight line appeared either side of Sorenson's mouth. 'She was very dedicated.'

'And the trouble she had? How did that affect her position here?'

'Oh, she told you about that?' Sorenson nodded, his face relaxing. 'Good move on her part. Excellent. It was investigated, of course, but no charges were laid. And I suppose we've all come close to blowing up a chemistry lab at times.'

'Deliberately?'

'I doubt it. When you're working with volatile chemicals, there's always an element of danger. Which is why students aren't supposed to do research by themselves. You'd have trouble reading people with speech impediments, I'd imagine.' Sorenson's face brightened. 'How did you manage with Duck Face downstairs?'

———

He drove straight back to the Bay and reached the outskirts of town around seven, eyes gritty, a buffeting wind flicking through the Mini's air vents and cracks, carrying topsoil from neighbouring farms. The arrow on the fire danger sign had edged up into 'extreme'.

The pieces were all there, he just had to fit them together. Portia was the key. She was the link to her father, to the Copperheads, to Jai, to Honey. To ice? She had a chemistry degree and a history of blowing up laboratories – meth labs were notoriously volatile places. But it didn't feel right. Portia planted trees and kept a photo of her beloved brother by her bed; a woman like that didn't turn around and start cooking meth for the man she blamed for his death. Did she? Too tired to make any sense of it now. Food and sleep, then more ideas would come. But first he'd see Ant and tell him that everything was nearly over.

Ant's car was outside the house, but there was no sign of Etty's. Damn, he'd hoped that the pair of them would have patched things up by now. He gave the door a cursory knock and went in, stopped a few steps inside. Something was wrong. Nothing in the hallway or on the stairs, nothing on the landing.

The bathroom at the end of the hall. Its door was ajar, a dark shape on the floor.

He sprinted down the hallway and flung open the door. Ant was slumped against the wall, limp and white, his lips blue.

41.

The needle was still in his arm, his palms raised to the ceiling. No, no, no, no. Kneeling on the floor, feeling Ant's neck for a pulse. Was that it? Yes, the barest of flutters. Phone. Ring for an ambulance. His phone was switched off in the car. Yell for help, keep yelling. He slapped Ant's face, rubbed his knuckles down his sternum. His chest wasn't moving. Oh God, he wasn't breathing. Pulling him onto his back, tilting his head. Nose. Had to pinch his nose. And blowing, trying to breathe life into him. Another breath. Another. Check his pulse again.

No pulse.

No pulse.

No pulse.

Gripping Ant by his shoulders, shaking him, screaming for help.

Please don't die. Pleasepleasepleaseplease.

A hand on his back: Mick. He was holding up a phone, words tumbling from his mouth. Ambulance. Help. CPR. He squeezed in beside Caleb and put his hands on Ant's chest, started pumping, driving the heels of his palms down hard. Caleb took up position by Ant's head and started the breathing again. Air in, air out. Don't look, don't think, just keep going. Air in, air out. Air in, air out.

EMMA VISKIC

Movement by the door. Two men in blue uniforms were pushing into the bathroom, carrying zippered bags and plastic cases. He scrambled to his feet and backed into the hallway, Mick by his side.

One of the paramedics was talking to him. Asking something?

'What?'

The man's lips moved meaninglessly.

'Just help him,' Caleb said. 'There's no pulse.'

The ambo kept talking to him, while his mate was shoving Ant's head back, sliding a tube down his throat. Have to be out of it not to feel that. Have to be half-dead. Dead.

Mick moved between Caleb and the doorway, signing with slow hands, 'Brother what take?'

'Smack,' Caleb told the ambo. 'It's always smack. He misjudged the dose. He's been clean. He's been clean for two years.'

The ambo was cutting Ant's T-shirt now, attaching patches with trailing wires to his chest. The flick of a switch and Ant's body spasmed. An answering jolt in Caleb's own.

Mick gripped his shoulders and turned him away, guided him past the waiting gurney towards the front door. People had gathered on the footpath: neighbours, Mrs Naylor, two of Mick's kids. Ant would be so embarrassed. Had to be alive to be embarrassed.

Etty was running up the pathway. She skidded to a halt beside him, chest heaving.

'Breathing?' she asked.

He shook his head.

'Pulse?'

Another shake.

He should tell her that everything would be all right. That Ant had done this before. That the ambos had given him a shot of Narcan and he'd got up and walked away.

Ant wasn't going to be walking away this time.

Caleb reached out and gripped Etty's trembling hand.

A thump. The paramedics were pushing the gurney into the bathroom. A flurry of movement, then they wheeled Ant out. He was still and pale, his eyes closed. Etty ran to his side. Words flew between her and the ambos; calm gestures, tears. They weren't hurrying.

'What's happening?' he asked, but no one seemed to hear him.

He said it again as they wheeled Ant past, tried to put some air behind the words.

One of the paramedics glanced at him. '…into… and… arrhythmia…'

And they were out the door. Ant didn't stir as they bumped him down the front step. Etty threw Caleb a wild look and followed them.

Caleb stood frozen.

Mick stepped in front of him, screwing up his face as he slowly formed the signs. 'Take brother. Good.'

'Is he OK?'

'Yes.'

'He's alive?'

'Alive. Yes. Alive.'

Sliding down the wall to the floor, all oxygen sucked from the room. Alive. He buried his head in his arms and sobbed.

There was a long wait on the hospital's hard plastic chairs. Mick had stayed for a while, then clasped him on the shoulder and said something about babysitters. Had the smack been another gift from Blondie? Had he held Ant down and shot him up? It was possible – someone had done that to Caleb last year. Possible, but unlikely. The person most likely to have bought the heroin and injected it into Ant's veins was Ant himself.

He'd been clean for so long. Stupid to be thinking how much it would have upset their mother. Even stupider to be missing your mother at thirty-one years of age. To be wondering what she'd say about your failings as a man, a friend, a husband. A brother. She'd stepped between Ant and the world on a daily basis, picking up the broken pieces and easing them back into a whole. Too soft, Ivan had said, too forgiving. And Caleb had agreed. It wasn't until she was gone that he realised she'd been doing the same for him, and that where her comfort had been was a raw edge. She'd died soon after his eighteenth – lain down with a headache and slipped into death as easily as she'd slipped through life. The abruptness of it had felt brutal at the time, but he knew now that fast was good. Fast is what he'd choose.

Ant was sitting on the bed when they finally let Caleb into the cubicle. Pale and hunched, the red needle mark glowing among the shadows of his past. He didn't look up.

'Ant.' An absence of any other words.

Ant pulled his T-shirt over his head, his movements cautious. He probably had a cracked rib or two. Caleb had been on that side of the pain, felt the stabbing shards, the vice squeezing his chest. It was worse on this side.

'You should stay in,' he said. 'They were worried about an irregular heartbeat. They'll want to monitor you, get you on a drip.'

Still no eye contact. Caleb spoke out loud to make sure Ant got each word.

'Stay. Let them look after you.'

Ant stood up and shoved his feet into his shoes.

'Where's Etty?' Caleb asked. She'd make him listen to reason.

Ant finally looked at him. His eyes were bloodshot and swollen. 'Gone.'

'Gone where?'

'Gone, left, pissed off. Zero tolerance to drugs. She was very clear on that from the start. Smart woman.'

'The ice wasn't yours.'

Ant's mouth twisted. 'No, but the smack sure as hell was.'

'So you bought it?'

'Of course I fucking bought it. Squirrel was right – it was like doing it for the first time.'

Caleb tried not to wince. 'I'll talk to Etty. She loves you, she'll come round.'

'Leave it alone.'

'She's upset. I'll tell her what –'

'I. Don't. Want. Your. Help.' Ant's bloodless lips spat each word.

He pushed past Caleb and was gone.

42.

He ran. Into the pine plantations, away from town. One foot and then the other, following the broken white line through the darkness. It was dense forest around here, the high branches blocking the moonlight, casting shadow upon shadow. Too dark to run; he should turn back. He should do a lot of things, most of them too late.

He looked at his phone again – nothing. Just a slim hope that Ant would text tonight, but he couldn't stop checking. The house had been empty when he arrived back from the hospital. No sign of Ant's car there or at Etty's, or anywhere else in town. He'd probably just gone to ground. He used to do that all the time: disappear for days or weeks on end, and then resurface, sometimes off the smack, sometimes on it. He'd be all right. He had to be all right.

'*You ruin everything you touch.*'

Headlights flashed as a car approached from behind. Like bloody peak-hour tonight. He'd run this way because it was the emptiest place he could think of, but there'd been a steady trickle of trucks and cars. He moved onto the verge and kept running. The car came closer but didn't pass. A nervous driver. He waved it on; it kept pace behind him. What the fuck?

He stopped running and turned, lifted his arm to shield his eyes against the glare. A boxy van, its headlights on high beam. Two figures climbed from it, vague shapes behind the bright lights. The driver was gesturing for him to stay still, holding something long and dark, raising it to chest-height.

A shotgun.

A moment of stilled disbelief. Run.

Into the forest. Sprinting through the charcoal landscape, one arm held in front of him, branches whipping at his face. A quick look over his shoulder. The two people were following, faint silhouettes in the darkness.

Smack. On his knees, stunned. Up, get up. Something warm dripping down his forehead.

He crawled across the pine needles, reaching blindly in front of him. Touching bark. Around the tree, sitting with his back against it, his knees to his chest. He wiped the blood from his eyes. Where were they? No hint of sound, not even the thump of his heart. He went to turn up his aids – no aids. Never wore them on a run. Shit. He pressed his palms to the blanket of pine needles, but the ground was mute. Were they sneaking up behind him? Following the sound of his ragged breathing, raising the shotgun?

A flash of light to his left.

And another one to his right.

Shit, he was caught between them. The light to his left was inching closer, sweeping over the pine needles and fallen branches. He held his breath and pressed himself against the tree. The light was an arm's length away. Stay still, don't breathe. It crept closer. Closer. On him.

He was up. Crashing through twigs and branches, the lights bobbing wildly as the figures followed close behind. Faster. He could outrun them. He could –

Falling. Into nothing. Slamming onto the ground. His scream caught in his throat. Arm. His arm. Up high, above the elbow, a jagged, savage pain. Hands grabbed him, pulling something over his head. Soft material, the stink of sweat and deodorant – one of their T-shirts. They hauled him up, one of them at his shoulders, the other at his ankles. Out through the forest, every movement jolting him. A pause, more jostling, and he was lying on his stomach, his cheek pressed against a metal floor. In the van. A knee on his back, and someone pulled his arms behind him. Crying out in pain. Tape wound around his wrists and ankles, his head, binding the T-shirt tightly across his eyes and mouth. A hand dug in his pocket for his phone. Then the slam of the door, the engine rumbling. Moving.

43.

It was a journey of wrenching potholes and sudden turns. Caleb lay on his stomach and tried to count the seconds. His right arm was wet, bleeding, a seeping flow that warmed then chilled. The van slowed when he got to four hundred, and the engine rumbled and died. They couldn't be too far from town, maybe still in the pine plantation or further over near the quarry. He braced himself and kicked out when they opened the doors.

They were ready for him. Hard fingers pinched his nose through the T-shirt, cutting off all air. Heaving, urgent terror. They waited until he'd stilled, then released his nose. He let them carry him. Across uneven ground, each step thudding through nerve and bone. Not in the pine forest; a strong scent of eucalyptus. A pause, then a subtle difference in atmosphere, the smell of cleaning fluid. They were in a building.

Inside was good. Inside meant they weren't putting him in a shallow grave. Yet.

A spasm of pain as they laid him on the floor. Don't vomit, don't vomit, might suffocate.

More footsteps around him, leaving him to shake. The

floorboards vibrating with thuds and the constant rumble of an idling engine, bigger than that of the van.

Hot, cold. Slipping in and out of the darkness.

The smell of smoke. Stillness, no footsteps or movement. They'd gone. Were they coming back for him? They'd been moving something. A big job involving four or five people; the slow tread of their footsteps going out, quicker footsteps coming back in. So they'd been carrying things from the building, not into it. More than one truck carting everything away – either two on a short turnaround or a fleet of them. And now they'd finished.

They weren't coming back.

Alone somewhere with no phone and the steadily growing scent of smoke. He rubbed his face against his shoulder, frantically scraping at the tape around his hood. It didn't loosen. He rubbed harder, his breath coming in shallow snatches.

Stop. Just stop. It wasn't going to work. Calm down and think it through.

He was in a building, so there had to be something in here he could use to cut the tape. He rolled to his side and got to his knees, pain radiating from his wrist to his jaw. A few attempts to stand, then he gave up and shuffled forward on his knees. His head banged against a wall. No plaster, just struts and an external wall.

Wooden walls and the faint smell of cleaning fluids – he knew where he was. The old school camp recreation room. Oh, thank God. He could picture the place: high ceilings and wide double doors. They'd dumped him near the doors, which meant the kitchen was a few metres to his left. There might be knives or sharp corners, or glasses he could break.

He shuffled around the room, using his shoulder on the wall as a guide. A sudden indentation: the kitchen door. He braced his shoulder against the doorframe and tried to lever himself to his feet. Burning, twisting pain. He bent double, nausea sliding up his throat. Try again. They weren't coming back for him. They'd dumped him here to get him out of the way, cleared their stuff out, and gone. He inhaled slowly and tried again.

And he was up. A little pause to catch his breath, then he pivoted so his back was to the door. Reaching for the handle, trying not to jar his arm.

Locked.

He lowered himself gently to the floor and curled onto his side.

He slept, woke, slept, pain the centre of everything. A growing need to piss, an equally desperate need for water. The smell of smoke was thick now, clogging the back of his nose.

Thud.

His heart thumped and then faltered. Someone was here. To let him go, or to kill him? He struggled to his knees. Another bang, then the quick beat of footsteps. A touch to his shoulder. He reared back and the hand patted his head reassuringly. Someone had come to help him. Thank God. A sawing movement against his head, tugging, more sawing, and the hood ripped away. He peeled open his eyes, squinting against the brightness.

Frankie.

She was kneeling in front of him. Dressed in a grey T-shirt and black jeans, her hair lying flat and darkened with sweat. He could have wept at the sight of her. Was weeping, tears streaming down his face.

'Cal. Mate. I mean, fuck.'

She held a water bottle to his lips, and he gulped at it.

'How –' His tongue felt too thick for his mouth. He swallowed and tried again. 'How close is the fire?'

'Over near Cockatoo Ridge, heading north.'

Cockatoo Ridge was a bit too close for comfort, but at least the fire was moving away from them. Frankie started hacking at the tape around his ankles with a pocketknife. It was packing tape, wide and brown, glistening in the light from the door.

'How'd you know I was here?'

She glanced up at him. 'I've been tracking you.'

Admitting it as casually as if she'd sent him a friend request on Facebook. Of course she'd been tracking him – she was still after her fucking key. But how? He had nothing on him. No phone or wallet, no watch, just his shoes and clothes.

His shoes. She'd put a GPS in his running shoes.

'My fucking shoes. Jesus, Frankie, full points for stalking.'

She gave him a quick grin. 'Thought it was a stroke of genius myself. They're always with you. Like a baby's dummy.' She ripped the tape from his legs and tossed it to the floor where it lay coiled like a brown snake. 'I figured even you weren't dumb enough to go camping in the middle of a bushfire, so I thought I'd come and see what trouble you'd got yourself into this time.'

She ducked behind him and started sawing on the tape around his wrists. He lurched as it gave way, and a hammering pulse started up in his arm.

Frankie came around to face him again, but didn't say anything. She sat back on her heels, examining his arm, a grey tinge to her skin. He looked down at it. Darkening bruises and blood, a pulpy mess of flesh halfway between his shoulder and elbow, a shard of something white sticking into it. No, not sticking into it, sticking out of it – bone. A swooping wave of dizziness. He leaned against the wall.

Frankie ran a hand through her hair, standing it on end. 'Guess I should make a sling.'

'Ambulance?' he asked. A faint hope.

'I've dumped the phone. Got sick of people being able to find me.'

'What are you using to track me, then?'

'Equipment for the seriously paranoid.' She rubbed her hands on her jeans. 'Maybe I should bandage the, ah, icky bit first. Stop the bleeding.'

'No!' A bit of bleeding he could handle, but the thought of her touching the splintered bone made him want to scream.

'Your call,' she said, looking relieved. She stripped down to her grey cotton bra and made a makeshift sling with her T-shirt. 'OK, this is going to sting a bit.'

She lifted his arm.

The touch of a live wire. His head slammed back against the wall. Another wrenching tug, and another. He turned his head and vomited up all the water. Panting, his eyes screwed shut. Fuck. Fuck.

When he finally opened his eyes, he found Frankie watching him.

He realised she was clutching his clammy hand and pulled it free. Bad idea. No more moving for a while.

'Who dumped you here?' she asked.

He shook his head.

'You must have some idea. Even you couldn't piss off that many people in a few weeks.'

'You'd be surprised.'

'Probably not. But I love a good list – run through it for me.'

If she was trying to distract him from the pain, it wasn't working.

'C'mon.' She tapped his foot, kept tapping.

Jesus, she was worse than Ant. A twist in his guts at the thought of him. Don't think about that now. Don't think about Ant or Kat. Or the thousand stupid decisions that had led him to this moment in his life.

'Maybe the Copperheads,' he said. 'Or a guy called Hirst. A local fuckwit called Dave McGregor.' He thought it through. 'No, not McGregor – he would have kicked me around a bit.'

Frankie's face settled into a familiar, distant look as she went through the possibilities, ranking and assessing each one. 'Not bikies, either,' she said. 'Blowing your head off is more their style. Bomb your house, kill your dog. Feels like a rush job, too.' She flicked a hand at the tape on the floor. 'Packing tape, not duct tape. T-shirt for a blindfold.'

'I think they panicked because they saw me heading this way. They were doing something in here last night. Moving something.' And twitchy about it: he'd been kilometres from the turnoff onto Snake Gully Road.

She shook her head. 'All the more reason to think it wasn't bikies. Bikies don't bundle you up if you get in their way, they just blow a hole in you. Hirst is Portia's father, yeah? Why would he dump you here?'

'He controls the local ice trade. I think he's been heavying the Koori community to buy his stuff, and they've been fighting back. He killed a young bloke and torched some houses.'

Frankie tapped her fingers on her thighs. 'Nah, none of this adds up. Someone went to a bit of effort tucking you safely away here. You know what I'm saying, right?'

That he knew his captors. Knew who'd dumped him, trussed and bleeding. Blinded.

'Arsehole move, leaving you blindfolded,' she said. 'Had to know you couldn't hear. The cunts.'

He laughed. Or maybe sobbed.

She glanced outside and wiped her palms on her jeans. 'That wind's getting pretty loud. You reckon you're up to walking now?'

No.

'Yeah, sure,' he said.

She grabbed his good arm and hauled him to his feet. A pause while the world span and dipped, then he shuffled to the door. There was a hazy, orange-yellow light, the air thick with smoke. He stepped into a swirling wind of heat and ash, and felt an urgent, animal need to be very far away.

Something was missing: the shipping container he'd seen here on his first visit. Maybe that was what all the movement had been about. It didn't matter now – there was a more pressing question.

'Where's your car?' he said.

'It's a code red. They've shut most of the roads.'

'How'd you get here, then?'

'How d'you fucking think I got here? I walked.'

Frankie hiking through the bush in her Doc Martens; he'd savour that image for a long time.

She looked up at the glowering sky. 'Head down the driveway and turn right. Keep turning right.'

'You're not coming with me?' Cold terror at the thought of being alone.

'I'm going back for the car. It's too far for you. Just head to the main road. The cops are diverting traffic – they'll get you to a hospital.'

Cops. That explained why she wasn't going with him.

'Cal.' Her eyes slid away. 'I know you found the key.'

It shouldn't have hurt. 'That's why you came? For the key?'

'That's right, just the key, I don't give a shit about you. Come on.' She clicked her fingers. 'Don't embarrass us both by making me beg.'

He undid the zip pocket on his hip and passed her his keys. She slipped hers from the ring, not meeting his eyes.

'A couple of people are looking for that,' he said. 'Looking for you. One of them says she's a fed.'

Frankie nodded.

'Is she?' he asked.

'Maybe.'

'Should I say hi from you next time I see her?'

'Turn right.' Frankie pointed to make sure he understood, then strode in the opposite direction.

44.

He lost the driveway after a few metres, or it lost him. He stopped for a piss the colour of beer. Not the VB that Mick kept serving him, but something dark and home-brewed.

Mick. Mick was going on fifty and slow to move on those football-ruined knees of his – a perfect match for the man Portia had described to Honey. Could it have been Mick, not her father, she'd been running from? Could Mick have been working for Hirst?

No. Not Mick: no way would he push ice onto his own community.

He'd been worried about Caleb talking to the police.

Please let it not be Mick. Father of four, friend, Kat's cousin. Oh God, Kat. She'd never choose Caleb over her family, never forgive him if he got Mick arrested. A laugh in his throat – Kat wasn't choosing him, anyway.

Caleb started walking again, one foot in front of the other, stepping in time with the drip, drip, dripping of his blood. Ash clusters the size of his palms whirled in mad dances around him. The wind was coming from his left now. Had it shifted, or had he got turned around? No sun to guide him – the sky dark and low.

And there was the camp. Shit, he'd been going around

in circles. He stopped walking, considered lying down and going to sleep.

A figure appeared up ahead, striding out of the haze as though she'd known he'd be here.

'For fuck's sake,' Frankie said. 'I said turn right.'

He walked with his arm slung across Frankie's shoulders. The blood was flowing down his arm now, each drop letting his head float a little higher. Smoke stung his eyes and throat, making him cough. He stumbled over a fallen branch and realised they were in the pine forest, not on the road. Lost? Or was Frankie just taking a shortcut?

'Where's the roadblock?' he said.

Frankie glanced at him, white-faced. 'We're heading for the car, not the roadblock.'

'Worried about the cops?'

'No. The wind's changed. We won't make it.'

And he understood why she'd been urging him to go faster for the past ten minutes – the fire was heading their way. They couldn't outrun a bushfire, couldn't even outdrive it. It would be on them before they reached her car: devouring trees and grass, sucking the oxygen from the air and melting steel. It would burn through timber and flesh and bone.

'Won't make it,' he said. He felt oddly neutral at the idea.

She didn't answer, just hoisted his arm higher and kept going, urging him on every time he sagged. They finally stumbled out of the trees onto a potholed road. Frankie propped him against a tree trunk and pulled the water bottle from her back pocket. He slid to the ground. So tired. Rest here. He had nothing to get back to. No Kat, no child, no home.

His father hadn't given up – fought right until the end, tendons tight, anger in his eyes.

Died just the same.

Frankie was squatting in front of him. Her mouth was moving but no words were getting through to his brain. Something ignited high in the canopy; the top of a pine tree flaming. Advance soldiers from the firefront. Soon there would be more, and then more, and then the fire would be on them. The song from Jai's funeral slipped into his brain.

For a world of lost sinners was slain.

The Auslan sign for 'sinner' was the same as the one for 'guilt'. A small sign for such a heavy burden, just a tap of the little finger against the shoulder.

Frankie smacked his knee. 'Concentrate,' she signed. 'Car long way. Know you...' She hunted though her fingers for the right letters and slowly spelt out 'Q.U.E.R.R.Y.'

'Query?' he said.

'No,' she signed. 'We on Q.U.E.R.R.Y. Road.'

Right, *quarry*. That made more sense. Frankie had always found fingerspelling tricky. Should give her another lesson one of these days.

Frankie waved a hand in front of his face. 'Big enough?' she signed.

'What?'

She switched to English. 'Is. The. Quarry. Big. Enough. To. Protect. Us?'

Big, small, it didn't matter. Just lie down and wait for the fire to come. The smoke would probably kill him first. A wonderful calmness at the thought: no more pain, no more nightmares, no more emptiness.

A punch to his shoulder, Frankie's face close to his. She was shaking, her greyhound ribs showing each rapid inhalation. 'Caleb, get the fuck up. What the hell's wrong with you? You can handle a bit of pain.'

'I killed a man.' The words came from somewhere deep within him, unplanned and unwanted.

Frankie jerked back. 'What? Who?'

'Last year. On the beach.'

'You're agonising over that? Mate, the fuck-knob was trying to kill you. And he was there because of me. If you need to blame someone, blame me.'

'I've been trying to.'

'Well, try harder.'

'I can still see his eyes. He was looking at me when he... I saw the light go out of them. He was alive and then he was dead and I can't... I can't get it out of my brain. I can't stop thinking about it.'

'OK.' She scrubbed at her hair. 'OK, I understand. We're gunna get you some help with that. We'll get you someone way smarter than me to fix you up. But right now you've got to get the fuck up and fight. Because I'm not going to fry in a bushfire and I am not leaving you here.'

He didn't answer.

'Cal.' She gripped his hand. 'I need you to be OK. Please. I really need you to be OK.'

He walked, staggered, Frankie half-dragging him. Chest heaving, ash choking his lungs. An orange-purple light, the wind grabbing and buffeting, sparks flaring on their skin and clothes. The heat a solid weight. He stumbled and almost fell, but Frankie yanked him up and pulled him on. Too fast. Feet missing the ground, lurching and slipping.

And they were out of the forest into open ground. The quarry. A bare expanse of dirt and rocks, with a hollowed centre of murky water. A shipping container sat a few metres away, its green paint blistering in the heat, turning brown, purple, black.

Frankie hauled him past the container towards the water. A slam of heat shoved him down. Falling, rolling. Onto his back. Something pressing against his chest, stopping his lungs from expanding. The container had ripped open. Snowflakes swirled from it, each one flaming as it fell, the labels turning as black as the printed names. He was lying a little way down the slope, looking across the rocky ground into hell. Flames rearing high above the canopy, reaching for him.

A tug on his hand: Frankie. She was yelling, tears cutting white tracks through her soot-stained skin. She pulled hard, trying to lift him. No. It was too much. Please let this be the end. Please.

He closed his eyes.

45.

Bright lights moving above him. People in blue uniforms. Crushing pain. Down a corridor and into a room: curtains, drips, machines. Where was Frankie? He tried to speak, but a plastic mask was covering his mouth. Hands grabbed him, wrenching his arm and splintering the bones. He cried out, trying to push them away. Someone leaned over him, her blue eyes visible above her white mask: Maria.

'You're safe now,' she signed. 'Breathe slowly.'

More tearing pain. Fire in him, burning through sinew and bone. A raw scream in his throat.

Maria smoothed back his hair. 'Sleep now. It's OK. Just sleep.'

And he was falling.

A long way down.

Not far enough.

46.

Hours, days, years submerged; swimming to the surface and sinking back down. His arm was the worst, but the raw patches on his legs and chest simmered with a constant eye-watering heat. Doctors appeared, talking about compound fractures and blood transfusions, second-degree burns. He gazed out the window and let their words go.

After the first couple of days, they took away the good drugs and gave him some pretty fucking average ones. Drugs that did little to dull the pain but sank him mid-thought into suffocating dreams. He was in a single room, thank God, with no one to glare at him when he woke, screaming, in the middle of the night.

Mick strode through the door at some point, carrying a sixpack of Boag's and a bunch of grapes. Caleb pretended to be asleep.

———

Sergeant Ramsden appeared on the fourth day, or maybe the fifth, his farmer's face squinting at Caleb's sling and bandages, the dubious-looking fluid draining from his arm. A vague memory of an earlier visit, half-caught words that had drifted into blankness. There had been something different about the cop's attitude, a slight warming, as though he'd stopped thinking Caleb was untrustworthy.

Ramsden made himself comfortable on the bedside chair. 'Are... today?'

He didn't have the energy to pretend. 'Slow down.'

'What?'

'I'm a bit dopey and I haven't got my aids here. You have to speak slower, maybe write some stuff down for me.'

Ramsden frowned. 'Are. You. Abitmore. Withit. Today?'

Oh great, now he'd made the cop self-conscious.

'Yes.'

'Still. No. Wordfrom. Yourbrother?'

'No.'

He'd begged every nurse who'd come into the room to make phone calls for him, but no one had seen Ant and he wasn't answering his mobile. Only days until Ant had to front up to the magistrate, and there was a fermenting sourness in Caleb's stomach at the thought of what would happen if he didn't. He was going to have to put a hold on dissolving the family trust, too. Yet another reason for Ant to hate him.

Ramsden tapped his pen on his notebook and shifted in his chair, looking uncomfortable. 'There might be. News on. That front.'

Caleb sat up; paused as the movement jarred his arm. 'Has someone seen Ant? Is he OK? Where is he?'

Ramsden held up a hand. 'No one's seen him, but the, ah, charges against him may be dropped.'

Oh, thank God: 'may be' in cop-speak meant 'will be, but we're embarrassed about it'.

'Why? I mean, that's great. But what changed your mind?'

Ramsden scratched his scalp with his pen. 'I guess you haven't seen the news lately. Dean Hirst was murdered on Tuesday afternoon. Evidence has been found to support your theory about his involvement in the methamphetamine trade.'

Caleb stared at the cop. Hirst dead. Hours before his kidnapping. Hirst hadn't sent the men to grab him. So who had? Not the Copperheads, not McGregor.

He was missing something important. If his brain wasn't so fogged, he might be able to work out what. He shouldn't have taken that last painkiller.

'What happened?' he asked. 'How was he killed?'

Ramsden paused, then said, 'I can tell you what's been released to the media, which is that it was an execution-style killing.'

'You think it was a falling-out with the Copperheads?'

'It's not their usual method.'

Ramsden was right; this felt very different from anything else that had happened in the past few weeks. No arson, no shotgun, just a professional execution.

'Do you think it was a hit by a rival supplier?'

'Hard to say.' Ramsden flipped to a new page in his notebook. 'Tell me about the men who grabbed you. Have you remembered anything that would help us to identify them?'

Drowsiness was creeping back, throwing a blanket over his thoughts. 'Um, they were driving a big van with a diesel engine.'

'And?'

'That's pretty much it. They covered my eyes straight away.'

'Any theories?'

Not Mick. Please not Mick.

'No. But they were clearing stuff out of the camp. Lots of things, some of it heavy. Big trucks – semis, maybe.'

'Clearing what out? According to you, there wasn't anything in the room the previous week, when you –' Ramsden checked his notes '– found the door open and happened to wander in.'

'There was a lot of metal shelving. I think they were setting it up as a warehouse. Either a permanent one or just for last night. It's an isolated spot on a logging road. No one would think twice about seeing trucks out there.'

'You think… there… ?'

Caleb blinked and refocused. 'What?'

'You think it was Hirst's meth lab?'

'No. There was no smell. At least, no strong smell, just a faint scent of cleaning fluid.'

An image floated into his brain, as insubstantial as mist. The quarry, the sheets of floating labels, burning as they fell. The shipping container had been full of them. His head slumped forward. He roused himself. Stay awake – something important there. What?

Ramsden was standing, tucking his notebook into his pocket. His gaze travelled over Caleb's bandages and bruises. 'You sure you don't know who did this to you?'

'Yes.'

'Well, have a little think. Because I get the feeling this isn't over. Whoever hurt you wanted you out of the way for some reason. Next time they might decide on a more permanent solution.'

He agreed, but couldn't summon any strong emotion.

Maria caught him coming back from the bathroom, a short-lived celebration of independence that had left him clammy-skinned and trembling. From what he could tell, she was on some kind of bushfire response team, but that didn't explain her continued presence in the hospital now the fires were out. She kept appearing at inopportune moments, checking his chart and leaving a string of straightened spines in her wake, never once mentioning Kat. He had a feeling she had something to do with his private room and view of the garden.

He wrestled himself back into bed, bare-arsed and sweating, trying unsuccessfully not to whimper.

'Do you need more pain relief?' Maria said once he'd stopped panting. 'I can speak to your doctor.'

'No. Just first time out of bed.'

'Ah. Perhaps wait for the nurse next time. I'll have a word with her.'

'Please don't.' The nurse on duty seemed star-struck by Maria. She was very young, with Bambi-like eyes and a tendency to drop things when she was nervous.

'Well, we'll see.' Maria unhooked his chart from the end of the bed. 'Now, your...'

He let his attention drift. There were too many words, none of them important. Movement had set up a steady throbbing in his arm, and the skin on his back was burning:

a wide band of gravel rash from when Frankie had dragged him to the water. Why hadn't she just left him on the rocks and run?

A touch to his shoulder. Maria was frowning at him. Shit, she'd caught him out. But her expression was of concern, not anger.

'Caleb,' she said. 'How can I help?'

His throat constricted. God, that was all he needed – to cry in front of his soon-to-be-ex-mother-in-law.

'I'm just tired,' he told her, then realised that he'd signed instead of spoken. He went to translate, but Maria was already nodding.

'Then I'll let you sleep,' she said.

A memory stirred: Maria signing to him after the fire. He hadn't realised how much Auslan she'd picked up over the years. And the thought dropped into his mind as solid as words etched in stone.

'You sent Portia to me.'

Her exhalation was like a sigh of relief. 'Yes.'

No. Maria couldn't be involved with the people who'd hurt him. Not Maria. For all her brashness, he'd always known exactly where he stood with her, always felt safe.

He'd thought the same thing about Frankie.

'I don't understand. Did you know that I'd been kidnapped? That I was hurt?'

'My God, Caleb, of course not. What do you think of me? I gave Portia your name and address, that's all.'

He believed her, breathed again. 'Why? What happened?'

She sat on the edge of the bed and seemed to think through each word. 'She rang the clinic from Melbourne the night she died. She was distraught, very difficult to understand, but I gradually worked out that a man was following her. She refused to go to the police, so I gave her your name and address and told her to wait with you until someone could come for her.'

Such a simple explanation, but it raised so many questions.

'Why didn't you just tell me? You knew I was looking into her death.'

She spoke slowly. 'Once I realised she'd died, I was nervous about becoming involved.'

No. Maria didn't shy away from involvement. She held gaping chest wounds together and resuscitated babies, told people they were going to die. She was protecting someone. Someone who worked at the clinic and knew what Portia had been up to – Honey. So Maria had intercepted Portia's frantic call to Honey and done what she always did: tried to fix things.

'I know about Honey,' Caleb said. 'I know she was involved in something with Portia and Jai.'

'Yes, I realised that when you interrogated her outside my house.'

'It's all right. I'm not going to get her into trouble with the police. I just want to know what she was doing with Portia.'

'I'm not concerned about the police, Caleb, I'm concerned about her being killed. They already tried once by burning down the clinic. They don't seem to care who might get hurt.'

Her silence suddenly made sense: she'd been worried about her family. Shops and homes had been destroyed, Jai killed, the clinic burned. Would fear be enough to shut

Maria up? Yes. She might be a fighter, but she was also too smart to take on unknown assailants who could hurt her family. And smart enough to know that he would. That he had.

Maria sat back, looking worn out and a little sad. 'Caleb, I'm incredibly sorry that I involved you. I acted without having all the details. It was a terrible error of judgement.'

'But you know the details now, don't you? You made Honey tell you everything after I saw her at your house. You're the one who told her to leave town.' It was a guess, but judging by Maria's expression, an accurate one.

'Some of it. Not all. But leave it now. For everyone's sake. Yours in particular.'

Yours in particular.

He took a breath and said the words quickly. 'Just tell me one thing, was Mick involved?'

'Goodness, no.'

The shock on her face was clear. But Mick had known something. Maybe not at the beginning when he'd been giving Caleb tips about Rat-tail Luke, but definitely by the end when he'd stared Caleb down and told him not to involve the police.

'How can you be sure?'

She examined his face. 'If Mick wanted to hurt you, he'd make sure you were facing him when he punched you. And then he'd tell you exactly why he'd done it.'

She was right: Mick either tackled things head-on or didn't tackle them at all. If he'd wanted Caleb out of the way, he would have grabbed him by the shirtfront and told him to get out of town.

Maria stood. 'Get some rest now. I'll see you in the morning.'

'Wait,' he called as she reached the doorway, 'did you teach Portia some signs?'

She turned. 'Yes. At least I tried to – it was a little difficult over the phone. Did she manage them?'

'Yes, but why?'

'Oh.' She frowned. 'I thought they might help clarify things. She wanted to catch you on the street. It was late and I thought there was a fair chance you'd be running without your hearing aids in – not the best conditions for you to be communicating with a stranger.'

Typical Maria, lining up all the boxes and ticking them. All except one.

'Then why send her to me? You must know dozens of people in Melbourne.'

She paused. 'Because I knew I could trust you.'

47.

Kat came the next morning. She strode through the doorway as though on a mission, but faltered when she saw him.

'God. Cal.' She pressed a hand to her mouth.

'It looks worse than it is.'

She was wearing a dusk-pink sundress with a lightweight orange cardigan, her hair freshly clipped. Tired. A tautness in her shoulders and face. He felt as though someone had scooped out his chest. Days hoping she'd come, but now he knew it would have been better if she'd stayed away.

She dragged her eyes from his bandages and ventured closer. 'I've got a message for you from Ant.'

It took him a moment to realise what she'd said.

'God, really?' Heat stung his eyes. 'Is he OK?'

'Hard to say. Have a look.' She passed him her phone.

—*Hey Kat. Can you tell C Im OK? He's not answering his phone. I've gone away for a bit*

Gone away. To get clean? To shoot up? His throat ached. Stupidly incapable of dealing with this; it wasn't as though it was the first time they'd been here.

Kat was watching him. 'Mick told me about the OD. I'm so sorry, he was doing so well.'

'I thought maybe this time... He'd been clean for so long.' Caleb rubbed his face. 'I fucked it up for him. I really fucked it up.'

Something like fear flickered in her eyes. She'd always had a soft spot for Ant.

'People make their own choices,' she said. 'Sometimes they're bad ones.'

'Yeah, but we don't have to make it easy for them.'

She hesitated, then sat beside him, taking off her cardigan and folding it in her lap. A moment to realise that the pattern on her arm wasn't another long-sleeved top, but the tattoo she'd designed. Artwork as fine as lace. An outstretched wing that started high on her shoulder and flowed down her arm, the head of the eagle nestling in the crook of her thumb. Dark ochres, browns, black; each feather drawn with a sure, strong hand. He reached for her arm and turned it over. The long white scar on her wrist formed the ridge of the wing. He ran a forefinger down it, felt its strength, the softness of the surrounding skin. Amazing, really, how well you could know someone without realising their true depths.

'Kat,' he said, and then ran out of words.

She pulled her hand away under the guise of signing. 'How are you doing?'

'Fine. Getting out tomorrow.' Nothing but weariness at the thought.

'I'm sorry I didn't come sooner. I was going to come, but...'

'You're busy.'

'No, I was avoiding you.'

Right.

'I mean, I couldn't come until I knew what to say.' She smoothed her dress.

Oh God, this was it. Did she have the fucking divorce papers in her bag? But there it was again, that flash of fear in her eyes.

He sat up, ignoring the warning jolt in his arm. 'What's wrong?'

'Nothing's wrong.' She was smiling now, but he hadn't imagined the fear: it was there in her clenched hands and stiff shoulders, the tightness around her eyes. 'I, um… We…' She moved her hand. A simple sign: one hand pressed to her stomach, then lifted.

Pregnant.

All thought suspended. Breathing suspended. Heart.

'I found out two days ago. I've checked four times since. Ridiculous, isn't it? It took us so long the last couple of times and this time we just…'

Pregnant.

God, please.

'It's early,' she said. 'Really early, just over two weeks. But I guess you can count.'

They'd got to seventeen weeks the first time, nineteen the second. They'd felt the first flutterings, had chosen names, imagined personalities, futures, dreams.

She was looking at him with an intense focus, her eyes too bright.

'It'll be OK,' he said.

Her smile cracked and then fractured. He reached for her, but she stood without speaking and left the room.

He lay back and waited, trying very hard not to think about statistics and history and the deep pain of hope.

She came back ten minutes later, lipstick applied, spine straight. She stood next to him, a faint tremble in her hands as she signed. 'I don't know how we're going to do this, but I need you to be part of it. If it goes well, or if it...' Her eyes darted away and then back. 'I need you to be there.'

'I will be.'

'Will you?' She stabbed out the words with strange urgency.

'Of course. How could you even doubt that? Of course.'

'Cal.' She paused. 'I spoke to Frankie.'

'What?'

'She came to me after they brought you here. She told me everything. About where she found you, about what happened. About the way you lay down and gave up.'

A prickling wave of heat rose up his face, making sweat break out on his forehead.

'She said she'd never seen you give up on anything before and that it scared the shit out of her. She said that you didn't want to survive. That you only moved to safety the first time because she wouldn't leave you. That you didn't move at all the second time.'

'Sounds like she had a fair fucking bit to say.'

'Yeah, we had a good talk. And you know what? She's not the only one who's scared.'

'You should know better than to listen to Frankie. I can't believe you let her in the door after what she did to you. I was hurt and bleeding, for fuck's sake. Of course I lay down.'

Kat dragged the chair closer to him and sat with her knees pressed against the bed. 'Look me in the eye and say you haven't thought about it. Haven't weighed the pros and cons, decided on a method. Was it pills? Or a bridge? Or maybe you thought you'd just drive off the road into a tree. Make it easier for us all by pretending it was just an accident.'

He stared at her. How could she know?

'Cal.' She touched his arm; her hand was warm against his clammy skin. 'Tell me you're going to be around for this. Tell me you're going to get help. Please.'

He closed his eyes against the tears. Only a tiny flame to light the way, a fragile, wavering thing. But growing.

'I will,' he said.

She took his hand and lifted it, drawing the signs in the darkness: a downwards brush of her hand from her chest, a tap towards him.

Two meanings to the first sign: need and want.

'I *need* you.' 'I *want* you.'

Impossible to know which one she meant.

48.

He surfaced from the dream in the middle of the night, the image of the burning shipping container clear in his mind, its metal lid curled open to the sky. It wasn't normal for a container to explode in a fire like that.

What had Portia's teacher said?

'When you're working with volatile chemicals, there's always an element of danger.'

A bushfire would add a pretty extreme element of danger.

And the puzzle pieces lined up and clicked into place. Portia's chemistry skills and marketing books, her unfathomable decision to live with her estranged father, her lack of tree-planting knowledge, her popularity with people like Dave McGregor. Coast Care wasn't a failed effort to grow trees in summer, but a front for a mobile drug laboratory. He'd seen that green shipping container everywhere – at the vacant block with Ant, the camp, the quarry. Portia had set up a business to rival her father's. But how? That vacant block had been next to a kindergarten. How could you manufacture ice metres away from pre-school kids and have no one notice the smell?

Because it wasn't ice.

The address labels swirling like snow, the printed

names blackening in the heat – not a mailing list, but the drug itself. Delivered like LSD on paper, the old-style ink jet printer spraying out each perfect dose. Portia must have used the alphabetised names to mark each new and improved batch. Not 'bee': B. The second batch. She'd put those marketing books to good use – that was an excellent gimmick. Easy to send, easy to identify, easy to hide. She'd taught her coworkers well, too. Jai had been killed, but someone had kept on with the work, moving the lab around and selling B, kidnapping Caleb and leaving him blindfolded in an empty room. And they were still out there. Ramsden was right: it wasn't over.

'Next time they might decide on a more permanent solution.'

He drifted back to sleep, accompanied by the image of McGregor waving the labels in the air and laughing.

49.

He shuffled out of the hospital the next morning to wait for Kat, the burns on his legs and chest smarting more than usual. Maria had popped by for one of her little visits when the nervous, Bambi-eyed nurse had been changing his dressings. After waiting until Bambi had inflicted maximum pain on him, Maria had announced that he was staying at her place until he could manage the drive back to Melbourne. He'd had so many mixed emotions at the idea that he'd just nodded.

He was easing himself onto a bench in the pick-up zone when a boxy van drove slowly past and pulled in a few metres away. A Coast Care sticker on the back bumper. The diesel engine vibrated through the bench. Motionless, pulse racing – he'd lain bleeding in that van.

A young man hopped out of the driver's side. One of the clenched-jawed blokes he'd seen arguing with Aunty Eileen at Jai's funeral. A slight hitch to the man's stride as he noticed Caleb, then he went around to open the passenger door.

Aunty Eileen climbed down from the cabin.

Aunty Eileen with one of his kidnappers. Aunty Eileen, who kept warning him not to pry, who avoided the cops, who was linked to Jai. Whose house was torched.

And Caleb knew. She was the one behind B.

He stood. She was shuffling towards him, leaning on the young bloke's arm. 'You look worse every time I see you.'

He could say the same for her. Her skin was a parched yellow, flesh hanging from the bones of her arms.

She seemed to read his mind. 'Chemo to go with the dialysis. I'm pretty much stuffed.'

'You're making B.'

'I don't know what you're talking about, love. Hope you're feeling better soon.' She turned towards the hospital.

'You're betraying your own people,' Caleb said. 'How can you live with yourself?'

She spun back at that, her dark eyes hard. 'I'm *saving* them.'

'You're selling them drugs!'

'I'm selling them a future.' Her chin raised as she spat the words. 'We've had two hundred years of the whitefella pushing brain rot onto us – alcohol, sugar, dope, ice – and I'm putting a stop to it. B's not addictive, not expensive and not-for-whitefella-profit.'

Her young companion tried to interrupt, but Aunty Eileen shushed him. 'It's all gone now – he can't prove anything.' She eyed Caleb, some of the fierceness fading from her face. 'Maria was right about you, you're a smart man. I hope you're smart enough to leave us alone. Not much you can do to hurt us now, but you're an easy target and not everyone's as patient as me. A lot of people reckon B's the best thing that's happened to this town.'

'Would the police agree?'

She shrugged. 'Not illegal. They haven't made laws for this stuff yet.'

'Then why hide it?'

But he knew the answer as soon as he asked. Because of Dean Hirst and his ilk. B must have hurt Hirst's profits badly, and he'd hit back with everything he could: vandalism, fires, murder. And when he'd discovered his own daughter was involved, he'd sent Blondie after her with a shotgun. Easy to imagine what had happened after that. Portia's realisation that her father was onto her plan, her hurried change of appearance, the trip to Melbourne – not just to get away from her father, but also to get a sample to his rival, William Walker.

Dear William,

The goods as promised. This is C.

C was the new and improved third batch, the label on the envelope 'the goods'.

'So you're letting Billy Walker run things now.'

Aunty Eileen's mouth twisted. 'Manage, not run. Whitefella's working for us now.'

'He killed Dean Hirst to wipe out the competition. Do you really want to be in bed with someone like that?'

'That's none of my business. I haven't hurt anyone.'

He gestured to his sling. 'What about this?'

'Yeah, the young fellas got a bit overeager.' She patted her companion's arm. 'Still, I can't really blame them – they had to think quick. We reckon we've finally managed to get you off to Adelaide for a few days so we can get on with the fit-outs, and there you are, running towards Snake Gully right in the middle of things. Warehouse full of equipment, all our bloody trucks comin' and goin'.'

'What fit-outs? I thought the lab was in the shipping container.'

'We're expanding, love. You can't take over the state with a single bloody container. Be a bit harder now we've lost our chemist, but Walker reckons he's got a few people who can handle it.'

The traffic on the usually quiet road; the constant rumble of trucks while he'd lain in the hall: carrying the empty shipping containers in, carting the fully equipped ones out. God, how many of them were there now?

Kat's Beetle pulled up in a cloud of smoke behind the van. He looked from it to Aunty Eileen's sagging figure. 'And now?' he asked.

'And now, I hope you're smart enough to stay out of it. We've had to change plans a few times because of you, and people are starting to get annoyed.' She nodded to the young bloke and they turned for the hospital.

Kat was out of the car and walking towards him, an easy sway to her hips, the hint of a smile in her eyes. The smile faded as she drew closer. 'Are you OK? You're looking really pale.'

Tell her now. It wouldn't get any easier. The bloodshed wouldn't stop just because Aunty Eileen thought she was doing the right thing. The world didn't work that way.

'What's Aunty Eileen to you?' he asked.

'What do you mean?'

'She related?'

'She's my cousin Tanika's aunt. Why?'

He pictured the intricate diagram she'd drawn for him all those years ago: blue for friend, green for stranger, red for family. Distant or not, Aunty Eileen would be one of the red lines. And so would most of the threads radiating from her.

There had to be dozens of people involved in the scheme, a network of eager young men and women fighting to control their own lives.

He held chaos in his hands.

A frown was tugging at Kat's forehead. 'What's wrong?'

He gripped her hand, her once broken fingers.

'Nothing,' he said. 'Nothing at all. Let's go.'

ACKNOWLEDGEMENTS

Thank you to all my Koori family, but particularly to my moodji, Gunditjmara elder, Jim Berg. Thanks also to everyone in the D/deaf and hard-of-hearing communities who have shared their stories and wisdom with me.

To the wonderful Janette Currie, who keeps lighting the way, and my eternally patient editor, Kate Goldsworthy, for going above and beyond. All the team at Pushkin Press, especially Daniel Seton, Adam Freudenheim and Tabitha Pelly. The eagle-eyed Tim Coronel for proofreading, Shaun Jury for typesetting and Tom Sanderson for his fantastic cover design, Sophie Viskich for being exactly harsh enough, Kate Morell for her expertise in hearing aids, and JM Peace for letting me pick her brains about police procedure (any mistakes are mine, either through artistic licence or ignorance).

To Sisters in Crime Australia and the Australian Crime Writers Association for their support and their ongoing efforts to promote Australian crime fiction. The character of Joy McKay was named for the winner of the Sisters in Crime Australia *Be Immortalised in Fiction* competition.

And, as always, to Campbell, Meg and Leni – this would be nothing without you.

DARKNESS FOR LIGHT

PUSHKIN VERTIGO

AVAILABLE AND COMING SOON
FROM PUSHKIN VERTIGO

Jonathan Ames

You Were Never Really Here

Augusto De Angelis

The Murdered Banker
The Mystery of the Three Orchids
The Hotel of the Three Roses

Olivier Barde-Cabuçon

Casanova and the Faceless Woman

María Angélica Bosco

Death Going Down

Piero Chiara

The Disappearance of Signora Giulia

Frédéric Dard

Bird in a Cage
The Wicked Go to Hell
Crush
The Executioner Weeps
The King of Fools
The Gravediggers' Bread

Friedrich Dürrenmatt

The Pledge
The Execution of Justice
Suspicion
The Judge and His Hangman

Martin Holmén

Clinch
Down for the Count
Slugger

Alexander Lernet-Holenia

I Was Jack Mortimer

Margaret Millar

Vanish in an Instant

Boileau-Narcejac

Vertigo
She Who Was No More

Leo Perutz

Master of the Day of Judgment
Little Apple
St Peter's Snow

Soji Shimada

The Tokyo Zodiac Murders
Murder in the Crooked Mansion

Masako Togawa

The Master Key
The Lady Killer

Emma Viskic

Resurrection Bay
And Fire Came Down
Darkness for Light

Seishi Yokomizo

The Inugami Clan
Murder in the Honjin